'. . . utterly gripping, ho[...]
We need more b[...]
www.theboo[...]

'Gibbons clarifies but never s[...]
The least escapist thriller imaginable, and yet as exciting,
and often as much fun as Horowitz.'
Jake Kerridge, *The Telegraph*

'*An Act of Love* is the most powerful book I have read
this year . . . This is a book about friendship and love: how
families work, how we grow up, and how violence can
change lives . . . It is a book about love and terror, about
how and why people fight. It is beautifully written and
the sharpness of the prose and utter skilfulness of the
storytelling should make this book a must read for young
men and women all across Britain.'
Catherine Johnson, *Armadillo Magazine*

'This book should be on every reading list in every
secondary school . . . An excellent, well-written,
hard-hitting book to make you sit up and take notice.'
Serendipity Teacher

'This, for once, is a young adult novel genuinely
meriting the description "thought-provoking".'
Robert Dunbar, *The School Librarian*

'There are not enough male teen novels, and this one
is of political as well as human importance.'
www.bookwitch.wordpress.com

'. . . a brilliant story and one that has been told
with excitement, compassion and honesty.'
www.thegreatthegoodandthebad.blogspot.com

An Act of Love

ALAN GIBBONS

Indigo

First published in Great Britain in 2011
by Orion Children's Books
This paperback edition first published in 2012
by Indigo
a division of the Orion Publishing Group Ltd
Orion House
5 Upper St Martin's Lane
London WC2H 9EA
An Hachette UK Company

7 9 10 8

Copyright © Alan Gibbons 2011

The right of Alan Gibbons to be identified as
author of this work has been asserted by him.

A catalogue record for this book
is available from the British Library

ISBN 978 1 78062 018 3

Printed and bound by CPI Group (UK) Ltd, Croydon, CR0 4YY

Author's Note

Eight years ago I wrote *Caught in the Crossfire*, a novel in response to the new political climate created by the 11 September terror attacks. It was a love story between Rabia Khan, a Muslim girl, and a white boy called Mike Kelly. It is a book that is read with great affection by many but which provoked some abusive letters and emails.

Writing about peace and love can, it seems, be controversial.

Since, there have been a disturbing number of terror attacks and plots. These have emanated from unrepresentative fringe elements of the Muslim community and from neo-Nazis. I thought it was time to return to the issues involved and tell a story of two friends whose lives are changed forever by the aftermath of 9/11. Why do I choose such bleak subjects? Well, you only enter a dark room if you think you can light the way out.

I would like to thank Salma Owen and students from Crownhills Community College in Leicester for helping me with background material. I have also had conversations with soldiers serving in Afghanistan but it would not be appropriate to name them. I have made every effort to ensure authenticity. Any errors are mine and mine alone.

Salaam Alaikum.

Shalom Aleichem.

Peace be with you.

Alan Gibbons
Liverpool
July 2010

One

Chris

You think you're invincible when you're a kid. Invincible, that's a laugh. We're easy to hurt, any of us, all of us. Physically, emotionally, we snap. Like a matchstick. Easy as that.

And the damage can last a day.

A week.

Forever.

I open my eyes. I crave daylight. There's darkness inside me, stifling, suffocating. It's always there.

Since it happened.

Since the explosion.

The sky is clear and empty. Sunlight hammers into my vision just as it did on that day of pain.

'Are you all right, son?'

It's Dad. He is here, by my side. He has been with me every step of the way. That's the thing about a parent's love. It's unconditional. My gaze drifts to his face and the

I

lines of concern that seem deeper now than in those first difficult weeks. He has a haunted look.

He has demons.

As I do.

I've seen that brooding shadow before, in men who've witnessed too much. I nod reassurance, first at him then at Mum. A smile trembles on her lips. Tears threaten. That's the other thing about love. It's what gets you through the bad times, but I tell you, it can hurt like hell. It can damn near break you.

'I'm fine.'

Kelly squeezes my arm and I know things are going to be all right. The sun *will* rise in the morning. The breeze *will* touch my face in the afternoon. I *will* have peace in the evening. If not for you, Kell . . . It doesn't bear thinking about.

'It's your leg, isn't it?' she asks. 'It's hurting again.'

It's not my leg, not this time. It's the past, a thing as physical and tangible as human flesh. Where there is memory there is joy . . . and there is pain. Pain. So many times, when I close my eyes I am back on the banks of that canal, resting in the pounding heat of a Helmand morning.

I remember I'd checked the time as I got to my feet, shouldering my pack. It was seven thirty. I'd been walking since before dawn. I'd taken a step. For an instant the ground was spongy underfoot. I knew right away. Improvised explosive device. IED. Simultaneously the world roared, belching dirt and fire. The earth lurched. It felt as if I'd been rugby-tackled. I would learn later that the shock wave had tossed me in the air like a scrap of rag. The explosion cracked in my skull. Grit and soil peppered my vision, making me blink wildly, gasping for breath. My comrades were shouting.

At me.

At one another.

'Don't touch the leg!'

'Oh, Christ! Christ, no.'

Somebody was administering an ampoule of morphine.

I tried to speak. Hurts like ... I bit my lip until the blood came. I was grinding my teeth, trying to contain the sensations surging up from my legs. I'd never felt pain like it. It was intense. Total.

Somebody spoke. 'Swear all you like, Hooky.'

So I swore. Over and over again. That had always been one of the things that separated me from the other guys. I didn't really swear all that much. Until that moment.

There was a hand on my shoulder. Somebody was trying to comfort me. 'Hooky. Chris mate, you're going to be all right.'

The soothing voice didn't fool me. It felt like my leg had just been forced through a giant meat-grinder. The speaker had a purpose though. He was holding me down, gently but firmly, making sure I didn't reach for the limb, trying to stop me contaminating it any more than it already was. He didn't want me making it worse. I was moaning and rocking my head. The morphine was beginning to kick in. The world was turning hazy, but I knew what had happened. I saw the mud walls of the compound, the fruit trees, the milky brown water of the canal. I had just become another victim of this distant war, another statistic on the evening news.

Minutes crawled by. I don't know how long I was lying there in the open. Time stopped having any meaning.

There was just endless present ... and pain. I was slipping in and out of consciousness. Powerful engines whined. Rotor blades throbbed. A Chinook helicopter, nose tilting forwards. It was hard to focus. I heard somebody say my name. Private Chris Hook. A face floated above me.

'Are you OK, son?'

I nodded yes, but I had a question. 'Am I still all there?'

The medic was used to that one. He nodded. 'Yes, it's just the leg. You'll be OK on your wedding night.'

With some effort I break the spell and return to the present. I swallow hard and grip Kelly's hand. I want that. I want to be married to you, Kell.

'You won't ever leave me, will you? Promise.'

See what I mean?

Easy to hurt.

Vulnerable.

Needing this girl so badly I can barely breathe as I speak.

'Don't be stupid, Chris,' she says, insulted that I'm even asking. 'We're for keeps, you and me.' She kisses me, full lips pressing mine, filling me with reassuring warmth. 'I'm in this for the long haul, you great lump.'

'I was back there,' I whisper, 'you know, the day it happened.'

I've been there every day since, in dreams and in nightmares. I've been there in sleep and in tortured waking moments. I wonder if there will come a day when I go a whole twenty-four hours without reliving the horror of that morning.

'Are you OK to do this?' Kelly asks.

'I'm ready.'

She gives a squint of sympathy. 'Are you sure?'

4

'I'm sure. I didn't go through all those months of rehab to fail now.'

She starts to answer but the clatter of rotor blades drowns her words. It's the prince's helicopter. He is attending in his role as colonel-in-chief. The chopper settles on the parade ground in a swirl of dust. Applause ripples through the crowd as the prince emerges in desert uniform. It is the same as the one worn by the soldiers he has come to decorate. I take a deep breath. 'This is what I've been working for.'

Two of my comrades approach. Dave Nugent is first. He's an Essex boy. Donavan Barrow follows. Black guy. Welshman. Dave nods a hello in the direction of Mum and Dad. 'Cent will take the wheelchair.'

Mum frowns. 'Cent?'

'The lads say I look like 50 Cent,' Donavan explains. 'He's a rapper.'

Mum pulls a face. 'How old do you think I am? I know who he is. But they don't call you 50 Cent. It's 40 Cent. I've heard them.'

Donavan grins sheepishly. 'I'm not so big, see. Forty, not fifty. So they call me Cent for short.'

I glance at the wheelchair. I can probably get by without it, but it is there as back-up. 'Thanks Nugget. Touch wood I won't be needing it.' I sway a little then steady myself. 'I just hope I don't fall on my backside when I go up for my medal. I'm still getting the hang of this new leg.'

Nugget is in no doubt. 'You won't.'

I'm about to add something when my mobile buzzes. I recognise the caller's name.

Imran.

What the hell does he want? Hasn't he done enough?

Dad is shaking hands with the lads. Mum strokes my cheek. I'm six two and she still treats me like her little boy. I move my hand over hers.

'I'm going to be all right, OK? Don't fuss.'

I look beyond her at the broad expanse of the parade ground. There is a strong police presence, both military and civilian, there to guard the prince. That's not the whole story. Nobody's forgotten what happened when the Anglia regiment returned home a few years back. Angry protests greeted them in Luton. The community was torn apart. The TV news relayed the story into every living room, screaming difference.

White against Muslim.

Red, white and blue against Islamic green.

At least, that's the way the media portrayed it. It made the evening news. Even though there were fewer than twenty protestors. Not enough for two football teams. But the words on those placards still dance through my memory, words that hurt nearly as badly as the IED.

British soldiers go to hell.

Troops are war criminals.

I imagine Imran's face in the huddle. He took their side. I can almost hear his voice coming from their mouths. How dare he call, in this place, on this day? After everything I've been through. I clench my fists until my fingernails cut half-moon shapes in the flesh of my palms.

Nugget and Cent are chatting with Mum and Dad. Kelly is linking arms with me, watching the prince with the senior officers. Nobody knows what's going through my mind. Nobody understands. How can they? They weren't there. Only a soldier understands. My phone buzzes again. It's a text. Imran again.

Stop the ceremony.

Oh, you'd like that, Imran. Imagine it. You think a text can succeed where a score of hate-filled protestors failed. Well, thanks for the advice, but no thanks. I want to tell him to drop dead. I'm not going to dignify his stupid games with a reply. I go to switch off the phone, but it buzzes again. The text is short. Two words from our childhood.

Blood brothers.

How low can he sink?

A lump rises in my throat. How dare he try to trade on our friendship? I scroll down and read the rest. The words chill me to the bone.

There's a bomb.

Imran

There are two Asian men in the white Lexus.

The younger man twists round in the passenger seat to talk to his brother. 'He won't take my call.'

There is panic in Imran's voice. He starts crushing the phone in his hand. He wants Rafiq to tell him what to do, like he did when they were kids. Rafiq doesn't return the look. He's got his eyes on the seething traffic. Imran wants him to speak, to say something, anything. All Imran's life, whenever there was something wrong, Rafiq had the answers. Not this time. The skin is drawn taut over his cheekbones. Imran wonders how much Rafiq resents him for what he's done.

'Keep trying,' Rafiq says finally, his voice tense.

Imran glances at the speedo. His voice rips back at his brother. 'What are you doing, Rafiq? Put your foot down. Can't you make this thing go any faster?'

Tower blocks slip by. Concrete walkways curve against the cobalt blue sky. Not far ahead the city centre clutter will thin and give way to miles of suburbs. Beyond that they will come to the barracks.

Rafiq snorts. 'Two Asian guys speeding? That's going to help. What do you think Five-O are going to make of that?' As if to back up his words, a police car sweeps past, going in the opposite direction. Blue lights flash. 'They'd pull us up for sure.'

'That's it then?' Imran cries. 'There's a bomber and we're worrying about the speed limit!'

'We've got no choice,' Rafiq answers. 'We play this wrong and we've got a bloodbath on our hands. Try texting him. So he doesn't want to talk. Maybe he'll read what you've got to say instead.'

Imran snorts in frustration. 'He'd better.' His thumbs start working the keypad. 'Why does he have to be so stubborn?'

Rafiq shakes his head. He's got something to say but he's trying to keep a lock on it.

'Say it, Rafiq.'

'Do you really want to know why he won't listen? It's down to you. You did this, Imran. You called him a kafir. You called him a murderer of Muslims. He was your best friend and you treated him like the dirt on your shoe.

8

What makes you think he's going to have any time for you now?'

There are things Imran could say in his defence. About the war. About British and American boots on Muslim land. About the way Chris made another life with his racist, gora mates.

But he takes Rafiq's accusation on the chin. He drops his eyes and gets on with the text.

'I'm not making excuses, Rafiq. This isn't about Chris and me. It's about people getting killed.'

Chris

1 FEBRUARY 2011. 10.05 A.M.

My fingers hover over the keypad. I think about calling Imran back. Can there be any truth in the message? Does he know something? Did he fly that close to the flame?

Dad sees me staring at my mobile. 'What's wrong?'

Nugget and Cent turn. They've picked up the crackle of tension in the air. I draw Dad to one side. I drop my voice and hope Dad follows suit. I don't want anybody else involved. 'It's Imran.'

The very mention of his name makes Dad scowl.

'What can you possibly have to say to him?' he says. 'No, I don't want to know. Just switch your phone off. Leave him in the past where he belongs. This is your day. Don't let him spoil it.'

'Dad, you don't understand.'

He gives a furious shake of his head. 'What's to

understand? Hasn't that lad done enough harm? Ignore him, Chris. Forget he ever called you.'

'That's easier said than done.'

He still doesn't understand. 'Why is it, Chris? He's always been able to twist you round his little finger.'

'Dad, that's not fair.'

'Isn't it? You've given him more than enough chances to be a friend. He threw them all back in your face.'

'It wasn't like that. It's … complicated.'

He snaps back. 'It's pretty black and white to me.'

The others are starting to look. Just calm down, Dad.

'Why can't you stand up to him, Chris? He's an extremist. He hates this country and everything it stands for.'

I know the speech inside out. I should do. I've had to listen to it a hundred times. What this country stands for. I would love somebody to tell me. I thought I knew once. That was before I went to war. Imran's face comes to mind. Friendship is like a piece of information in a computer's memory. You can try to delete it but it always leaves an imprint.

'Well?'

When I hesitate he has another go.

'All those months you were recuperating, who was there for you? It was me, your Mum, Kelly. Imran didn't come near.'

Who's arguing? 'I know, Dad. I know. That's not it. There's something you've got to see.'

I hold up my phone and he reads the message. Blood drains from his face.

Imran

The traffic has slowed as they crawl towards one of the city's most congested junctions. Rafiq glances at his watch. 'Come on!'

'Why don't we phone 999?'

Rafiq laughs. 'You're unreal, you know that?'

Imran is offended. 'It's an emergency, innit?' Then he feels stupid. Innit. Like a kid.

'I don't believe what I'm hearing,' Rafiq says, shaking his head. 'Oh, this is some turnaround, Imran. I thought you were the big man, preaching jihad, mouthing off about the dirty kuffar. Now all of a sudden you want them to bail you out!'

Imran retorts, fury boiling out of him. 'Don't keep throwing my past back in my face, Rafiq. If you're expecting me to crawl on broken glass, forget it. Look, I know I got myself into this, but I got myself out too.'

'I know you did,' Rafiq retorts. 'I gave you a helping hand, little brother. Or have you forgotten?'

'I haven't forgotten.'

There is a moment of silence, then Rafiq softens. 'You're right. You're right. We all make mistakes. Just look at my track record.' He sighs. 'So many wasted years. But think what you're saying. You didn't want anything to do with the gora state. Now you're hoping the police can help you. Nice one. Just perfect.'

Imran tries to answer back. His words come out wrong, a pathetic admission of defeat. 'It's better than doing nothing.'

Rafiq tightens his grip on the steering wheel. 'Here's how it goes. You'll get through to some operator. Do you know anything about the people who answer the phones? Are they civilian staff, or trained officers?'

Imran pulls a face. He doesn't know.

Rafiq doesn't expect his brother to be an expert. He keeps talking. 'Say this person transfers you to some office plod. How do you think that's going to play out?'

Imran doesn't know.

'This one thinks you're some kind of prankster.' Rafiq hangs a left, making his point in the same machine-gun delivery. 'They must get crank calls all the time. He doesn't believe your story. There's a shedload of stupid questions.'

'You think?'

'How should I know? I don't do this kind of thing every day. You're the one who was going to bring down the state. You tell me. How long do you think you're going to be on the phone trying to convince them?' He gestures at the road ahead. 'Get real, Imran. What are we, ten, fifteen minutes from the barracks? Chris is there. He's our best chance.'

'And if he won't listen?'

Rafiq gives a weary shrug. 'We go straight to the barracks. We move in as close as we can. If we get that far, our story might just make some kind of sense. We look them in the eye. It beats a phone call.'

'Do you think they'll listen?'

Rafiq laughs bitterly. 'We're relying on the same police who've been shaking our people down for years. Get out of the car please, sir,' he mimics. 'Is this your vehicle? Where do you live? Are you now, or have you ever been, a terrorist? It doesn't give you a lot of confidence.'

Imran leans back against the headrest. It's a gesture of despair.

Rafiq carries on talking. 'I don't believe I'm saying this, but try to see it through their eyes. A couple of Muslim guys appear out of the blue and walk up to the gates of an army barracks. We say our piece and they call in our details. Who've they got standing in front of them? Oh yes, it's a jailbird and a radical. Sound about right?'

About right.

In their eyes.

Rafiq drives the point home. 'I think they're going to lock us up and throw away the key.' Finally, he meets Imran's gaze. 'But what else are we going to do? There are lives at stake. Tell me if you've got a better idea.'

Imran doesn't speak. He sees a group of kids in a park and he remembers two excited boys kicking through the autumn leaves. It seems so long ago. What happened to us, Chris? he wonders. How did we screw things up so badly?

Chris

1 FEBRUARY 2011. 10.17 A.M.

There's a round of applause from the crowd. It makes me turn. For once there's no press scrum moving in on royalty. The reporters have had their orders. Dignity. Respect. This is the soldiers' day so they hang back. The press pack is sticking to the rules for once. Wouldn't it be great if that's what we all did – stick to the rules? Any of us: the angry men, the politicians, Imran. Me. But nobody sticks to the rules, not really, not even the people who make them.

Dad leans forward and hisses in my ear. 'This is exactly the sort of nonsense you'd expect from Imran.'

But I can't get the doubts out of my head. 'What if he's telling the truth?'

Dad looks at me as if I'm insane. 'Don't be ridiculous. Just look at the security. Everybody's been vetted. It's nonsense. Forget about him.'

Forget about him? For years we were inseparable. He wouldn't call me out of the blue just to stir up trouble. 'I know what makes him tick, Dad. We're talking about my best friend.'

Dad isn't in any mood to listen. 'He *was* your best friend, Chris. Was. Past tense. Over. Finished.' His words sting like wasps. 'Are you so sure you know him? When he found out you were in the Army he called you a murderer. I'll tell you what I make of Imran. He was a great kid, but his mind got poisoned somewhere along the way. He turned into a tinpot Islamist. Do I think we've got anything to worry about? No. He makes a lot of noise but he hasn't got the guts to do anything about it. It's his sick idea of a joke, son. It's rubbish. Forget it.'

I know exactly what happened to Imran. I was part of it. My skin burns.

Dad presses on. 'You go with your mates, Chris. There's no way anybody could get past the checks. Look around you. It's the police, the military and their families. Can you see anybody who looks like a terrorist?'

I'm tempted to ask what a terrorist looks like, but I know what Dad means. He looks and there's a sea of white faces, a few black guys in uniform, some Gurkhas: surely nobody who could pose a threat?

'Time to get a move on,' Nugget says, interrupting my thoughts. 'This is us.'

The boys from C company are among the uniformed ranks massing on the far side of the parade ground. Cent is speaking.

'They're on the way.'

DEATH OF A SON
Twelve-year-old Muhammad-al-Durrah
shot in his father Jamal's arms.

Two

Imran

NEW YEAR'S EVE 1999.

'They're on the way.'

The same four words, but from a different time – an age, if not of innocence, at least of not knowing. Those were the days before the world went crazy, before the phrase 'the clash of civilisations' was on every reporter's lips.

Imran's father's sister and her family had just arrived. Aunt Haleema was locking the car. Imran's cousins kicked off their shoes and made their way into the living room. There were hugs and kisses on foreheads. Uncle Syed followed and closed the door behind him.

Imran had just celebrated his eighth birthday. There were fireworks at his party. He had watched them wide-eyed and begged Abbu and Ammi to hold a millennium party ... with more fireworks. The family was gathering to see in the millennium. Naturally Aunt Haleema had to remind everyone that the Muslim calendar is different. As if nobody else knew. Ramadan fell in January that year. People had fasted until sunset. Now they were exploring the tables of food and drink. There was a spread made up of samosas, pakoras, Karahi dishes, daal. The rich fragrance of ginger and coriander hung in the air. Imran's cheeks were already bulging with half-chewed samosa.

'Hey,' Rafiq said, 'leave some for the rest of us.'

Imran grinned impishly. His father appeared and clapped his hands. 'The fireworks are all ready. Does anybody have a reliable watch?'

Rafiq had something to say as usual. 'You can't trust watches these days, Abbu-ji. Didn't you hear the news? It's the Millennium Bug. It's going to change everything.' He raised his hands in the air in a gesture that said *be afraid, be very afraid*. Imran was giggling already even though he didn't know what his brother was talking about. 'The computers can't handle all the numbers. On the stroke of midnight planes are going to fall from the sky.'

Dad pretended to throw out a hand to slap Rafiq across the head. 'My eldest, everybody. He's my joker in the pack. Just look at the grin on his face. He takes nothing seriously.'

Imran glanced up at Rafiq. Rafiq winked.

Aunt Haleema insisted it might be true. 'It is all over the newspapers. The man on the TV said my washing machine is going to stop working.' When Rafiq rolled his eyes, she shook her head. 'You think you are so clever. The reporter must have done his research. He said it's all this software in the machines. The dates confuse it.'

'That's right,' Rafiq said. 'The year 2000 has scrambled the poor machines' brains. Your Zanussi won't know what day it is.' He lurched robotically around the room. 'I'm

Rafiq. I'm a washing machine.' He cocked his head to one side. 'What day is it?'

Imran was giggling fit to burst. Mum rapped her knuckles on the table to introduce a little calm to the proceedings. 'Does anyone have the right time? We don't want to set off the fireworks too soon.'

Imran turned on the TV. His jaw dropped. An amazing display was taking place. 'We've missed it!' he cried. 'Look, their fireworks have already started.'

Rafiq grabbed him round the waist and threw him up in the air. 'That's Australia, you lulloo. Don't they teach you anything at that school? That's the Sydney Harbour Bridge.'

Rafiq swung Imran round and round. He did it so fast the room started to spin.

'That's the news you're watching. They've already had their celebrations.'

'The lights are still on in Sydney,' Dad observed. 'It looks like your washing machine is going to work after all, Haleema.'

Rafiq was still swinging his little brother. 'That's Australia,' Imran squealed. 'It's on the other side of the world. I bet the lights are working because everything is upside down.'

Rafiq flipped him over so his head was facing the carpet. 'Now you're the one who is upside down, my wriggling friend. Are you still working? Say tick tock.'

Imran yelled for him to slow down. 'I think I'm going to be sick.'

'He's still working,' Rafiq observed as he turned Imran the right way up. 'You can tell because he never stops whinging.'

Dad wagged his finger. 'Put him down, Rafiq. You're getting him over-excited.'

Imran pulled a face. Why did Dad always have to tell everybody what to do? There would be no fun if he had his way. Over-excited! There's no point being *under-excited.*

Mum was growing impatient. 'So what is the time?'

'Four minutes to go,' Aisha said. 'It is right there on the TV.'

Everyone started to file out into the small garden. The air was crisp. The night was fine and clear. There were only a few milky clouds at the edges of the vast darkness. It was a night that seemed to promise so much: a night to remember.

Imran wondered where Chris was. He was leaving it late. Imran glanced over the wall, expecting to see his best friend making his way round. The lights were on, so where was he? 'He's going to miss the fireworks.'

Dad squeezed his shoulder. 'Chris can't come. His mum told me earlier.'

'But they're in,' Imran protested. He refused to believe Chris wasn't coming. 'Look, the lights are on.'

'Of course the lights are on,' Rafiq said. 'They leave them on so they don't get burgled.'

Imran was disappointed. They'd been best friends since they could walk. Chris had said he was coming. He'd promised. He was the one who'd said the millennium was such a big deal, not Imran. Rafiq slapped his little brother on the shoulder.

'Come on, the fireworks are about to start.'

Right across the neighbourhood, rockets were climbing

into the heavens. Lights streaked back and forth. Explosions cracked and fizzed.

Mum smiled and adjusted her hijab. 'It's going to be a great New Year, a great new century too. I feel it in my bones.'

Imran smiled. Ammi-ji felt all kinds of things: the way the weather would turn out, the university careers her three children would have, prosperity for everyone. Her bones even knew the Millennium Bug was rubbish, way before anybody else did.

Dad looked down at her and smiled. 'May there be many years of peace and happiness.'

Mum echoed the sentiment. 'Inshallah.'

The word fluttered from the lips of the guests then all eyes turned back to the sky where more rockets were racing ahead before bursting in great star flashes of colour, illuminating the narrow streets below. Imran wondered if the fireworks Chris was watching were as good.

Chris

NEW YEAR'S DAY 2000.

Everything was about to change but we didn't understand. We were just kids, me and Imran.

I remember the way Imran described his night, turning me green with envy. 'Are you kidding? You had a proper display. How long did it last?'

'About ten minutes. Rafiq organised it.'

'Ten minutes!' I was sure he was exaggerating but it was obvious he'd had a better evening than I did. I had to go to my grandparents. 'You know what we had? One lousy box!'

Imran put on his superior look. 'Grandparents are no good at fireworks.'

'You're right there,' I told him. 'Grandad spent the whole evening telling everybody how people only used to set fireworks off on 5 November and how nobody ever set them off on birthdays or New Year the way they do now. It wasn't a party. It was a history lesson!'

Imran had a big smirk on his face.

I got the message. Serve me right for not going to his party. As if I had any choice!

'It was so boring,' I told him. 'Dull as the dullest thing in Dull Town. Even when Grandad set them off he must have taken half an hour to do it.' Now I was the one who was exaggerating. 'He kept moving us back, saying somebody was going to lose an eye.'

Imran said that's what happened to that Nelson guy – fireworks. 'Put his eye out.'

I laughed. 'Yeah, right.'

'It's true,' Imran insisted. 'Captain Hook too. Banger took his hand clean off.'

'Long John Silver,' I said. 'Catherine Wheel whipped off his leg.'

I thumped him on the arm. He thumped me back. I wrapped my foot round Imran's calf and tripped him up. Imran came back shoving his head in my stomach. We wrestled for a few moments then Imran asked me if I wanted to see his birthday present.

I told him I'd seen them all.

Imran led the way upstairs. 'Not this one. It's the big one.' He threw his bedroom door open. 'Ta da!'

'You've got a computer! They're letting you have your very own computer. That's so cool!'

'I have to keep my door open when I'm on it,' Imran explained. 'You know, my dad doesn't want me watching anything I shouldn't.'

'Like what?'

Imran shrugged. 'I don't know, naked ladies or summat.'

I was still staring at his computer. 'So are we going to have a go?'

Imran declared that it was only for education. I stared at him dumbfounded. Then his face crumpled and he burst out laughing.

I shook my head. 'What games have you got?'

'Let's play Doom. It's Rafiq's.'

I watched it loading. 'This isn't the Doom I've played.'

'This is Final Doom. It's better.'

I tried to blag him. 'Yes, I've played it.'

'No, you haven't. Liar.'

'OK, I haven't, but it's not new. It's been around for ages.'

'I never said it was new, did I? What's important is, I've got it and you haven't.'

Doom was the breakthrough first person shooter game. The player saw through the shooter's eyes. The blood splashed when he made a kill. It looks dated now but back then it was state-of-the-art and we couldn't get enough of it.

I gunned down the first enemy. 'Do you think this is what it's like in real life?'

'Nah,' Imran said. 'Real life's better.' He blasted away. 'But not much.'

'Do you think we'll have to fight wars?' I asked. 'Men fight. That's what they do.'

Imran shrugged. 'Who are you going to fight?'

'Our enemies.'

'Like who?'

I had to think for a minute. 'It used to be the Germans, but my dad says we don't fight them any more. They just beat us at football.' Something unpleasant occurred to me. 'You don't think we'd ever fight each other do you?'

Imran pulled a face. 'Don't be stupid. We're blood brothers. Besides, I'd kick your butt.'

Chris

10 JANUARY 2000.

We were sitting in the cinema.

Imran nudged me. 'Told you Rafiq would get us in.'

I shook my head. 'What do you mean, get us in? It's only a PG.'

'We couldn't have come on our own though, could we?' Imran demanded.

Rafiq told us to settle down. An hour and a half later we were jostling through the crowds leaving the cinema. Imran loved the feeling of coming out of the dark into the light. We hurried out of the cinema dark into the rain-slicked city dark. Tyres hissed on the damp, gleaming streets as we made our way home. Headlights sprayed through the showers. Cold rain dripped down our necks while we had a play fight up the road. Rafiq spotted a bus coming and the three of us ran, spilling through the doors, shouting and laughing.

'If you could have a super power, any power,' I panted as I tumbled into the seat next to Imran. I fought to get my breath after the mad sprint down the street, 'what would you pick?'

Before Imran could answer, I interrupted him. 'Oh, and you can't claim the power to have any power you want.'

Imran grinned. 'How did you know what I was going to say?'

'I can read your mind. Go on, choose one.'

Imran gave it some thought. 'Invisibility. No, fire.' He changed his mind again. 'No, levitation.'

I howled in protest. 'Only one power, you cheat.'

Imran thought hard. His credibility as a superhero depended on what he said next. One mistake and the forces of evil would rule the Earth. 'Flight,' he said at last. 'I would fly like a bird.'

'OK,' I said. 'It's my turn. I would have super-strength so I could beat up the bad guys.'

Rafiq was sitting behind us. 'Which bad guys are these?'

'Any bad guys.'

Rafiq smiled. 'It's best to know who the bad guys are before you start fighting them. What if you go beating up the wrong side?'

'When you find the bad guys, I'll fly over them,' Imran said, 'and poop on them from high up.'

I was laughing and pulling a face. 'You're disgusting.'

The old woman sitting next to Rafiq thought so too. She pulled a face. Rafiq apologised. Then he told Imran to say sorry to the lady.

'Sorry, lady.'

She looked right through both of them. Imran felt uncomfortable. He knew that look. Sometimes people would squint down their nose at him as if he was a little bug that had crawled out of a tree. It would be a few years before he understood it. 'What's your power, Rafiq?'

Rafiq shrugged.

'Go on,' I said. 'You've got to pick one.'

'I'll think about it. Ask me when we get home.'

But as we walked through the door we froze. It was what Imran's dad, Mr Hussain, was watching on TV. A boy and his father were sitting with their backs against a wall. There was something about their faces and the way they tried to make their bodies small. There was a burst of gunfire. The boy slid to the ground. His father tried to protect him.

I didn't see any blood.

Somehow that made it worse. As if he had been struck down by some invisible force.

Imran watched in horror. 'Did he just get shot? Is it real?'

Rafiq rested a hand on his shoulder. 'It's real.'

The firing continued. The boy was hit and his father slumped on the wall. I could feel Imran's body jerk involuntarily.

Mr Hussain told Rafiq to get Imran upstairs. 'He shouldn't be watching such things.'

Imran refused to go, planting his feet. He demanded to know what it was about. 'Why did they shoot them?'

His dad didn't want to discuss it. 'Go to your room, Imran. This is not suitable for either of you. Show Chris your computer.'

Imran didn't move. 'Why did they shoot that boy?'

A boy like him.

With black hair like him.

And brown skin like him.

'Why, Abbu-ji?'

That's when Rafiq spoke. 'Why don't you tell him? He should know what the Israelis are doing.'

Mr Hussain reacted angrily. 'You be quiet, Rafiq. Don't put ideas in the boy's head.'

Rafiq didn't listen. 'He is a Palestinian, Imran. He is a Muslim like us.'

'But why did they shoot him?'

Rafiq had the answers. 'The Palestinians are standing up for their rights.' He pointed to the crowds of young men on the TV screen. 'They fight the soldiers. They throw stones.'

I could see from the look on his face that that made no sense to Imran. 'But the soldiers have guns. What good are stones when they've got guns?'

'No good at all,' Rafiq replied.

Mr Hussain had had enough. He went to the TV and switched it off. 'No politics in this house, Rafiq. I won't have you ramming things down your brother's throat. He looks up to you. You must be careful what you say.'

Rafiq shook his head. 'You tell me not to talk politics. Why? You are in the Labour Party, Abbu. Isn't that politics?'

'We live in Britain,' Mr Hussain said. 'That makes us British. We should discuss British politics.'

Rafiq pointed at the TV screen. 'What do you think when you see something like that, Abbu? Tell Imran what is in your heart.'

'There must be justice. There must be a homeland for both the Palestinians and the Jews.'

Rafiq snarled something back. Imran watched them. Their voices were raised. Their faces contorted. He loved them both and it tore him in two to watch the scene.

'We are Muslims. We must never forget our brothers and sisters across the world.'

At that moment Mrs Hussain came in from the kitchen. She had heard the shouting. 'Enough! No more politics. You should listen to your Imam. Islam is an act of love, not anger.'

Rafiq threw up his arms. 'You always say that, Ammi-ji. What does it mean? What good is love when you are looking down the barrel of a gun? What good is love when a child can be gunned down without mercy?'

Mrs Hussain didn't answer directly. 'You will not raise your voice against your father, Rafiq. This quarrel is over.'

Rafiq hesitated, not wanting to lose the argument but, seeing the expressions on his parents' faces, he accepted defeat and stalked out of the room.

Mrs Hussain noticed me standing in a corner. 'I think it is time to go home,' she said, guiding me to the door.

As I went on my way, I heard Rafiq say to Imran: 'I know the super power I want.' He made the shape of a gun with his thumb and forefinger. 'I would make guns and give them to the boys who throw stones. I would help them fight back. I would help them win.'

Three

Chris

I know this moment. This is when feet shuffle, stomachs clench, hearts thud in chests. I get ready for action. It takes me back to Afghanistan. Weapons are stripped, cleaned and oiled. Eyes squint down barrels. Grenades are primed and placed in pouches. Links of machine-gun ammo are distributed. Medical packs are inspected. Sons speak to mothers on the satellite phone, husbands to wives. The Chinook's turbines whine. The rotors turn.

But this day, here on a parade ground in the north of England, I'm not preparing to be flown into the Green Zone. I'm not expecting a tense patrol through the compounds, a walk past watching eyes in some dustbowl of a town with the ever-present menace of a suicide bomber, or a firefight. This is something more insidious. I'm preparing for the unknown.

I can't get Imran's message out of my head. *It's a bomb*. Imran's been hanging round with some pretty iffy characters, but a bomber? No, it's impossible. Not Imran. Forget it.

But I can't forget. Eleven years ago it was all so different. We were kids.

Chris

12 FEBRUARY 2000.

We were out in the street. There is a broad paved area halfway down where we used to play sometimes. Others used it. There was a crowd of teenagers who used to hang out in the evening. Whenever they turned up Mum shooed us inside. Sometimes the older boys tossed empty cans of Red Bull on the ground and flicked stuff at passers-by. Other times it was booze. Mum said they set a bad example.

The paved area had other uses too. When there was no room anywhere else, drivers mounted the kerb and parked their cars. Some of our neighbours got worked up about it from time to time. They went to their councillor. I only knew about it because the councillor was Imran's dad. You're supposed to represent us, they said. So get something done.

Mr Hussain was soon on the case. He promised to get bollards put in, or alley gates, something to stop the nuisance. We didn't care if we were a nuisance or not. We were wearing our new Manchester United kits. I was Ryan Giggs. Imran was Paul Scholes. I chipped the ball across. Imran met it with his head and peeled away to celebrate. It was his turn to cross it. I got my shape all wrong and the ball thumped into the window of the corner house. A face appeared at the window. He was new, a black guy by the name of Mr Bankole. He came stamping out of his front door.

'What's wrong with you kids?' he grumbled. 'Can't I get some peace on my day off?'

'Sorry, Mr Bankole.'

He wasn't interested in an apology. He had a face like he'd swallowed a bee. 'Hit my window again and you will be.'

He kicked the ball back. 'It's your last chance, you hear?'

The door slammed. Imran scurried to retrieve his ball.

'Last chance?' he said. 'I thought you were supposed to get three strikes.'

Mr Bankole looked like a one-strike kind of guy. We kept the ball on the ground after that. Pass and move across the paved area and down the alley. Then back again. It worked for a while but nobody can keep the ball on the ground forever. Not even Ryan Giggs. Imran hit his pass a bit too hard and it skewed off my trainer. Straight into Mr Bankole's window. The door burst open.

'What did I tell you kids?'

He grabbed the ball and went back inside.

Imran stared at the closed door in disbelief.

'It's not his ball. It's mine.' Imran knocked on the door. There was no answer. So he knocked harder, rapping till his knuckles hurt. It was a few seconds before Mr Bankole reappeared.

'Can we have our ball back, please?'

Imran had to be polite. He was Mr Hussain the councillor's boy.

But Mr Bankole wasn't impressed. 'No.'

'Give us our ball back!' Imran was furious that Mr Bankole could just pick up his ball and walk away with it. He hadn't even hit the window. I had.

Mr Bankole disappeared inside for a few moments and came back with the ball in his hands. It was flat.

'You punctured it!' Imran yelled. 'You burst my ball.'

'I didn't burst it,' Mr Bankole said. 'It was already like that.'

'No it wasn't,' Imran cried. 'You did it. You burst my ball. Tell him, Chris.'

I didn't want to get involved, but I owed him.

And Imran knew it.

I finally broke my silence. 'He's right, Mr Bankole. It was fine when … when I kicked it against your window. Sorry about that.'

My grovelling didn't have any effect on Mr Bankole. He tossed the useless football on the pavement. 'No more kicking it against my window. Of course, chance would be a fine thing.' He thought he was a funny guy.

Imran yelled as he closed the door. 'I'll get Rafiq on you.' Then he changed his mind. 'No, I'm going to get him back myself.'

That was ominous. I knew he'd get his revenge. The only question was how.

Chris

26 FEBRUARY 2000.

Two weeks later it snowed. I watched the big, fluffy flakes fluttering down like a million white butterflies. I shouted to my little sister. I wanted her to share the wonder of the moment with me. 'Look Jess, it's snowing. It's going to settle.'

She clambered onto the back of the couch to peer through the blinds. 'Mum, can we go out in it?'

Mum insisted we dressed up warm. I took no time at all. I grabbed my new jacket, the leather gloves Grandma got me for Christmas and a Man U bobble hat. Jess took longer. She squirmed like an octopus as Mum wrapped her up in her coat, hat, scarf and mittens. It wasn't long before Imran joined us staring up at the fat flakes and the blue-black sky. There was already enough snow to have a snowball fight. Imran threw one at me. I ducked and it hit Jess on the side of the face. She ran to Mum, bawling her eyes out.

'Why do you have to be so rough? You threw it too hard.'

Imran stood his ground. 'It's not my fault. You ducked, you coward.'

'Who threw it in the first place? You're going to get me in trouble.'

'It was only a snowball,' he said.

'Yes, and Jess is six. You've got to be careful with little kids. You do that again and I'll punch your lights out, even if you are my best friend.'

Imran saw that I meant it. 'Did I really hurt her?'

'Yes, you did.'

'Sorry man. I didn't mean it. I'll make it up to her.'

'Are you all going to play nicely together?' Mum asked. 'Jess is younger than you two so don't be so rough. I want you boys to take care of her.'

Imran set about making a snowman, but it wasn't a

man. It was a bunny. Jess loved the snow bunny. She'd been pestering Mum and Dad to get her a rabbit since forever. Now Imran had made her one. It had big ears and a plump, friendly face. He took so much care, smoothing it into shape. He even went in for a jug of water so he could make the outer surface tough as a shell to protect it.

Jess's face lit up. 'I'm going to kiss you.'

Imran danced away laughing. 'You are not!'

'Am too.'

For a few minutes they raced around. Jess didn't come close to catching him. Imran was as lean and agile as a cheetah. He was the fastest kid in the whole year. After maybe half an hour Mum brought us a plate of chocolate brownies. We were munching our way through them when a van parked down the street.

Imran was curious. 'What are they up to?'

There were two council workmen in green, fluorescent jackets. One was brushing away an area of newly fallen snow. The other was hauling a drill from the back of the van.

'What are you doing?'

'We're putting a line of bollards in,' the first man said.

'Why?'

'It's to block access to the alley and to stop drivers parking on the pavement. One of the councillors has been getting hot under the collar about it.'

I pointed at Imran. 'That's his dad.'

'So your dad is Councillor Hussain?'

Imran stuck his chest out, proud as punch. 'That's right.'

All afternoon we watched them working. Jess stayed for a while, but she got bored.

When she had gone Imran said, 'You know I was going

to pay Mr Bankole back for bursting my ball? Well, I've got an idea.'

It snowed again about four o'clock. The workmen had finished.

Imran rubbed his hands together. 'Right, let's get to work.'

Within an hour we had built snowmen around the three bollards. We inspected our work.

'Are you sure about this? Won't he be angry?'

'Of course he'll be angry. That's the point.'

I must have looked doubtful.

'Oh, come on. Don't wimp out on me now, Chris.'

Half an hour later it was getting dark. Snowflakes were still floating in the light from the streetlamps.

'What time do you think he gets back?' Imran asked.

I shrugged. 'I don't know. An hour maybe.'

It turned out to be less. Mr Bankole's car turned into the road, the beam of his headlights picking out the snowmen. The bright gleam washed over them.

'Here he comes!'

Mr Bankole saw us. He was braking, getting ready to pull into the empty space in front of his house. He saw me and Imran and peered through the windscreen. Imran shouted something and he wound down his window.

'What did you say?'

'I said you owe us a ball.'

Mr Bankole rubbed at the end of his nose. 'You're not getting anything from me.'

He glanced at the line of snowmen. Imran made a show of trying to protect them. He played his part well. He put himself between them and the car. It was all the invitation

Mr Bankole needed. He put his foot down on the accelerator and mounted the pavement. He targeted the first snowman. Imran stepped out of the way, a huge smile on his face. Too late Mr Bankole smelled a rat. There was the crunch of buckling metal. Mr Bankole leapt out of his car. He saw the concrete beneath its covering of snow. His jaw sagged. We were already on our toes.

The damage cost my parents and Mr and Mrs Hussain seventy-five pounds each. I had to go round to Mr Bankole and apologise for what I did. Imran went with me. I saw him standing there, looking really upset and I knew he was laughing inside. As we walked away he nudged me in the ribs.

'Abbu has stopped my pocket money for two months. What about you?'

'A month.'

Imran thought that sucked, but he was the one with a councillor for a father. He was supposed to be A GOOD BOY. The smile wasn't long returning. 'Don't you ever tell anybody I said this,' he whispered, 'but it was worth it.'

Four

Chris

4 JANUARY 2001.

A year passed. The snow thawed and retreated until all that was left were a few white stripes on the distant hills. Summer followed spring and we left our home streets behind and went looking for adventure. Imran had discovered a great place behind the trading estate. Just a few minutes from the roaring dual carriageway we had to cross to go to school we could hear birdsong and the city streets retreated so far it was as if they had never existed at all.

We stepped into a different world up there. There were woods and tangles of withered briars, thistles and nettles. Dozens of purple flower heads nodded, reminding us of advancing aliens. There were squares and rectangles of concrete where there used to be buildings. They were knocked down long ago. Every year the weeds and grass reclaimed a bit more. We gave it a name. We called it The Wilderness.

We had a favourite part where a rope swing dangled

over a rubbish-choked stream. We zipped back and forth all summer. The sunlight flickered through the trees turning the world around us into a shadow play. When we were done we would wander down to the lake. Autumn came and rain and falling leaves drove over The Wilderness. That's where, that winter, our friendship was sealed.

The lake had been frozen hard for weeks and the ice still glistened under the watery sunlight. We stood there with our breath misting. Imran liked the ice. It drew him like a moth to a flame. He went right up to the edge of the lake where the ice whitened and formed bubbling patterns. 'I bet you I can walk all the way across to the other side.'

I was appalled at the idea. Mum was always telling me about kids getting drowned playing on the ice. Dad made it a bit racier. He told this story he'd heard about a boy playing ice hockey. He fell through and the current caught him, dragging him along under the ice. His mates could see him staring up at them, screaming as he drowned.

I begged Imran not to do it. 'Don't be stupid. It's dead thin in the middle. That's how kids get themselves drowned.'

Imran thought for a moment. 'You could be right. The middle's too much of a risk.' But that wasn't the end of it. 'Tell you what. I'm going to walk out to the count of ten then I'll come back.'

I tried to talk him out of it, but Imran shrugged and set off across the ice anyway. When he's in that kind of mood he doesn't listen to anybody. I paced up and down, willing him to get off the ice.

He saw me watching. His eyes were sparkling. 'Start counting,' he said.

So I counted. Imran walked. I heard the ice groan and creak. 'Imran, I really think you should come back.'

He looked over his shoulder and started to bounce up and down on the ice.

I begged him to stop. 'Just come back.'

He took no notice. 'Not till you finish counting to ten.'

My heart was pounding. 'You don't need to do this.'

'Yes,' Imran said, 'I *do*.'

I will never forget that look. It wasn't just defiance. There was something self-destructive about him. I would see it again. 'Eight, nine, ten,' I said breathlessly. 'Now come back, you idiot.'

He came swaggering across the ice as if he had all the time in the world, but he wasn't done with the lake yet. He wanted to put my courage to the test. He dared me to go next. 'What's wrong?' he asked. 'Turned chicken?'

I stood at the edge of the lake. All I could think about was the story of the kid who drowned, staring up at the world above through a pane of ice. Imran wouldn't let the idea drop. He started clucking and flapping his arms like wings.

'I'm not chicken.'

'Prove it.'

So that's what I did. I knew it was stupid. I knew it was dangerous. But I did it anyway. I did it because Imran was my mate. I did it for a very simple reason. I did it because he was brave and I wasn't. Each step I took, the ice sheet creaked. 'No counting slowly, OK?' My voice was shaking. 'You've got to do it the same speed I did.'

I put my feet down carefully, willing the ice to take my weight. But I was taller than Imran. Heavier too. The ice groaned. It was telling me to get off. My throat tightened with fright. I could feel the tension in the frozen sheet. I knew it was going to break but I couldn't move. Cracks were appearing under my feet.

'Imran, it's going to go!'

Suddenly he wasn't counting any more. He knew it was serious. He didn't hesitate, not even for a moment. I was numb with terror. He set off the instant he saw I was in trouble. There were two of us on the ice and things were threatening to get a whole lot worse. Imran didn't care. He stepped on the ice and reached out an arm. 'You've got to get off!'

But the noise of the breaking ice had me spooked.

'Can't move.'

I felt Imran's hand strong round my wrist. 'I've got you. Chris. Move. Do it!'

But I didn't move. I couldn't. There was a loud crack and I plunged into the icy water up to my waist. The shock of the cold thudded into me like a baseball bat. I fought for some kind of foothold on the bed of the pool but my trainers were slipping. I couldn't get out and the cold was hammering into me. My legs buckled and water was bubbling into my nostrils.

'Imran!'

Then he had me. All these years later I still wonder where he got the strength from. At nine years old Imran was short and scrawny. The wind could have blown him away. But he was decisive. He didn't think about his own safety for a single moment. He risked everything to save me.

He went out there in the grinding cold, one hand clamped round my wrist, the other round my wheezing chest. The pair of us struggled through the icy shallows, gasping and panting. I was sucking in breaths against the slashing cold. I fell back against his strength and we sprawled side by side on the rutted, frost-hardened earth. The cold punched into my legs but I was on solid ground and it was down to him. I twisted round.

To this day, I don't know why but my first reaction was anger. 'You could have got us killed!'

Imran looked away. 'Sorry man.'

Then I just felt gratitude. 'There's no need to be sorry. I mean, you saved me. You got me out.'

Imran didn't want thanks. 'It's no big deal. It wasn't that deep.'

I was starting to realise just how much I owed him. 'I would never have got out on my own.'

He was riven with guilt. He knew what could have happened. 'I don't know why you're thanking me, Chris. It's my fault you were out there in the first place.' His eyes were afraid. 'I knew you didn't want to go.'

'It's OK.'

I saw something in his eyes, a kind of desperation. That's something I got to know about Imran: he needed people – his parents, Rafiq, Aisha, me – so much more than any of us needed him. 'You sure?' There was something plaintive about those words.

'I'm sure,' I told him.

'I'm an idiot.'

I laughed. 'You got that right.'

We walked home in squelching trainers. Imran was wet. I was wetter. He was cold. I was colder. My jeans hung heavy on my legs. The wet material slapped and clung. I was trembling, my arms wrapped round me, teeth chattering. I never knew people did that in real life.

'I didn't think it was possible to be this cold.'

'Are you going to be all right?' Imran asked. 'You haven't got frostbite or anything? Frostbite is really bad,' he explained. 'Your toes and stuff go black and drop off.'

'Don't be stupid!'

'They do! Imagine if I got you home with loads of bits missing.'

I wasn't sure whether Imran was being serious. 'I hope not. It hurts though. Hurts like hell. Did you see *Titanic*?'

He looked at me as if I'd gone crazy. 'Of course I did. Everybody's seen *Titanic*. My dad read somewhere it's big in Afghanistan.'

I didn't know anything about Afghanistan. 'Leonardo DiCaprio turned blue in that film. Am I blue?'

Imran thought that was funny. 'You're a bit grey.'

When we got home I told him not to come in. For his own sake. Mum was bound to think he had put me up to it. Which he did. Mum liked Imran, but she thought he was a bit wild at times. I was sparing him some serious grief.

From her.

From his own parents.

I sat drying off in front of the TV. I let the numbness ebb from my limbs and watched the news. I was reaching for the remote when something caught my attention. People were throwing eggs at a black limo. I read the banners the protestors were waving.

Lord Help Us.

They had to be protesting about something scary.

'What's that about?' I asked.

Mum handed me a mug of hot chocolate. It was

steaming and the silky, sweet aroma filled my senses. 'That? It's the new American president.'

'Why are people so angry with him?'

Mum shrugged. 'They're always angry about something. That's the way the world is these days.'

I was still curious. 'What's his name, this new president?'

'George Bush.'

There was nothing more to say. 'Can I turn over to *The Simpsons*?'

Chris

17 FEBRUARY 2001.

A few weeks later Imran came round. His eyes were wide and he was gasping for breath. He'd been running.

'What's the matter with you?'

He was hopping from one foot to the other. 'You've got to come with me.'

'What's wrong?'

'It's an emergency. It's a matter of life and death.'

He'd found a dog in The Wilderness.

Not a person.

A dog.

'I thought you were scared of dogs.'

'Abbu always says they're dirty. But it's hurt. There's all this blood on its leg. If we don't help it, it's going to perish.' That's the word he used.

Perish.

He peered over my shoulder. 'Is your mum in?'

'No.'

'Your dad?'

'No, I'm on my own.'

'Good.' He was in a hurry. He had a dog to save. 'You can help, Chris. Quick, boil a kettle.'

'Can I get some stuff?'

'Of course. Help yourself.'

He grabbed some cotton wool balls out of the jar in the bathroom. He shoved a tube of antiseptic in his pocket. He rummaged in the cupboard under the sink and tore off a big sheet of tin foil. He folded it and slipped it inside his jacket. 'Do you know what you're doing?'

'No. You?'

'No.'

I locked up and we carried the kettle to The Wilderness. Carefully. By the time we got to the dog, the water was cooling. Imran dipped the cotton wool balls in and started cleaning away the dried blood. It had glued the dog's damaged leg to the frozen ground. Imran's patient was a little black and tan terrier with huge, scared eyes. The dog was trembling the same way I did the day at the lake. And there was Imran again, sorting things out. He cleaned away the frozen blood and the dog started trying to lick him. The tiny, flicking tongue darted out. Imran pulled away. He didn't like the idea of getting licked, but he giggled anyway.

I smiled. 'He's saying thanks.'

Imran didn't answer. He was over the giggles and busy concentrating. He kept wiping away the dirt and the blood until the wound was clean. He was gentle.

'You should be a doctor.'

Very carefully, he touched the damaged leg.

'I don't think there's a break. He would make more noise if there was.'

'What do you think happened?'

Imran shrugged. 'Most likely a car's hit him. He must have crawled here from the main road. I think he's been here all night.'

'So what's the cooking foil for?'

Imran wrapped the dog in it.

'You're not going to put him in the oven!'

Imran gave me daggers. 'Don't be stupid. I'm keeping him warm. I saw it on TV. It helps if you've got hypothermia.'

I wanted to know hypo-what? Sometimes I think Imran swallowed dictionaries whole.

He explained. 'It's what you get when your body temperature is really low.'

I was impressed. 'How do you know all this stuff?'

Imran shook his head. 'How do you *not* know all this stuff? I read, Chris. You should try it sometime.' He picked the dog up and carried him gently in both arms. The dog kept trying to lick Imran all the way home. We were turning into our street when I noticed the nametag on its collar.

'Hey, he's called Lucky.'

Imran didn't think the dog had been very lucky.

Imran kept Lucky for two days. Mr Hussain said the dog couldn't come in the house so they made a place for him in the garden shed and wedged the door open so he could come and go in the small yard. Aisha helped Imran make some posters and they tied them on lamp posts in the nearby streets. He finally tracked down the owner. The postman had heard about an old lady who had lost her dog. One Wednesday night after school me and Imran walked the three streets to one of the old folks' bungalows near school. Fully recovered, Lucky trotted along beside us.

'I bet you're going to miss him.'

'Of course I am,' Imran said, 'but he isn't mine. Besides, Abbu doesn't want a dog.'

He knocked and the old lady appeared. The moment she saw Lucky she squealed with delight. She hugged him while his little pink tongue fluttered round her ruddy cheeks.

'Where did you find him?' she asked.

Imran explained how he had discovered Lucky in The Wilderness. I filled in the details, how he had cleaned away the dried blood and put antiseptic on the leg and wrapped him in tin foil.

'Like a Christmas turkey, only we didn't cook him.'

Imran glared at me. Maybe that wasn't the right thing to say.

The old lady was called Mrs Neal. She had eyes that smiled when she was speaking. She gave us a chocolate biscuit each. She offered us money. Imran refused it so I did too. As we walked away, she called after us.

'You can come and see Lucky any time.'

'I'll come every week,' Imran told her. His parents wouldn't let him have a dog so he was excited about the invitation. 'Or is that too much?'

'Come round whenever you like,' Mrs Neal said. 'I'll look forward to it. So will Lucky. Promise you won't forget.'

Imran kept his promise. He went every week just like he said. He's loyal like that.

Five

Chris

16 MAY 2001.

We had our good times, but there were bad times too.
No matter what happened Imran was true as steel. One
evening we were walking home from football practice. It
was a mile and a half, but the weather was fine and we
were busy talking about the latest transfer gossip. We
turned the next corner and Imran stopped dead. I followed
the direction of his stare. It was a group of boys. They
were older than us. They were all white and they weren't
interested in me. They were staring at Imran. One of them
stepped forward. He was the leader of the gang. I think
he was about twelve. He held out his hand, palm up as if
he was expecting us to give him something.

He snapped his fingers. 'Have you got your passports,
boys?'

Imran frowned. 'What are you talking about?'

'You're crossing my turf, Abdul.' He was smirking. 'I'm
Link, by the way, Jack Lincoln. Some people call me the

46

Missing Link.' His mates started giggling behind him. 'But you can call me Sir. It's like this. You've got to show your passport if you want to cross our turf.'

Imran's eyes went hard. 'My name isn't Abdul.'

'Don't talk back to me, Paki boy,' Link said.

Imran wasn't about to back off. 'My name isn't Abdul and I don't let anyone call me Paki.'

The smile drained from Link's face. 'Your name is whatever I say it is. Paki!'

I wanted to put out the flames before they turned into a fire. 'Look, we don't want any trouble.'

Link looked round at his mates. It was four onto two. Bad odds.

'Now there's me talking to Batman and Robin chips in. Here's a piece of good advice. Butt out, Robin.'

I could feel Imran bristling next to me. Things were going to kick off.

'We just want to go home.'

'Yes?' Link was playing to his little crowd. 'Well tough.' His gaze flicked from me to Imran. 'You a reverse coconut or something?'

I didn't know what he was talking about.

'He means you're white on the outside and brown on the inside,' Imran told me.

Because I was mates with an Asian kid.

'That's right, Robin. Now, here's the way I see it.' Link took a step towards Imran. 'We've got ourselves a big-mouthed Paki.' Then he turned and pointed at me. 'We've got ourselves a Paki-lover, too.'

So that's what it was all about. I tugged at Imran's sleeve. He shrugged me off. Oh great, I thought, he's fixing to take them on. On his own, if necessary.

'Don't be stupid, Imran. There are four of them. Let's go.'

I started backing away. Imran hesitated for a moment, then followed suit. But it was never going to be that easy. Link gestured to his mates. They started to outflank us. There was no point trying to reason with them. I looked for an escape route.

Link caught my eye. 'You can go if you like.'

I couldn't believe my luck. 'Really?'

'Yes, off you go.'

I started walking. So they were just winding us up. Then I heard Link's voice. He had his hand on Imran's chest.

'Oh no,' he said, eyes narrowing. 'This one stays.'

Imran did his best to hide his feelings. 'Do as he says, Chris. There's no point both of us getting a kicking.'

'Aw, did you hear that?' Link sneered. 'Abdul doesn't want his girlfriend to get hurt.'

I started to go. I took one step. Two. Then I heard scuffling behind me. They had Imran against the wall. I half-turned and saw them laying into him. There was only one thing I could do. I turned and gave Link a shove. 'Get off him!'

Link burst out laughing. 'Want to play the hero, do you?' He butted me in the face. 'Now clear off!'

I reeled back holding my nose. They got Imran on the ground. All four of them were booting him in the ribs. He was lashing out, trying to get them off him. I stumbled forward.

'Leave him alone!'

Link turned. 'You again.'

I saw the way he was looking at me. More by instinct than anything I crashed my head into his face, returning the compliment. After that the world exploded. There was shouting. Pain. The sky spun. Link was on top of me, raining blows down on my face and chest.

How long did it last? A minute. Two? It felt like forever. When they were done they stood gobbing on us. I could feel it running down my face. There's something about spit. It's not just the gluey wetness on your face. It's the shame. It cuts tracks deep inside you. I could hear them laughing as they walked away.

Imran tapped me on the shoulder. 'You OK?'

One of his eyes was puffy and his lip was swollen.

'Your face is a mess.'

Imran shrugged. 'So's yours. But what's new?' He prodded at his teeth with his thumb, one by one.

'Did you lose one?'

Imran shook his head. 'I think it's a bit loose. Rafiq says you just press it back in.'

'How does he know?'

Imran chuckled. 'How do you think?'

'This kind of thing's happened to him?'

'Of course it has.'

'When?'

'A few months ago. It happens. But Rafiq's had more trouble with aapnay than with racists.' Aapnay. Our people. I grew up with this stuff. 'It's mostly a guy called Majid.' He looked at me. 'Did nobody ever tell you about this?'

I was starting to understand that I had lived a pretty sheltered life. Imran explained a few home truths. 'Some white guys get their kicks beating up Asians.'

'Why?'

'How should I know? Ask them.'

'And it still goes on?'

'Not like it did. Abbu says it used to be really bad round here. You must have heard of Paki-bashing.'

I hadn't. My ignorance made me feel pretty stupid.

Imran looked at me as if I had just grown fins and crawled onto land. 'My grandad got attacked a few times. These days we don't take it like his generation did.' He laughed. 'Plus there are more of us now.' He pulled a packet of paper tissues from his pocket. 'Ammi said they'd come in handy. She wasn't kidding. You want one?'

I took the tissue and cleaned off the blood. But it was the spit that bothered me. I could still feel where Link gobbed on me, sticky tendrils of humiliation on my skin. Weeks later, when I remembered that night, I would still be able to feel it.

Imran dabbed at his nose. 'Hey, look at that. We still bleed the same colour.' He cleared his throat. 'This proves we are blood brothers.'

He offered his hand and pulled me to my feet.

I grinned. 'I like that.'

That evening it felt like me and him against the world.

Chris

7 JULY 2001.

The warm nights of spring turned into the hot nights of summer. We were shooting baskets in Imran's yard. Rafiq fixed a backboard and basket on the wall for us. Imran did a jump shot. The ball dropped in sweetly.

He danced round. 'You lose. Loser, loser, loser.'

I told him to quit showing off. 'So you're good at basketball. Big deal.'

'I'm better at football too. And cricket.'

I grabbed him round the neck. 'Yes, but I can wrestle you.' Imran started to howl so I let him go.

He rubbed his neck. 'Fine, so you're better at fighting, you big gorilla. Remember when you butted that Link kid?'

'Yes, and he butted me harder.'

The back door opened. It was Imran's mum. My mum was with Mrs Hussain.

'What's up?'

'It's time to go, Chris.'

'But it's only seven o'clock.'

'Just come home, OK? No arguments. Please.' There was something in her voice. And her face.

Mr Hussain appeared.

'Why's Chris got to go, Abbu-ji?' Imran asked. 'What did we do wrong?'

'It's not you. There's going to be trouble.'

I didn't understand. Neither did Imran.

'What kind of trouble?'

'Fascists,' Mr Hussain answered. 'We don't want extremists in this town. The council told them not to come. They took no notice. They wanted to stir up trouble. Now they've got it.'

Worry was etched on Mrs Hussain's face. 'Where is Rafiq? I hope he is not getting involved.'

Mum smiled sympathetically. 'I'm sure he'll be all right, Fozia. He's a sensible boy. Come on, Chris.'

I could still hear Imran protesting as Mum opened the front door. Half a dozen Asian lads ran past. They were pumped up about something. They vanished into the dusk until they were only blurs in the distance.

'Chris. Come inside.'

I followed her in. Reluctantly. The night promised excitement. 'What's going on?'

Mum pulled a face. 'All sorts. There was a demonstration in town.'

I had all kinds of questions. She didn't have many answers.

'Mr Hussain says there are fascists. That's Hitler and stuff, isn't it? This sounds pretty big, Mum. They started World War Two. We did it at school.'

'I don't think it's quite the same,' Mum said indulgently. 'Look, I don't want you worrying. This isn't World War Three. There were a few hooligans hanging round the pubs in town. Groups of Asian lads and some other protestors started to gather to confront them. There was a bit of shouting and fighting. I wish they would all just go home.'

'They're not going to, are they?'

Mum went over to the window. Strange flashes were staining the darkness scarlet and gold. There were loud thumps and more flashes.

'No, I think this is just the beginning.'

My eyes strayed to the street outside. 'Is that what's happening now? They're all fighting with each other?'

'No. The hooligans went home hours ago. They got what they wanted. The trouble is between the Asian boys and the police now. Your dad called on his mobile. He says it's all kicking off. There's a car showroom burning. He's seen lines of riot police.'

I felt a rush of panic. 'Is Dad going to be all right?'

Mum took my hands to reassure me. 'He's on his way home. Don't worry about your dad.'

It was another hour before Dad made it home. He was agitated.

Mum wanted to know what was happening.

'I worked my way round the worst of it,' he replied. 'I could see the flashes of the petrol bombs.'

I stared wide-eyed and waited for him to explain.

'They're milk bottles with petrol in them. The thrower shoves a cloth wick in the top and sets fire to it.'

'So it blows up?'

My parents looked at each other. They didn't want to have this conversation. They didn't want Dad coming home through a riot. They didn't want me to know about such things. 'When it hits the ground it does. It showers people with flaming petrol.'

'That's terrible,' I said.

But exciting.

'I ask you,' he says. 'Molotov cocktails. On an English street.'

That night I watched from my window. The main action was three or four streets away. Occasionally shadowy figures would appear, silhouetted against the firelight. The shouting echoed under a starlit sky. I was nine years old and I watched the place where I had grown up being consumed by flames. I suppose I found it more exciting than scary. It was the firework party I had missed. But the night of fire was only the beginning. As the summer of 2001 turned to autumn my life, and Imran's, changed forever.

Six

Chris

1 FEBRUARY 2011. 10.22 A.M.

I said things were simple then. I look around me at the regimental colours snapping in the breeze, then at my comrades in their desert-issue uniforms. In my hand I have a mobile and a text that says there's a bomb. That's simple enough. Either Imran is playing a grotesque game, some kind of black propaganda, or hundreds of lives are in danger. How the hell did I end up here, on this parade ground, with this kind of responsibility?

There was a time when I trusted Imran with my life. We didn't think about our friendship. We didn't talk about it. We didn't need to. It was there the way the air is, the way the sun is. It was a fact of our existence, like our homes and families, something so permanent and true we didn't have to examine it or explain it.

Now it is a name on a phone and a message as blunt and monstrous as gunshot. Or a bomb.

I think about the effect of an explosion in this crowd.

I try to imagine the impact of the shockwave, the heat, the torn, twisted shards of metal. How did it ever come to this?

Imran

7 JULY 2001.

There were footsteps on the landing. Imran scrambled down from the window from which he'd been watching the running battles outside. Burning with curiosity, he padded across the room. Rafiq was there. His hand was gripping the doorknob. The smell of smoke hung on his clothing. He registered Imran's presence and turned.

'Do you have to sneak up on people, you little creep?' His voice sounded strange: part croak, part whisper. There was a smudge of soot on his face.

There was a knot in Imran's stomach. 'What's wrong, Rafiq?'

Somebody stirred. Rafiq gripped Imran's elbow and spun him round. He shoved him towards his room. 'Get in there. I don't want Abbu to start on me.'

Imran felt a rush of alarm. 'I know something's wrong. What have you done?'

'Get in there.' He gave Imran a push. 'Ammi and Abbu will hear you.'

'Hey, you're hurting!'

'Look,' Rafiq said, elbowing the door shut behind him, 'here's the deal. There's been some trouble.'

'I know there's been trouble,' Imran said. 'I've been watching it all night from the window.'

Most of the time he hadn't seen much at all. The front line was a few streets away, tantalisingly out of sight. Only occasionally did the rioters stray into view. But Imran had heard it. The thump of the bottles. The thud of stones against shields. The clatter of the mounted police as they moved to confront the young men massing in the darkened streets. For half the night, firelight flared behind the curtains.

'Everybody's talking about the riots. There were bombs.'

Rafiq stared at him with big, startled eyes. 'Keep your voice down, Imran!' He leaned closer. 'Not real bombs, you lulloo, not like in a war. They were petrol bombs.'

'What's the difference? They explode, don't they? That makes them bombs.' The moonlight caught Rafiq's face. Imran saw the worry there. Now he understood. 'You were part of it, weren't you?'

Rafiq started nodding then he ran his fingers through his hair.

'What happened?'

Rafiq swallowed. 'Things got out of hand. Everybody was pumped up. We were angry about those goons. It was the thought of them strutting through the streets, abusing us. It made us crazy, man. Most of them were from out of town. The fascists were taunting us. If they were trying to get a reaction they succeeded. We were all pointing at them and yelling. That's when the police moved in. They went for us.'

'Why did they do that?' Imran asked. 'You said the fascists were the ones causing trouble.'

'Try telling that to the police. They had riot shields, crash helmets, the works. I mean, we were giving as good as we got, but it felt like the Feds wanted confrontation as much as we did. Some of the mosque committee came out trying to calm things down, a few of the councillors too. It didn't work.' He paused. 'I saw Dad down there.'

'Did he see you?'

Rafiq shook his head. 'No, I kept out of sight. You know what he's like. If he'd seen me he would have lost it. The eldest son is supposed to be a prince.'

'But you didn't come home?'

'No.'

'What did you do, Rafiq?'

He turned away. Shadows stole across his face. 'I didn't do anything.'

'You said you were there.'

'What's with the third degree, Imran? Give me a break. I was there, that's all. I was in the crowd. It's like this. You kind of stop being yourself. The moment you join the crowd you're part of something bigger. It eats you up. I was the claws of the beast.'

Imran frowned.

'What I mean is, I did what everybody else was doing.'

'Were you throwing things?'

'Don't be stupid!'

The answer was too quick, too angry. Imran smelled a lie. 'It's two o'clock. Where have you been till now?'

Rafiq stalked to the door. 'Running mostly. They had mounted police. You don't argue with a man on horseback. Don't tell anybody, especially Abbu.'

'What if he asks me?'

'He won't.'

'But if he does?'

Rafiq looked desperate. 'You know nothing. You say

nothing.' He made a zipping gesture across his mouth. 'Promise.'

It was a while before Imran answered. 'OK, cross my heart. I promise.'

It was only after Rafiq had gone that Imran realised he didn't know anything anyway.

Next morning the stench of burning was still in the air. It was the same aroma Imran had smelled on Rafiq's jacket. He came across a burned out car less than a hundred yards from his front door. The road was littered with broken glass, stones, half-bricks. He looked around and wondered what Rafiq had got up to the night before. Did he throw any of those stones? Did he hurl the bottles? Ghosts seemed to flicker around the wreckage. Imran's skin prickled. He remembered what Dad said once. Actions always have consequences. Life will find you out.

Imran saw Chris staring at the scene. 'It looks like a war zone.'

His words disturbed Imran. Everywhere he looked there was evidence of the troubles. The debris left by the riots was a reminder that Rafiq had come home late. What had he done?

His fears for his brother came out as irritation. 'Don't exaggerate, Chris.'

Chris looked confused. 'Who's exaggerating? Just look around you, Imran. Dad took an hour to get home last night. He said it was terrifying.'

'What do you expect us to do, Chris? It was self-defence.' He had to stick up for Rafiq. 'The police turned on the crowd. Racists came to cause trouble and the police turned on the local lads. They charged on horseback. Where's the justice in that?'

Chris said that wasn't how his dad saw it. 'He read out the newspaper report. It said three hundred police officers were injured.'

Imran lost his temper. 'What about our side? They got hurt too! Five-O were lashing out with batons. They were cracking heads.'

'How do you know? You weren't there. You were already in bed, same as I was.'

Imran's neck burned. He couldn't say too much. On account of Rafiq. 'I've heard people talking.'

'Which people?'

'Just people.'

There was a long silence before Chris spoke. 'My dad says the rioters are being stupid. They're destroying their own area. Did you know they burned a car showroom last night? It was Asian-owned. What's that about? Those people weren't racists or policemen.'

Imran repeated something he had heard Rafiq say. 'It wasn't meant to be that way. Things got out of hand.'

Imran joined the crowds standing around after Friday prayers. The mood was one of shock. All the talk was about the riots. The older men shook their heads and muttered about the price the community would have to pay. Dad was with Imam Nawaz. The Imam had spoken at length about the riots. He had told the worshippers that violence breeds violence. He said that they would not love God until they loved one another. They should spread Salaam. Islam was nothing if it was not an act of love.

There was little evidence of peace or love outside the

mosque. Debris littered the street. Council workmen were brushing it up. Imran turned back to his father and Imam Nawaz. The two men were shaking their heads as they surveyed the scene.

You don't know, Abbu-ji, Imran thought. You are shaking your head, but you don't know where your eldest son was. You must never know. The councillors and the mosque committee were calling for calm and reconciliation. Some of the rioters had already given themselves up to the police. The euphoria of battle had given way to a sober reckoning. The police wanted the names of everyone who had fought them on the front line. Imran sought out Rafiq.

He whispered a question. 'Did you see the posters?'

The police were circulating requests for information. The posters and leaflets showed the faces of the rioters. There were twenty mug shots on each one. Imran was there when the young men crowded round and peeled away one by one. Some wore looks of relief. Others came away knowing they were about to pay a heavy price for their defiance. They had seen friends in the police brochures ... or themselves.

Rafiq finally answered Imran's question. 'I saw them. My face is not there. Alhamdulilla. Praise be to God.'

Imran had another question. 'So is it over?'

Rafiq dropped his eyes. 'I don't think so. There will be more posters. The police had cameras.' His breath caught in his throat. 'I am scared, little brother. We took a stand. I swear, we did it for the right reasons.'

Imran looked at some of the discarded leaflets lying at their feet. 'The police don't see it like that.'

Rafiq tousled his brother's hair. 'You're right. The

newspapers and the police treat us like criminals. Suddenly we're all looking over our shoulders, wondering who will be next. It wasn't meant to be like this. Everybody is afraid. This is bad, really bad.'

Imran didn't want things to be bad and definitely not really bad. He said what was in his heart. 'Do the police have your picture? You must tell me if they do.' He had tears in his eyes. 'I couldn't stand it if you had to give yourself in.'

Rafiq tried to reassure him. 'I would tell you if I could. I saw the police filming. There were officers with camcorders. In the heat of the moment I didn't even think about it. I don't know if I'm on any of the footage. Imran, I just can't say.' He gazed at the heavens. 'This is horrible. I can't think about anything else.'

Imran glimpsed his father out of the corner of his eye. 'Don't say any more. Here comes Abbu.'

He looked as weary as Rafiq. 'The word is the police are going to come down heavy on the rioters.' He ran his hand through his hair the way he always did when something was bothering him. Rafiq had the same mannerism. 'Our parents spent years establishing ourselves in this country. We work to create respect. Then something like this happens. A moment's loss of control and now there are boys from decent families walking into police stations to give themselves up. Promise you will learn this lesson, both of you.'

Imran was the first to speak. 'I promise.'

Rafiq took longer. 'Of course, Abbu-ji.'

Dad had the reassurance he wanted. 'Let us find your mother and Aisha. It is time to go home.'

*

Next day Chris dropped his bombshell. 'I hate those stupid riots. My parents are talking about moving.'

Imran stared back. Had he heard right? 'They can't! I won't let you go.'

Chris could hardly speak. 'I don't think there's anything we can do. It sounds like a done deal.'

'Where will you go?'

'Only across town, but that's far enough.'

Imran felt sick. First it was the worry about Rafiq. Now this. The thing that made life worthwhile was his family. And Chris. 'This is crazy. We've got to do something.'

'Like what?' Chris asked.

Imran was stuck for words.

Chris put on a brave face. He gave Imran a playful poke on the arm. 'Cheer up. Nothing is decided yet. They'll get over it. When things settle down they'll forget all about it.'

It sounded to Imran as if he was trying to convince himself. A week ago everything was fine. Then his world had caught fire.

'No, you watch,' Chris said, 'it'll die down. They'll forget all about it.'

That's what they did. As the days ran into weeks, there was no more talk of moving. Imran managed to convince himself that Chris was right. The school year ended and they had a carefree summer. They went swimming. They played football and cricket. The long games stretched late into the evening. They headed home with a big, red sun hanging over them and silhouetted figures bobbing in the distance. For Imran, the days were punctuated by trips out, the call of the muezzin, the distant tolling of a church bell.

There was no more trouble like the night the gang had jumped him and Chris. Imran was growing up. He knew the places he could go and the places that were out of bounds. Some days he accompanied Chris on long walks through The Wilderness. Swarms of flies hung over the lake and the stream. Bees flitted lazily to and fro, cutting zigzag patterns in the heat haze. One August afternoon they kicked off their shoes and went running through the grass. Chris was cautious. Not Imran. He raced ahead, feeling the warm earth underfoot and the dry grass prickling between his toes. It felt good. He was free. He careered down a slope and Chris shouted a warning.

'What if someone nicks our shoes?'

'Then we go home barefoot.'

'If you stand on rusty metal and you get blood poisoning and die, your parents will yell at you.'

Imran laughed. 'If I stand on rusty metal and die, it won't matter.'

There was a Mela that July, a festival of music and dancing. There were floats and costumes. The slogan was One City, One People, One Mela. The organisers wanted to show that the city was about more than riots. But the first court cases were just weeks away.

Imran
11 SEPTEMBER 2001.

The summer holidays came to an end. Soon it was the second week of school. There was a display about the Mela in the main corridor. In one of them Imran was on stage with Chris. They had joined in with the dancers. All the other kids pointed and laughed. They were starting year five. They were making Viking longships. That morning they were gluing milk bottle tops to the hulls. It was hard to get enough of them for the whole class. Lots of families bought their milk from the supermarket in plastic cartons.

The teacher, Mrs Bradshaw, was checking how everyone was doing. The teaching assistant, Miss Aziz, was booting up the computers. The kids who finished first were going to do some research about the Danish invaders. Imran wanted to be in that group. He loved computers.

Imran said Chris's name. Chris turned round and Imran dabbed a blob of glue on his nose. Chris wiped it away with a paper towel.

'Knock it off, you.'

Chris wasn't really angry. He was already planning ways to get Imran back. Imran was about to say something when he heard Miss Aziz gasp. Heads turned. She told the kids around her to get on with what they were doing. There was a buzz of anxiety in her voice, as if she'd seen something disturbing. Once she thought the pupils had their heads down she called Mrs Bradshaw over. Together they stared at the screen. Imran leaned to one side to see what they were looking at. It looked like a computer game. He jabbed his elbow in Chris's ribs.

'Are they watching a movie?' he asked.

'Don't be daft,' Chris said. 'Teachers don't watch films in class. They'd get the sack.'

'Well, they're finding something interesting.'

Mrs Bradshaw looked over her shoulder and shushed them.

'What are you watching, miss?'

She stood back from the screen so the whole class could see. 'You can have a look one group at a time. If there's any pushing you will have to sit back down again.'

'What is it, miss?'

'There's been an air crash. A plane has struck the World Trade Centre.' She saw the blank looks. 'It's a big building in New York – well, two big buildings.'

Imran wanted to know if the World Trade Centre was bigger than the Empire State Building.

'Yes Imran,' Mrs Bradshaw answered, 'even bigger.'

Only the adults understood the significance of the images on the screen, maybe not even them. Mrs Bradshaw was trying to listen to the commentary. 'They said it was an air crash at first. Now they're talking about a terrorist attack.'

Imran said what he was thinking. 'It just doesn't look real.'

Miss Aziz answered. 'Oh, it's real. Horribly so.'

After that, Mrs Bradshaw kept the computer on all day so she could follow developments. There was non-stop coverage of the events. By the time afternoon lessons started there was no talk of accidents. Everybody knew what was happening. America was under attack.

News kept filtering through. By home time everyone knew that two aircraft had crashed into the twin towers of the World Trade Centre and another had come down in a field near Pittsburgh. Yet another had hit a place called the Pentagon. Imran was puzzled. Wasn't that a shape in the maths corner? Both of the twin towers had collapsed in an enormous cloud of grey smoke. It was hard to take in. But this wasn't a movie. It was for real. Suddenly a world that had always seemed so solid and permanent was crumbling before their eyes.

Chris's mum always picked Jess up so the boys walked back with her.

She told them it was definitely a terrorist attack. 'The north tower has collapsed. The south tower fell earlier. It's awful.'

'But who did it?'

Mrs Hook shook her head. 'I don't know, Imran. I just don't know.'

That night Imran called on Mrs Neal. Chris tagged along. They passed a group of older boys. One of them shouted Imran's name. Imran glanced back to see who it was and ignored him.

'He said hello,' Chris said.

'Yes,' Imran answered, 'and I ignored him.'

'How come?'

'That's Majid. He's trouble.'

Chris wanted to know how Majid was trouble, but Imran was in no mood to explain. When they got to Mrs Neal's front door he rang the bell. She didn't answer right away. He flipped the letterbox.

'Are you all right, Mrs Neal?'

They heard her voice and Imran started to relax.

'Is that you, Imran?'

'Yes, I've got Chris with me.'

The chain rattled and a bolt slid back. Imran swapped glances with Chris. She wasn't usually this cautious. It was another thirty seconds before her face appeared.

'Hello lads. Do you want to come in?'

Lucky scampered up the hall behind her.

'What's with all the security, Annie?'

'Some boys have been hanging around,' she explained. 'They just stand across the road watching the house. It's not just that.'

'What then?'

'Oh, I've been nervous ever since the riots. I know I'm a silly old woman but it doesn't take much to scare me. I've lived here for a long, long time and I've never seen anything like that.'

They followed her down the hall.

'Isn't it awful about New York? The world is going mad.' She waved the boys through the door. 'I think I'm going to stop watching the news. It's always bad. Do you want some orange juice?'

'Yes, great.'

'And some biscuits?'

'Wouldn't say no. You buy great biscuits, Annie.' Imran winked at Chris. 'She gets me these great coconut ones.'

The boys followed her into the living room. They were surprised to see packing cases. 'Are you going somewhere?'

Annie patted her lap and Lucky jumped up. 'I've been meaning to talk to you, Imran. My daughter doesn't think it's safe for me to live on my own. There have been a lot of break-ins lately. You hear such things.'

'Where are you going?'

'Lauren's found me sheltered accommodation a bit nearer to where she lives.' She scratched Lucky's ear. 'It's hard for her to get down here all the time because of her job. I think it makes sense to be a bit closer.' She glanced at the window. 'Look, I'm not judging anybody but I was very scared during the riots. At my age you just want some peace and quiet.'

Imran felt a knot in his stomach. He wanted to know when she was going.

'Next Wednesday.'

His stomach turned over. He'd got used to calling in to see Lucky. 'That soon?'

'It's for the best.' She met his eye. 'I want to ask you a favour. I want you to have Lucky.'

He looked at the little dog. 'Isn't he going with you?'

'They don't allow animals. I do hope you can take him. I don't want him to go into a home. Or worse.'

It was a few moments before Imran realised what she meant. 'You wouldn't have him put down!'

Tears welled in Mrs Neal's eyes. 'That's why I want you to have him. Do you think it's possible?'

'I'll ask my parents the moment I get home.' He couldn't make any promises but he was determined to win them over. He'd make it possible.

Imran's mum said yes to the dog. Which was a surprise. Maybe it was because her mind was elsewhere.

'He is one of God's creatures,' she said. 'We wouldn't let him get put down. You still can't have him in the house.'

Imran fell over himself to agree. 'He stayed in the yard last time. He can be a guard dog.' The world's smallest guard dog. He stared at his mother. She seemed distracted. She just stood resting her hands on the sink, gazing out into the yard. It hadn't even been two years, but it seemed a long time since they had all watched the millennium fireworks together and saw the coloured lights climbing into the winter sky.

'What's wrong?'

'Something happened this afternoon.'

The back of Imran's neck prickled. 'What was it?'

Rafiq and Aisha were at the table eating roti and daal. Rafiq was listening in on the conversation. He seemed to be biding his time, waiting for his moment. Aisha carried on eating. She'd decided to leave the explanations up to Mum.

'Forget it,' she said. 'I shouldn't have said anything.'

Imran was worried. 'Something bad has happened,' he said. He looked around. 'Is it Abbu?'

Mum smiled. 'Don't be silly. Your father is still at work. It's nothing like that. Have something to eat. There is nothing to worry about.'

Rafiq chose that moment to say his piece. 'If you don't tell him, I will. He should know the way the gora think.'

'That's enough, Rafiq. I want you to respect my decision.'

Imran was fighting back the tears. 'Please tell me.'

Aisha was the one who spoke. 'You and your big mouth, Rafiq. Look what you've done now.' She turned to her mother. 'You'll have to tell Imran now, Ammi-ji. You know what he's like. He's only going to worry.'

Mum sighed. 'Maybe I'm making too much of it. It's like this. I was on the bus. The seat next to me was empty. There were three people standing.'

Rafiq chipped in. 'They didn't want to sit next to Ammi.'

Imran examined the faces of his mother, brother and sister. 'I don't get it.'

Rafiq spelled it out. 'They saw an Asian woman in a scarf. They saw it as a threat.'

'A headscarf can't hurt you.'

Rafiq pulled a face. 'Tell those morons.'

Mum nibbled at her bottom lip. 'They treated me like a leper. It was the look on their faces. I'm a Yorkshire girl. I was born in this town and they treated me as if I was an alien.'

Rafiq had heard the story once. It didn't stop him being equally angry the second time round. 'What do you think of that? Terrorists fly a plane into a building in New York and these people won't sit next to a woman on the bus! That's not all though, is it?'

She gave a shake of the head. 'As I was getting off, one of them told me to go back to Pakistan. I told him I was born here. That's when he said something to me, a filthy word.'

Rafiq clenched his fists. 'I wish I'd been there.'

'And what would you have done?' Mum asked, her eyes flashing. 'Do you think it would do any good if you started a fight? When did violence do any good? You would only get arrested.'

Rafiq caught Imran's eye. Imran saw something in the look. He imagined the glow of flames on his skin and the smell of burning on his clothes. He was scared for Rafiq.

Aisha stopped eating. 'How can they think she's responsible for something like that?'

Rafiq's face was angry. 'They're ready to blame any Muslim.'

Mum was annoyed with Rafiq. 'That's enough. It was just a few narrow-minded bigots.'

Rafiq got up and shrugged into his jacket. 'Are you sure about that? What if those three were the honest ones?

I bet they're not the only ones who think like that. I'll see you later.'

Mum wanted to know where he was going.

Rafiq headed for the door. 'Out. I need to get some air.'

Imran ought to have been feeling good about Lucky. But some people had crashed four aeroplanes. The shock wasn't just being felt in America.

Imran

MARCH 2002.

The first court cases were getting underway. Rafiq had started to beat his father to the evening paper. He went straight to the court reports. He read them from start to finish. Sometimes he would return to the paper later, scrutinising every detail a second time just to be sure.

'Did you see this?' he cried after a forensic examination of one report. 'Sabir Khan's got two years. He didn't do anything!'

Dad glared over his glasses. 'He must have done something, Rafiq. He was involved in violent disorder. I was there that night. There was so much rage. Our young men were out of control. We tried to persuade them to go home, but they wouldn't listen to us.'

There was the usual drawing of swords.

'They wanted to stop the racists.'

'The troublemakers had already gone by this time. This wasn't about standing up to racists. It was about relations between our young men and the police.'

'But they gave him *two years*, Abbu. For throwing stones.'

Dad treated Rafiq to that sceptical stare of his. 'It wasn't just stones, was it?'

Rafiq's eyes ran down the columns of newspaper print. There were other names he knew: Haris Ahmed, Sadik Ibrahim, lads he had known all his life.

'These sentences are crazy!'

This time Dad agreed. He was training to be a magistrate. 'You're right on this issue, Rafiq. If a football hooligan did a similar thing he would probably get no more than community service.'

There was horror in Rafiq's eyes. This could so easily be him. 'This is political. The courts are sending out a message. They're telling us we must know our place.'

Dad remained calm, measured in his response. 'The verdicts are very harsh. I spoke about it at the Labour group meeting. We are going to make representations ...'

Rafiq burst out laughing. 'Representations! What are you going to do this time, send a strongly worded letter?' He wagged his finger mockingly. 'That will have the judges trembling in their boots.'

Imran watched his father's expression. Rafiq wasn't showing him proper respect. Dad was just managing to keep a lid on his temper. 'There will be a letter, yes, and much more. We will gather evidence and put our case. That is how you get things done, not by running round the streets goading the police.'

Rafiq was angry. 'Is that right? You're always so *reasonable.*'

There was the same dogged answer from their father. 'If they had listened to us, there would not have been a riot. Two hundred families would not be living in fear right now.'

Rafiq got to his feet. 'If we had listened to you and the mosque committee, the fascists would have been left to run amok in our streets.'

'They were a handful of idiots, Rafiq. If our boys had ignored them, they would have gone away.'

'You think? If you lie down, people walk all over you.'

Dad folded his arms. 'Sit down, Rafiq. Let's discuss this calmly.'

'Calmly!' Rafiq shook the paper in front of his face. 'Do you not see what they are doing? They are trying to turn us all into criminals.'

The argument continued for some time then Rafiq stormed out. Dad grumbled about his behaviour. Imran knew what lay behind Rafiq's show of rage, even if Dad didn't. He was scared.

Seven

The White Leopard

'The Crusader armies are raining their bombs down on the Muslim lands,' the speaker, Arshad explained. 'They call it Operation Enduring Freedom.' He waited a beat. 'What freedom? The imbecile Bush loves to talk about freedom and democracy. Does he not understand that democracy is haram? It is forbidden in Islam. Democracy is idolatrous.' He pointed his finger upwards. 'It does not allow for one God to rule mankind, but allows human beings to decide their destiny. Remember what Bush said after the martyrs struck their blow in New York. He vowed to hunt down and punish those responsible. It was always going to come to this. The kuffar, the non-believers, have launched their attack on Afghanistan. They demand the sheikh's head on a plate but he was ready for them.'

At the mention of Bin Laden people burst into applause. At that moment I knew that I had crossed a threshold.

'This is the man who broke the Soviets' hearts when

they launched their war on the Afghans. The sheikh has thwarted their desire to parade him in the American courts by melting away into the mountains. Bush promised to bring his followers the head of Osama bin Laden. Did he deliver?'

No, the audience rumbled.

Arshad nodded approvingly. 'They will not find him now.' He pointed to the TV screen. 'America has unleashed its fury. Here it is, the great bullyboy of the world, backer of Israel, exporter of McDonald's, globalisation and imperialism, puppet-master of Arab dictators, pouring down fire on the heads of the innocents.

'Let them search for their Muslim terrorists,' he continued. 'They will be disappointed. Why will they be disappointed?' He allowed the question to hang. 'Because such a thing does not exist. They will find only resistance fighters. Is it not the duty of all Muslims to support their brothers in Palestine, Bosnia, Kashmir, Chechnya and the Philippines? In the face of overwhelming odds, when the soldiers of the Muslim states are held back polishing their rifles in their barracks, can it be wrong for the fighters to undertake martyrdom operations?'

Arshad's delivery was quick and authoritative. He had everyone sitting on the edge of their seats, hanging on his every word. It was as if he knew each and every one of them. He understood their grievances. Most of all he sensed their fury. Somehow, he spoke to me too, even though I was so very different from those around me.

'It is not just in the Muslim lands that we face the wrath of the kuffar,' he declared. 'Look what happened in this city.' His finger stabbed the air. 'Yes, brothers,' he repeated, 'this very city. Almost two hundred people were charged with riot, fifty with violent disorder. For what? For defending the Muslims in their homes! Do you want to know the meaning of British justice? The courts have handed out two hundred jail sentences. How many young men does that represent? It is maybe one fifth of those who came onto the streets that night to confront the enemies of Islam. The sentences add up to six hundred years.' He leaned forward and dropped his voice. 'Here is the key question: how many racists were convicted?'

Some members of the audience anticipated the answer.

'That's right. None. We will not have justice until we establish the worldwide Muslim state, the khilafah. We will not have law until the flag of Islam rises over Downing Street.'

Arshad concluded his speech to loud applause. I started to shuffle towards the exit. I had attended the meeting on the strength of a leaflet handed to me at the college canteen. I who am nothing wanted to be someone. But I was too different. This wasn't for me. As I left the meeting two men who had been acting as stewards confronted me. 'Do we know you, friend?' one asked, hostility dripping from his lips.

The raised voices attracted Arshad. I told him I wanted to help. Arshad examined me with a clinical stare. 'How do you wish to help?'

My heart thumped. 'I'm not sure. I hoped you would tell me.'

There was pleading in my voice. I could hear it. The man on my right tried to bundle me away but Arshad stopped him with a slight shake of his head. I tried to explain.

'I have been alone too long. I am too unimportant, too weak.'

I explained how, in the milling crowds of the city I was a small worm. In that audience I felt like a great lion. The stewards started to laugh. Arshad silenced them with a snap of his fingers.

He pondered my words for a few moments. 'A lion?' He closed down the laptop he'd used in his presentation. He studied the screensaver for a second, then looked up at me. 'I have a better name for you, my friend. I will call you the White Leopard.'

Eight

Chris

1 FEBRUARY 2011. 10.24 A.M.

When you lose your home you lose part of yourself. I'm fortunate. When I look at the regimental colours, when I see the comrades who fought alongside me, I realise that I have had two real homes in my life. Oddly, neither of them are the semi-detached house on the edge of town. That's where I put my head down. That's where my parents live. Somehow, because of the circumstances of the move, I never felt as if I belonged there.

My first home was the squat terraced house where I spent my early childhood. The second was every fly-blown patrol base in Helmand where I dropped exhausted onto a bed. That probably sounds crazy to most people. Cent would understand. So would Nugget. My comrades are my cause. My comrades are my home.

I have all a man needs, a sense of home, identity, belonging. But from the day I left the street, from the day they banged Rafiq up in prison, from the moment his father turned in on himself, I honestly think Imran lost everything. In some strange way, he became homeless.

Chris

11 NOVEMBER 2002.

They were the words I didn't want to hear. I was jogging upstairs when I caught Dad's voice.

'Look Carol, if we're going to move, we might as well do it now.'

Mum was a while replying. Maybe she was going to put Dad straight about what was best for the family. This was my home. I didn't want to live anywhere else.

'I think you could be right, Steve.'

I sat down on the top step.

Mum finished. 'Chris is in year six already. He's growing up fast. If we move now we can get him into a good high school. Jess is fine. She doesn't have the same attachment to this place. I think she's quite excited about moving to be honest. Thanks to Brownies, she's got friends all over town.'

Dad fastened on her words with undiluted glee. 'That's decided then. We start looking tomorrow.'

Tomorrow.

I felt my gut clench.

Dad went on and on.

'I tell you, Carol, I've been restless for a while now. I want us to make a new start.'

I couldn't hold myself back any longer. I burst into the living room, choking with frustration. 'Is that it? When were you going to tell me? When the bags were packed? I bet you've told Jess.'

It took a moment for Dad to answer. 'I think you need to lower your voice, son. Who exactly do you think you're talking to?'

'Don't make us move, Dad. Please. I won't be near any of my friends.'

Dad didn't care what I said. 'You'll make new ones.'

'It's not that big a deal,' Mum said. 'You will still be living in the same city. You can stay in touch.'

Dad didn't seem so sure. He wanted to make a clean break. He would never forgive the city for making him drive home from work staring anxiously at the arc of petrol bombs through the evening air. He had always been comfortable in his own city. After that night he would never feel the same.

Something occurred to me. 'If we move, which high school will I go to?'

Dad saw where the conversation was going. 'We don't know until we find the right house. Don't worry, it will be a good one.'

My heart hammered. I could see what was coming. 'But I'll be at the same school as Imran?'

'Maybe, maybe not.'

I felt sick. 'So it's not about moving across town at all! You're cutting me off from my best friend.'

Mum was trying to calm me down. 'Don't go on, Chris. This is a great opportunity for the family. We'll be able to afford a proper garden. The house will be bigger so there's more room for you and Jess.'

But I didn't care about any of that. 'I don't want more room. I'm fine the way I am. I want to be with the friends I've known all my life.'

In her own way, Mum was as determined as Dad. 'You've got your mobile. You'll be able to call Imran any time. I can drop you off whenever you like. Or Dad can run you.'

'But I don't want to go! What's wrong with where we live now?'

Dad finally spoke his mind. 'You want to know what's wrong? I'll tell you, son. Rioting is what's wrong. Trouble-makers chucking bottles at the police is what's wrong. It's only a minority of troublemakers, but the press make a big deal of it. Put this postcode on a job application and they'll toss it straight in the bin. Once a place gets a bad name, it sticks. What kind of future do you think you'll have round here?'

'What about Rafiq?' I protested. 'He's got an offer from Newcastle University. Living round here hasn't stopped him.'

'The Hussains are a good family,' Dad answered. 'There are a lot moving in round here who aren't made of the same stuff.'

I tried to protest but Dad put his foot down. 'Listen son. There's no point going on. We're not going to change our minds. We've got to do what's right for the family. The moment we find the right house, we're moving. End of story. Now go and get your homework done.'

I slunk away defeated. I didn't sleep much that night.

Chris

Me and Imran were sitting on the bollards. Lucky was at our feet. Mr Bankole's face appeared at the window from time to time but he didn't come out. Lucky barked and wagged his tail at the same time.

Imran knew something was wrong. 'Spit it out,' he said.

'Come again?'

'Whatever's on your mind. Come on, cough.'

I decided I might as well come right out with it. 'We're moving.'

Imran's shoulders sagged. 'It's the riots, isn't it? Abbu says a few other families have moved out – not just white, Asian too.' When I didn't answer, he said it again. 'It *is* the riots, isn't it?'

I nodded. Since the night of fire and broken glass the strands linking my family to the neighbourhood had been fraying one by one. Each blazing petrol bomb burned another link.

'Yes, the riots are part of it. Then there's people like him over there.' There was a sapphire blue Subaru Impreza parked opposite. Dad had been pointing out the cruising vehicles for a few weeks. The driver was talking to a group of teenagers.

Imran saw who I was looking at. 'You mean Majid.'

'Yes. My dad's got a notebook. He keeps a record of everything he sees happening. He's talking about calling the police.'

'Your dad doesn't still trust Five-O, does he?' Imran had started hating the police. He was beginning to sound like Rafiq. He watched the driver working the crowd. 'Majid thinks he's the big man because he's selling a few kilos of heroin and making thirty k.' There it was again, Rafiq talking. 'Look at all that bling. All he needs is a gold tooth.'

Majid saw Imran looking and winked. He rolled a toothpick from one side of his mouth to the other. Imran spat through his teeth and looked away. Majid burst out laughing and said something to the lads surrounding the car. They turned to look.

Imran had a word for Majid. 'Scum.'

Majid heard. He was meant to. 'You got something to say to me, little boy?'

Imran got up off the bollard. 'Let's go, Chris.'

Majid shouted after Imran. 'You're Rafiq's brother, aren't you?'

Imran frowned, stopped, turned. 'So what if I am?'

Majid leaned on the vehicle. 'Tell him I want to talk to him.'

'I'm not your messenger.'

'Tell him.'

'There's no point. Rafiq isn't interested in anything somebody like you has got to say.'

'Somebody like me?' The same superior smile lingered on Majid's lips. 'You might be right. Well, this is the message anyway. He's going to listen whether he wants to or not. Tell him he'd better watch his back. The word on the street is he's been badmouthing me. Your big brother had better put a lock on that mouth of his. You hear? Make sure you tell him.' He raised his voice. 'Tell Rafiq Majid's looking for him.'

Imran's face was a mask. How was he keeping his cool?

This guy made my flesh crawl. The moment we got round the next corner Imran let out a long, shuddering breath.

That was when I realised it was all an act. 'So you *were* scared?'

Imran rolled his eyes. 'Of course I was scared. I was bricking it. Rafiq must know what he's doing. Inshallah.' He changed the subject. 'So when do you move?'

'I'm not sure. Soon.'

'Next week? Next month?'

'Yes, something like that.'

'Rubbish, isn't it?'

I caught his gaze. 'Yes, rubbish.'

Lucky wagged his tail. Goes without saying. Rubbish.

Imran stuck out a fist. We bumped knuckles. Blood brothers. We set off in silence. Everything had been said.

Chris

14 NOVEMBER 2002.

Not everything was rubbish. Two days later Imran had a tale to tell. Majid finally caught up with Rafiq. The details poured out on the way to school. 'Majid rolls up in his flash motor. He's cruising with his gora mates.'

I reminded Imran that Majid wasn't the only one with gora friends.

'Nah,' he said. 'It's not the same thing. You've lived here all your life. You're sound, white boy. These guys are real boneheads. Now, do you want to hear the story or not?'

'Yes, I want to hear it.'

'Majid stops the car and gets out, right. No salaams,

nothing. He wants to get right down to it. He says he's going to kick Rafiq's head in for calling him a drug dealer.'

'But he *is* a drug dealer.'

Imran gave me a pitying look. 'He's not trying to clear his name. That's not why he was after Rafiq. It was about reputation. It was about losing face. Can I finish the story?'

'Go on.'

Imran finished the tale. 'Well, Majid comes over. He's sticking his chest out all macho. Big man. Hard man. He waves Rafiq forward. You want a piece of me?'

'And?'

'I'm coming to it. This is tension, innit? Rafiq isn't interested so it's down to Majid. He marches up fast and throws a punch, real sudden like, but Rafiq isn't there any more. He's quick as lightning, dodging out of the way. Then his fist crashes into Majid's face. Poum. The scumbag's nose is gone, man. It's like a squashed tomato. Rafiq follows up with a combination. Poum. Poum. Majid's rocking.'

'You saw this happen?'

Imran shook his head. 'I know people who did. I got reports. Next thing you know Majid's bent double. He's like this.' He mimicked Majid. He was leaning over protecting his head with his hands. 'There's sick dribbling from his mouth.' He put on a whining voice. 'He's all: *Lay off, Rafiq. No more, Rafiq.*'

I liked the story. Everybody wants the bad guys to get what's coming to them. 'I wish I'd seen that. What happened next?'

Imran was beaming. 'Rafiq drags Majid over to his gora mates. He tells them: throw this piece of rubbish on the dump where it belongs. He humiliates him in front of his crew. I think we've heard the last of Majid.'

Bad call.

Imran couldn't have been more wrong.

Chris

16 NOVEMBER 2002.

The following Saturday I was having a sleepover at Imran's. It must have been three or four in the morning. There was a loud crash and heavy footsteps came pounding up the stairs. I was in the camp bed by the window. Imran was in his own bed, so he was first to the door. He peered into the corridor. 'It's the police.'

I scrambled out of bed and watched over Imran's shoulder. The police looked huge in their dark overalls and helmets. Shouts threshed around the walls of the cramped house. The noise was deafening. Three officers were pinning Rafiq's arms. He was wearing shorts and a T-shirt. Rafiq struggled ferociously until he saw Chris and Imran staring from the doorway. The fight went out of him.

'It's all right,' he panted. 'I'm not going to resist.' His face twisted with pain. 'You're breaking my arm!'

The nearest policeman told him to shut his mouth.

Rafiq acknowledged the warning with a compliant nod. 'I'll come quietly. Just go easy, yeah?' His eyes pleaded with me and Imran to return to the room. 'Go back inside, you two. There's nothing to see.'

Mr and Mrs Hussain were at the end of the landing.

They were comforting each other in the doorway of their room.

Rafiq finally met their eyes. 'I'm sorry.'

The senior police officer told him he was being arrested for riot and violent disorder and Mrs Hussain started to sob. After that, everything was like a dream. Mr and Mrs Hussain exchanged words in Urdu so the police couldn't eavesdrop. The police were going through Rafiq's things. Soon after – it's hard to say how long – Dad appeared.

'You're coming home.'

There were no protests from me. I wanted to go. In their overalls and helmets the police were like something out of a movie. They looked like an occupying army.

Dad put his arm round my shoulders and sat me down on the sofa next to Mum. 'Are you all right?'

That was the first time I realised I was crying. I saw my hand. My fingers were trembling. Mum made a mug of hot chocolate. I sipped it, trying to break through the early morning cold. I looked around.

'Where's Dad gone?'

Mum patted my arm. 'He's gone next door to see if there is anything he can do.'

Dad was back in a matter of minutes. He reported on what he had seen. 'Mohammed is on the phone arranging a solicitor. Fozia is distraught. God, what a mess.'

Mum made tea for her and Dad. 'I just don't understand why it's taken so long to make an arrest. I mean it's eighteen months since all that trouble. I thought it had blown over. I didn't see him in any of the photos.'

'I asked Mohammed about that before he left,' Dad told her. 'It seems somebody passed Rafiq's name to the police. They had CCTV footage showing him throwing a bottle.

It wasn't very good quality. That's why they didn't publish the photograph. They hadn't been able to put a name to the face until now.'

'So it was an informer?'

'Sounds like it. They think they can build a case on his evidence.'

Mum brought in two mugs of tea. 'It's such a close-knit community round here. I wonder who turned Rafiq in.'

I drank my chocolate. It wasn't hard to work out.

Chris

17 NOVEMBER 2002.

The conversation round the breakfast table the following morning didn't come as a surprise. Dad had a bundle of property magazines. 'That's the last straw. We're moving. The sooner the better.'

'You know I want the move too,' Mum said, 'but I don't see how last night makes any difference. Rafiq is a fine young man. He's never put a foot wrong until now. Steve, we've known him all his life. Don't get things out of proportion.'

'I've nothing against the Hussains. Mohammed and Fozia are good people, the best.' He drained his tea and wiped his mouth with the back of his hand. 'But Rafiq's got in with a bad crowd. They're losing the young ones. I don't want Chris mixing with the wrong sort.'

I couldn't believe what I was hearing. 'Do you mean Imran? What did he do?'

'Chris is right,' Mum said. 'Imran's only a lad. He hasn't done anything wrong. Steve, you can't tar every young person with the same brush.'

Dad didn't look at either of us. 'Imran follows Rafiq like a sheep. It's only a matter of time before he goes the same way.'

'Steve,' Mum snapped, 'don't say another word.'

Dad backtracked under pressure. 'I'm just saying the kids are getting out of control. I don't want our Chris growing up in the middle of all this.'

It was time for school. I left the house with a heavy heart.

I knocked for Imran as usual. He seemed different somehow.

Subdued.

I struck up a conversation. At least I tried to. 'Have you heard from Rafiq?'

'They've charged him.' Imran could hardly speak. 'People have been getting two years for what he did. It's scary.'

I told him he was worrying himself over nothing. 'He won't get that long. He was only throwing things.'

Imran wasn't convinced. 'Yes, but he was fighting the police. They come down on you for that.'

Chris asked a question. 'It was Majid, wasn't it? He grassed Rafiq up.'

Imran nodded. Of course it was. 'We should have known he was going to get his own back. Why don't the police go after the bad guys? All Rafiq did was lose his temper with a few lousy racists and throw a few stones.'

'I thought it was a bottle.'

'OK, a bottle. That's not the point. Drug dealers go free. It isn't fair.'

I tried to think of something to say that would make it better. The words didn't come. The important ones never do.

Imran wasn't finished. 'Everybody is really worried. Rafiq could lose his place at uni over this.'

'You're kidding! But he's done all that work. Could he really lose his place?'

Imran nodded miserably. 'That's what Abbu says.'

He didn't make it through the day. He was so upset that Miss Aziz had to sit with him outside the head's office until his mum came to pick him up. I walked home alone. It was a taste of the future.

MARCH AGAINST
WAR WITH IRAQ
in London and around
the world.

Nine

Imran

1 FEBRUARY 2011. 10.25.

The Lexus is picking up speed. Rafiq breaks the silence. 'It's not far now.'

Imran looks round. The barracks occupy a large area on the edge of the city, just off the main route east. It is an area of post-war suburban houses standing in a grid system of broad, tree-lined avenues. Imran wonders out loud what will happen if the police don't listen.

Rafiq grunts. 'We've got to make them.'

Signs for the barracks have started to appear and there's a knot in Imran's stomach. With every second the threat comes closer. The bomber is there, within those walls, preparing. His brothers will hail him as a shaheed, a martyr.

Rafiq checks his mirror and accelerates. 'Anything from Chris yet?'

Imran shakes his head. 'Nothing. Maybe we didn't have such a great friendship after all.'

Rafiq tells him to stop feeling sorry for himself. He wouldn't let anyone else talk to him like that. Imran owes Rafiq. It isn't too much of an exaggeration to say he owes him his life. They went after him: the police, the courts, scum like Majid. No matter what life threw at him, he stood up for what he believed. But a man who sticks up for himself attracts enemies.

He stands tall and falls far.

Those years could have destroyed Rafiq. But he stayed strong. He's the strongest person Imran has ever known in his life. So many times Rafiq has been the rock on which he stood, the man who was both brother and father. Whenever Imran was in trouble, Rafiq was the one he went to.

Imran remembers the big fight. Rafiq had promised to take him on the Stop the War march in London.

Imran

14 FEBRUARY 2003.

Dad pounded the table. 'You are not going to London, Rafiq.' He pointed at Imran. 'And you are not dragging him along with you.'

Imran protested that he had to go. He wanted to stop the war.

Dad was dismissive. 'You are eleven years old. What can you know of such things?' He turned on Rafiq. 'Do you see what you are doing? Do you see how he copies everything you say and do? Stop putting ideas in the boy's head. He is a child.'

Imran hated the way Dad spoke about him as if he wasn't there.

Rafiq was angry. 'But you keep telling us you're against the war, Abbu. Bush and Blair attacked Afghanistan. Now it's Iraq. They're killing Muslims. Why do you want to get in my way? It's my duty to go.'

Dad was incensed. 'It is your duty to stay out of prison, you young fool! Look at your mother. The worry is destroying her. Do you want to break her heart? In this house you will show respect. Don't you see where your defiance has got us? I can't lift my head up in the street.'

'So that's it. You're worried about *your* standing in the community,' Rafiq shouted. 'I'm the one who's going to do time. I'm the one who'll rot in prison. It's not about you.'

Dad let out a growl of fury. 'Don't ever talk to me like that! When did I ever put myself before my children?'

Rafiq had gone too far. A pained silence then: 'I'm sorry Abbu-ji.'

Dad waved the apology away as if swatting a fly. 'Everything I do, I do for this family. You listen to me, Rafiq. You have a court case coming up. It will decide your future. What if there is trouble in London? Have you even considered that possibility? Think about your studies. What if you get yourself arrested? How do you think that's going to play with the jury?'

Mum put in a word. 'Your father is right, Rafiq. What about university? What about all your hopes and dreams? Do you want to ruin your life? It is only one day.'

'This is not about one day, Ammi-ji,' Rafiq cried. 'It is about the future. The Americans and their puppet Blair are going to wreck millions of lives in Iraq and Afghanistan.

Are you asking me to stand by while that happens?'

Dad was adamant. His sons weren't going. 'Others will be marching, Rafiq. There will be many tens of thousands on the streets of London, possibly hundreds of thousands. Your presence will make little difference. Think of yourself. There are many ways to make your views known. By your actions you could destroy this family.'

Rafiq looked round for support.

Finally, Aisha spoke. 'Don't look at me, Rafiq. You know my opinion of this war. I will be in London with my friends. Nobody is asking you to change your views or give up your principles. We all love you so much. Your freedom is the first priority. Just wait until the court case is out of the way. Then you can do anything you want.'

Rafiq was bitter. 'What's the point? Everybody knows I'm going to prison anyway.'

Mum sat next to him and took his hands. 'Why do you talk like this, Rafiq? Are you trying to hurt us? It is your first offence. Your teachers have given excellent statements about your character. Your solicitor says that if you plead guilty you will get a suspended sentence, maybe just community service. All you have to do is express regret for what you did.'

'I am prepared to show remorse for throwing things,' Rafiq said. 'That's the only apology I will make.'

Dad scowled but held his tongue.

Rafiq spat his defiance. 'I will not apologise for opposing the racists. I will not say sorry for standing up for my community. Just because I fight injustice, that doesn't make me an extremist. I will admit to this, and this alone. I wish I had never picked up that bottle. When everybody is running and shouting you get swept along. I never

94

understood how easily that can happen. Will you forgive me, Ammi-ji?'

Mum embraced him. Suddenly she was crying. So was Aisha. Imran managed to hold back the tears. Big boys don't cry.

Dad alone showed no emotion. Somehow he stood aloof. Even when he made his last plea to Rafiq it sounded like a sermon. 'We will support you no matter what happens. We know you did not go out that night intending to hurt anyone. You are young. You made a mistake. The court will listen to what you say. I ask only this: do not go to London. Trust the law, Rafiq. I know this country. We have a good case. You will not go to prison.'

Imran seized on his father's words. He was desperate to believe them. His family was being pulled apart in front of him and it made him so frightened for the future. Mum was stroking Rafiq's cheeks and looking pleadingly into his eyes. Her face was shining with tears. 'Tell me you will obey us in this.'

Rafiq gave in. 'I will stay.'

Imran

15 FEBRUARY 2003.

Imran accompanied his father to the mosque to wave Aisha goodbye. Rafiq stayed away. The buses were drawn up along the pavement waiting to leave. There were so many people milling around: Asian, black and white. Imran read the posters that people had sellotaped to the window.

George Bush, world's number one terrorist.
Tony Blair=Liar
No War.
Not in My Name.
Dad told Aisha to be careful.

'Don't worry,' she said. 'There won't be any trouble. Just look at all these people. It's going to be massive. This is a people's revolt.' She embraced them both. 'If we all blew at once the Houses of Parliament would fall right over. They would topple right into the Thames. Nothing can stop us. You'll see.'

As the buses started pulling away Imran looked up at his dad. 'I've been feeling really bad since Rafiq got arrested. Seeing all these people, I feel better. Everything is going to be all right isn't it? Promise it is.'

Dad smiled. 'Rafiq is being very responsible. He has good legal advice. Yes Imran, everything is going to be all right.'

'And the war?'

'If the people take to the streets in great numbers, the government will have to listen. This is a democracy, Imran. When the people are united, they are unstoppable. The government will have to go back to the United Nations. A way will be found to resolve the matter. It won't come to war.'

He was wrong.

A month later bombs were falling on Iraq. Imran watched it all on TV. He heard the crump of the explosions. He watched the red flashes in the night. Rafiq pointed to the screen.

'Two million people marched against this. Still they

don't listen to us. It's all down to your Mr Blair. Do you still think you know this country, Abbu?'

Imran hated the images. He felt humiliated. All those people marched. There were so many it seemed impossible that they would be ignored. But the war was going ahead anyway.

What would it take to make the government listen?

Imran

22 MARCH 2003.

The question came up again when Imran was round at Chris's house. The TV was on. He saw the same bombs. He heard the same loud cracks and bangs. But the interpretation of events was very different. Mr Hook was there.

He said there were two sides to every story. 'Saddam Hussein is a dangerous man, Imran.'

Imran was confused. All he could see were the bombers in the sky. All he could hear were the explosions. Sometimes it was as if he was right there on the ground in Baghdad. He gazed up at a sky on fire. He felt the ground shudder beneath his feet. At that moment he was an Iraqi.

He didn't know what to make of Mr Hook. What was wrong with him? Everybody Imran knew was against the war. 'You don't think the war is right, do you?'

Mr Hook tilted his head this way and that as if he was weighing up the pros and cons. 'I wouldn't go that far, Imran. I'm no politician. I do know it's not as black and white as some people think. Our newspaper says Saddam's a modern Hitler. Did you know he gassed the Kurds at a town called Halabjah?'

Imran listened patiently before answering. 'Rafiq says the ordinary people living in Baghdad didn't gas anybody, Mr Hook. The bombs don't ask if you are for or against Saddam. Many people who hate Saddam are also against the war.'

Mr Hook was uncomfortable arguing with an eleven-year-old boy. 'Is that right? You seem very well-informed.' He gave a crooked smile.

'It's true,' Imran told him. 'I've met them. There was a big meeting—'

Mr Hook interrupted him. 'Saddam's police torture people, Imran. They kill them. He's destroyed the lives of three hundred thousand people. You can't justify that.'

Imran wondered why Mr Hook seemed to be blaming him for it. 'I don't.'

'So maybe it's right to get rid of him. The way I see it, the Americans should have finished the job last time, in the first Gulf War. Saddam invaded Kuwait, his fellow Muslims. This president's father was in charge then. He could have marched on Baghdad but he let Saddam off. He could have saved us all a lot of trouble.'

'I don't know about any of that that,' Imran admitted. It was news to him that there had been two Gulf Wars.

Mr Hook was trying not to get into an argument. 'I thought the bombers had guided missiles, you know – smart bombs. Technology has changed a lot since World War Two.'

Chris tried to get Imran to drop it.

Imran ignored him. 'They call it Shock and Awe. That

doesn't sound very smart. That sounds like they're giving it all they've got.'

'Maybe, but—'

Imran's dad was bound to tell him off if he heard he had interrupted an adult, but he couldn't help himself. 'Rafiq says there will be thousands of civilian casualties.' At the mention of Rafiq's name, Mr Hook's expression changed.

'What's happening with Rafiq?' he asked.

Imran repeated what Abbu had told him earlier. 'We're waiting to hear. Everybody has given him a good statement. The solicitor says he will get community service. The worst that can happen is a suspended sentence. We're feeling much better about the case.'

Mr Hook frowned. 'Are you sure, Imran? They've given out some pretty hefty sentences. They're not treating this as mere hooliganism.'

Mrs Hook heard what he'd said and cut him dead with a stare. 'I'm sure the solicitor knows more about the law than you do, Steve.'

Imran's face crumpled. In that moment all his worst fears come flooding back. Tears stung his eyes. He remembered all those other cases, the ones Dad used to read out day after day. The house of hope Imran had built brick by brick came crashing down.

Mrs Hook was furious with her husband. 'Look what you've done.' She slipped her arm round Imran's shoulders. 'It's going to be all right, Imran. I promise. If Rafiq is telling the truth he's got nothing to worry about. I'm right, aren't I Steve?'

'Yes. Yes, of course.'

Imran stammered a few words through the sobs. 'He is pleading guilty. That will make it better.'

Imran saw the sympathetic faces around him.

'It will, won't it?'

They smiled, but they couldn't bring themselves to say yes.

Imran

MAY 2003.

The boys were halfway through their tests. They were walking home.

'Easy, wasn't it?' Imran enjoyed school. It took his mind off his worries.

Chris was quiet. Imran saw the expression on his face. He'd said the wrong thing.

'Chris?'

'I didn't finish the paper.'

'You're kidding!'

'I didn't get any of the problems at the end.'

Imran asked which ones and explained how to break them down. Chris's face fell as he realised how badly he'd messed up.

'It's all right for you, Imran. All this stuff comes to you naturally.' He dug his hands in his pockets. 'I just don't see patterns. I'm rubbish at maths. My dad will kill me.'

'No he won't.'

Chris's face twisted in misery. 'He will, you know. He wants the ideal family. His son the doctor. His daughter the lawyer.'

'Sounds like Abbu too.'

'You're dead clever, Imran. That's the difference. It could happen for you.'

Nothing Imran said was going to help. He kept quiet.

Eventually Chris spoke. 'You know what makes it worse? Our Jess is just like you. She's good at everything. My sister is Little Miss Perfect.'

'Is that what your dad says?'

Chris booted an empty drinks carton along the pavement. 'He doesn't have to. It shows in his face. I'm a big disappointment. I'm the family thickie.'

Imran gave him a shove. 'I bet it isn't as bad as you say.'

Chris didn't respond. As they turned the corner into the street Imran invited him in. 'It'll give you time to get over the grumps.'

The moment they walked in the house Imran became the one with the grumps. Mum was watching BBC 24. President Bush was standing on an aircraft carrier. He was wearing a zipper jacket and he had that smug look on his face. He was claiming victory. There was a banner behind him announcing *Mission Accomplished*. 'In the Battle of Iraq, the United States and our allies have prevailed.'

Imran stared at the scene. Their side had won. His side had lost. 'Come on, Chris. Let's go round yours for a bit. I've heard enough.'

They knew they should have stayed where they were. There was a bottle of wine on the table. Jess was asking if she could have a taste. The boys swapped looks.

Mrs Hook smiled. 'Just a sip.'

Jess grimaced and shook her head.

Mr Hook turned. 'Oh, hi lads. How was maths?'

Imran caught Chris's eye. 'It was so-so.'

'Yes,' Chris said, taking his cue from his friend. 'So-so.'

Chris's dad didn't push for more information. His mind was elsewhere and that rang alarm bells.

'What's the wine for?' Imran asked. 'Are you celebrating something?'

Mr Hook raised his glass. 'We certainly are. We've got the house. We exchanged today.'

Ten

Chris

3 SEPTEMBER 2003.

That was the day it finally sank in. I shrugged into my new blazer, knotted my tie and set off for the bus. My uniform still had that straight-out-of-the-carrier smell. The High School was five stops down the busy main road. I was late but I just caught the bus at the entrance to the estate. I glanced back at the house. My new home was a three-bed detached property on a quiet close.

I had been there for two months but it still felt unfamiliar. My eyes still stung when I compared it to the old neighbourhood. It looked open and airy compared to the narrow streets where I had grown up. When I think back – this sounds stupid – I see a world with too much sky. It's as if people didn't belong there, just houses and cars. Years later the word home still conjures the cramped terraced streets on the edge of the city centre.

I missed the old community with its hustle and bustle, its halal butchers, its mosques, the stores selling saris and shalwar kameez, its barbershops. There was nothing on the new estate, and I mean nothing at all. It was soulless. It was a ten-minute walk to the nearest row of shops, though most people drove to Tesco or ASDA, even if they only wanted to do the lottery or pick up a newspaper. Suddenly almost everything the family did involved a car ride.

As I boarded the bus I couldn't help wondering what Imran was doing. Starting my new school without him felt wrong. We still played football at the all-weather five-a-side pitch once a week. Most Saturdays we met in town. It wasn't the same. I don't know why, but it just wasn't. Only last year we'd attended the same school, played out in the same streets, shared the same hopes and dreams day in, day out. Late at night we would send texts.

Wuu2?

Nuttin.

Me 2.

That we could still do, but there was no nipping next door on a whim. There had been a time when we could read each other's thoughts. It was getting so we weren't even on the same wavelength when we met.

As I boarded the bus, I could only see two empty seats. One was next to an old lady. She had her bag covering half the seat next to her. The other space was next to a lad my own age. He'd been at the bus stop as I came panting up. He was wearing the same school blazer. I slid in beside him, taking care to look straight ahead. I was surprised when he started talking to me.

'Don't you live across the road from us?'

'Yes,' I replied. 'We moved in a few weeks ago. Have you been living there long?'

'A year,' he says. 'I'm Joe, Joe Latham.'

'Chris Hook.'

'So people call you Hooky, I suppose.'

'Yes, they do.'

Outside the family, there was only one person who didn't. That was Imran. I was always Chris to him. Joe pointed out a girl about the same age three seats in front. She had long, blonde hair and the most vivid blue eyes. Her suntanned face was dotted with freckles. 'That's my dorky twin sister Kelly.'

She heard him say her name and stuck out her tongue. He did it back. 'I'm five minutes older.'

Kelly was talking animatedly to her friends. I liked what I saw.

'You didn't get those tans in England,' I observed.

'We just got back from a fortnight in Turkey,' Joe answered. 'Have you been?'

I shook my head.

'Where did you live before you moved here?' Joe asked.

I told him.

Joe rolled his eyes. 'Must have been a bit like Turkey living there.'

'What do you mean?'

Joe laughed, not in a good way. 'You know, Allahu Akhbar.'

I felt disloyal letting the comment pass unchallenged. 'Was it hot out in Turkey?'

'Roasting. Where did you go?'

'Nowhere this year.'

Joe nodded, thought, moved the conversation on. 'Do you box?'

I told him I played football. 'I'm in a five-a-side team.'

A frown. 'Football's all right but you should give boxing a go. You don't rely on anyone else. It's you and your opponent. It's like being gladiators. I can introduce you to the coach if you like. Charlie's always looking for new talent.'

'I don't know. Maybe.'

'It's on Wednesdays.'

Football was on Thursdays. So it was possible. Joe seemed all right. 'I'll think about it.'

'What year are you in?'

'Seven.'

'Me too.'

'Cool.'

It was. Cool.

That night my mobile rang. It was Imran. I didn't get to say hi. I didn't get to say anything at all. Imran's voice sobbed out.

'Rafiq is going to prison,' he cried. 'They didn't listen to a thing he said. Chris, they gave him four years. *Four years!*'

An hour later I was lying on my bed. I laced my fingers behind my head and studied the ceiling. Dusk gathered and I watched the odd headlight wash across the smooth white plaster. I was angry with Dad, with what he'd said. I needed to talk after Imran's call, so I'd told him about Rafiq. I'd expected him to be sympathetic. I couldn't have been more wrong. He agreed with the judge.

'Rafiq must have done more than he said. You don't get four years just for throwing stones.'

'It was a bottle.'

'Yes,' Dad replied, 'and what was in the bottle? Don't

forget three hundred policemen got injured in the riots.'

That was the start of the quarrel. What did Dad know? I stormed out of the room. I would never let this stuff come between Imran and me. But I knew it already had. I lay there wondering how people can be friends so long then drift apart so quickly. How did it come to this? I crossed the room to my laptop and brought up Imran on MSN.

What's on your mind? You OK?

It was a few minutes before he replied. *Not really*.

It blows. How's Rafiq?

What do you think? He's lost his university place, everything.

Do you want to talk? Properly. Not here. Not on the phone either. What about Saturday? Then I remembered. We were going to a wedding, one of Mum's cousins. I felt bad but I had to change it to the Saturday after.

Yes, that would be cool. Where?

The bollards. Eleven o'clock.

Chris

13 SEPTEMBER 2003.

The bollards. I'd been there a few minutes when Imran came striding down the street. Lucky raced round him in ever widening circles, yapping and jumping up, then he saw me. His ears twitched as he ran me through his doggy database, then he ran forward and leapt into my lap. I tousled the untidy fur that made him look like a very small mad professor. I fought off the wildly flicking tongue. I managed to calm the little dog down long enough to look across at Imran sitting on the next bollard. His face was blank. It was as if something had broken inside him. We were eleven. Nearly twelve.

Too young to be broken.

'Have you been to visit Rafiq yet?'

'Last weekend.'

'How's the family?'

'Not good. The solicitor made it worse. He promised us Rafiq would get away without a prison sentence. We went into court thinking he would walk free. Abbu has changed. He doesn't want to be a councillor any more.'

'What happened?'

'He resigned as soon as he heard the news. People have tried to change his mind but he won't listen. I don't know why he's got to beat himself up over it. It was a stitch-up.'

'What did the judge say?'

Imran stumbled through his reply. It came in snatches. 'It started fine. He said Rafiq had a flawless character reference. He said he didn't go looking for trouble.' He took a ragged breath. 'He thought it was good that Rafiq said sorry to the police.'

'So how could he give him four years? I don't get it.'

'It goes like this,' Imran said. 'He says he's going to give Rafiq a tough sentence to send out a message. He wants to stop other people doing the same. Rafiq calls it victors' justice.'

'What does that mean?'

Imran shrugged and pulled a chocolate button from his pocket. Lucky started to tremble with excitement. 'Watch this.'

He told Lucky to sit. He put the chocolate drop on

Lucky's nose. Lucky was whimpering and long trails of saliva spilled from his mouth.

'Wait for it.'

Lucky scratched at the pavement with his claws.

'Wait.'

Lucky stared at the chocolate drop and drooled.

'Wait.'

Lucky was quivering with such intensity I thought he would explode. Imran took pity on the poor mutt.

'Take it.'

Lucky tossed it into the air, swallowed the chocolate drop and started nosing at Imran's pocket.

'You can have another one later,' Imran told him.

He pounded me on the shoulder blade.

'Let's go.'

'Where?'

'The Wilderness.'

We stood by the lake. 'Did this place get smaller, or did we just get bigger?'

It was a magical place when we were little. Already, after such a short time it looked shabby. Litter-strewn and overgrown, it was disappointingly ordinary.

'Honestly Chris, you've only been gone a few months.'

'I know. It's just …' I watched the birds wheeling over the trees. What was I expecting? A world that was an ocean, trees that were a petrified forest, a friend who was a hero? Whatever I was looking for, I didn't find it. 'Forget it.'

Imran threw a stick for Lucky.

I laughed. 'The stick is bigger than the dog.'

'There's something I didn't tell you,' Imran said. 'Abbu

didn't see Rafiq.' His voice cracked. 'He wouldn't go in the room.'

'How come?'

'He drove us to the prison. He got as far as the main gate then he turned round and went back to the car. He sat waiting for us. Ammi tried to persuade him but he just sat there with his arms folded. He's stubborn like that.'

'Why didn't he go in?'

Imran took the stick from Lucky and threw it again. 'He said he couldn't stand to see his son in that place. Those were his words. In that place. He couldn't even bring himself to say the word prison.'

'Rafiq must have been devastated.'

Imran swallowed. 'He was. Abbu drove all the way there and all the way back. That's a three-hour round trip and he didn't even go in.'

I tried to imagine what was going through Mr Hussain's mind. He was always so proud of Rafiq. His first-born. His joker in the pack. 'Is he angry with Rafiq for what he did?'

Imran collected the stick from Lucky and scratched his ears. 'He was. Now he's ashamed … of himself. That's why he stopped being a councillor. The way he sees it he has always helped other people. Now he can't help himself. He's resigned as a magistrate too. How could he be a community leader when he couldn't keep his own son out of jail?'

'But Rafiq shouldn't even be in jail. It's not fair.'

'That's what I keep saying. Abbu won't listen. I think he wants to punish himself. He doesn't smile any more. It's ripping our family apart.'

Chris watched Lucky gulp down the chocolate drop.

'It's not right. Somebody should do something.'

Imran clenched his fists. 'If I knew who was to blame I'd kill them, Chris. I'd kill them.'

Every time I think about how Imran changed I remember that moment.

Chris

DECEMBER 2003.

It was as if I was born to box. That autumn I finally found something I was really good at. I belonged in the ring. I was strong but it wasn't just that. I found a hunger inside me. I was a fighter. One time Joe's dad was working late so I arranged the lifts – Mum dropped us off. Dad picked us up. Joe was saying how he wanted to go into the Army when he's older.

Dad sounded interested. 'Why the Army?'

'My dad was a soldier,' Joe explained. 'He served in Northern Ireland when it was really kicking off.'

'That must have been tough.'

'It was.'

'And that doesn't put you off?'

Joe shook his head. 'No, not a bit. You want it to put you to the test. Then you see what you're made of.'

Dad said he'd thought about joining up once.

I was surprised. 'You never mentioned that.'

Joe looked at me. 'Have you ever thought about it?'

I hadn't. I hadn't really thought about any job.

Dad jumped in. 'The Army is all right for some, but you need to keep your options open, son. Get a decent education, then you can sort out what you want to do with your life.'

I reminded Dad I was in set four, same as Joe. 'I'm not going to book a place on University Challenge quite yet.'

Joe asked if I wanted to go to his for a while. We went over and sat talking. Kelly walked through the living room at one point and I followed her with my eyes.

Joe nudged me. 'Do you like my sister?'

I pulled a face. 'Don't be stupid.'

'You do, don't you? I'm going to tell her she's got a fan.'

He shouted Kelly in.

'Joe, don't you dare.' I tried to cover his mouth with my hand. Kelly saw us wrestling on the couch. She rolled her eyes and walked out again, shaking her head.

'Silly boys.'

'Did you hear what she said?' I cried. 'That's your fault! Thanks, Joe.'

Joe squirmed out of my grip. He wouldn't let it go.

'I thought you didn't care.' He saw the wounded look on my face. 'You *love* her,' he teased, putting on a weird, falsetto voice.

I told him to knock it off but Joe just kept getting louder.

'Pack it in, will you?'

I finally got him to drop it. 'I don't care about your stupid sister.'

But who was I kidding?

Of course I cared.

Eleven

The White Leopard

I saw the images from Abu Ghraib today. I saw the treatment of my Muslim brothers. It wasn't the brutality that twisted my gut. It was the humiliation: the dog lead, the touching of private parts by a young woman with a cigarette dangling from her lip, the grins, the gleeful thumbs up gestures, the fact that this girl treated adult men like pieces of meat. These American soldiers think Iraq is one big theme park, Disneyland with electrodes. They get their kicks from ridiculing proud, devout people. The photographs invite you to ride the prisoners, mock them, strip them, have your fun at their expense.

Because they are only Muslims.

I attended a discussion today. It was at Arshad's flat. After all this time he is beginning to trust me. He lives on the ground floor of a run-down Victorian house. It has been converted into flats. Nobody really knows each other. There is a weed-choked garden out front.

There were two other men in the room. Arshad's friend

had a heavy beard. He wore tinted glasses that partially shaded his eyes. He was also wearing black jeans and shoes, a white shirt, a red and white chequered keffiyeh round his neck and a leather jacket. He had his eyes fixed on the television screen. Arshad glanced at him from time to time. It was an act of deference. Finally the newcomer spoke.

'This is their war of liberation,' he declared. 'They promised the people of America that hundreds of thousands of Iraqis would toss flowers on the street in front of their troops. It would be like the end of World War Two. It would be liberation day. Did either of you see the flowers? Did anyone hear cheering?' He didn't expect an answer. 'When the people refused to play their allotted role, the Americans turned the country into a prison camp. This is the result.'

For the first time he looked at me. He introduced himself as Nabeel. He spoke with a pronounced London accent.

'Let's get down to business. Arshad tells me you want to prove yourself.'

I felt a buzz of excitement. I was nothing. In this man's eyes I have begun to matter. I nodded. 'I want to serve Allah.'

Nabeel pointed at the TV and asked for my opinion. He was putting me to the test, just as Arshad had once before.

I chose my words carefully.

'It is ... evil.'

He nodded. He was pleased with me. 'Evil. Yes, it is the work of Shaitan. There is only one way to prevent such acts. We must destroy the West and their puppets in the

Muslim lands. Tell me, have you come to any further conclusions?'

I thought for a moment. What did Nabeel want now? I had already said it was evil.

'I see the occupation of the Muslim lands.'

Nabeel touched his temple to acknowledge agreement. 'The infidel aggressors murder the Muslims in Iraq and Afghanistan. They arm Israel so that they can kill the Muslims in Gaza. They carry out these crimes in our lands. What must we do?'

There was only one answer possible. 'We must take the war to their lands.'

Nabeel glanced at Arshad. There was satisfaction in their eyes. 'That is it exactly. We must take the war to their lands. We must infiltrate their security. Do it at home. Do it in your backyard. It is your obligation as a Muslim.'

Nabeel was watching my reactions. 'Do you have a question?'

'I have been attending the mosque ...'

'Which one?' Nabeel demanded.

Arshad provided the information. 'He means the central mosque.'

Nabeel digested the information. 'So what troubles you?'

'The Imam's message is very different from yours. He tells the congregation to respect and love the country they live in. He says this is the duty of a Muslim.'

Nabeel listened to what I had to say then he posed a question. 'Do you have any doubts?'

I shook my head. 'I am only telling you what the Imam says.'

Nabeel wanted to know his name. Arshad told him it was Nawaz.

'Let me tell you about this Nawaz,' Nabeel said. There was contempt in his voice. 'He is a sell-out, a puppet of this godless government. He talks of inter-faith dialogue. He sits down with Christians, Hindus, Sikhs. After the riots he allowed the kuffar police to put their posters up inside the mosque. How dare he allow the same police that cracked Muslim heads to meddle in our affairs? The mosque committee is made up of men with defeated minds.'

I listened in silence while Arshad and Nabeel denounced their fellow Muslims. For a moment I wondered what had happened to the idea of brotherhood. But Nabeel had all the answers. There was no room for doubt or introspection, no room for disagreement.

'Don't listen to men who are lackeys and lap dogs of the British government,' Nabeel said. 'We do not accept their democracy. We stand for the re-establishment of the Muslim state, the khilafah, the caliphate.'

'Then the Muslims will rule?'

Nabeel shook his head as if correcting a naïve child. 'In Islam, men don't rule. Allah rules. You must understand,' he told me. 'Being a Muslim is not about going to mosque when you feel like it. From now on Islam is who you are. The Muslims will fight. They will win and rule the whole world. Are you with us?'

'Yes.'

Nabeel was pleased. 'Then we have work for you to do.'

LONDON
BOMBINGS
SHOCK
56 people die in
bus bombing
and on tube.
US attacks Iraq.

Twelve

Imran

7 JULY 2005.

When Dad finally agreed to visit Rafiq in prison, Imran thought the family would mend. Ten months later however he was still letting everybody know how he felt. While the family waited to see Rafiq, Dad looked round at the other families. Some were laughing. Others were having a smoke. He glared at the carefree way they behaved and shook his head.

'Do none of them feel any shame?' he demanded in a low voice.

Aisha gave him a piece of advice. 'Don't be too quick to judge, Abbu-ji. You can't go round hanging your head forever.'

'Do not expect to see me laughing and smiling. I will never get used to this terrible place. I will never accept the idea that my son is a prisoner and ... a criminal.'

Three people were allowed to visit at a time. The family members took it in turns to go. This time it was Mum who stayed at home. They took their places round the table and waited. Dad picked nervously at his knuckles. Everything about him said that he wished he was somewhere else. It made Imran uncomfortable. Why couldn't his father make an effort for Rafiq? He seemed to have shrunk since they put Rafiq away. When he sat on committees in the Town Hall he meant something. Now his son was in prison and he felt like nothing. Soon Rafiq appeared. Dad didn't even look him in the eye.

Imran got the message. Everybody did. As the eldest son Rafiq was meant to set an example. He had failed. He had got into trouble with the law. Once Dad's pride and joy, Rafiq was now the source of his humiliation.

'How are you?' Aisha asked. Her voice betrayed her, shaking slightly.

'I am better,' Rafiq said. 'I have made friends.'

For the first time Dad looked at him. His eyes were unforgiving. The idea of making friends with criminals offended him.

Rafiq ignored the reaction and told them about his cellmate. 'He's called Luke. He's a decent guy.'

Out of curiosity, Imran asked what Luke did to end up inside.

Rafiq gave his father a sideways glance. 'He's in for assault. He found a guy in bed with his wife. He completely lost it and put him in hospital. He beat him to a pulp.'

Dad raised his eyes to the ceiling and let out a long sigh. It shuddered along for a moment then died away in his throat.

Rafiq ploughed on. 'It's good having somebody like Luke around. He can handle himself.'

Dad folded his arms. His eyes had a hooded look. 'Evidently.'

Aisha changed the subject to avoid a quarrel. She wanted to know what Rafiq was doing with his time.

'I work out,' Rafiq told her. 'They've got a decent gym. They've got a library. I spend a lot of time reading.'

At this Dad brightened up. 'So you're studying?'

'No ... well, kind of. Look, I'm not talking about college. I try not to think about what I've lost. That just makes me feel worse.' He laid his hands flat on the table. For some reason that made one of the prison officers move forward. 'When I close my eyes, I imagine myself in a lecture theatre, or discussing ideas in a tutorial.' His voice thickened as he struggled with his emotions. 'But I'm not, am I? I'm stuck in this hell-hole.'

Aisha told him he must not become bitter.

Rafiq looked away. 'Easy to say when you're on the outside,' he reminded her.

Aisha persisted. 'You will endure. This will come to an end. You're my big brother, Rafiq. Don't let this place change you.'

The words had an effect on him. He told them about the books he got from the library. 'I'm reading novels, biographies, history. I'm reading *Malcolm X* at the moment. I do it for the sheer pleasure of it.'

Dad announced that Aisha had some news.

'I've got an offer from Manchester University,' she told him. 'An A and two Bs.'

Rafiq smiled. 'You'll walk it.' There was pain in his smile. 'What about you, Imran?' Rafiq asked. 'Still in touch with Chris?'

'Not much,' Imran answered. 'He keeps missing football practice.'

'Why's that?'

Imran explained about Chris's boxing. 'He's good. He's qualifying for tournaments. He's too busy to even return my calls.' He looked away. 'Who needs him?' He didn't want to sound like a loser so he told Rafiq his news. 'Do you remember Mrs Neal?'

'Annie? Yes, of course.'

'She died last week. I got a letter from her daughter. She thanked me for taking care of Lucky.'

'Aren't we gloomy today?' Aisha said. 'Let's find something more cheerful to talk about.'

That's the way it was. Visiting somebody in prison is like sitting at a sick person's bedside in hospital. They run out of things to say after a while, then it's a matter of filling the silences.

Not with things that matter.

With anything.

They drove away from the prison. Nobody spoke. What was the point of trotting out the same tired observations about Rafiq's appearance, his state of mind? He was beginning to cope with life inside. He had become familiar with the prison's routines. Aisha spoke for everyone when she pleaded with Rafiq not to change. What kind of man would he be when he came out?

The thought scared Imran. Rafiq was strong, his rock. But there were thoughts that Imran couldn't drive from his mind. He'd always thought he could rely on Chris and he barely saw him anymore. What if Rafiq changed too?

Fingers of shadow curled round the future. Everything used to be so simple.

Dad grumbled about the music on the car radio and changed channels. A presenter's voice faded into a familiar signature tune. It was the news on the hour. There was a report about power cuts on the London Underground, something to do with an unexplained surge on the Grid. They didn't pay much attention.

But by the time the family pulled into the motorway services a very different picture was starting to emerge. News updates were reporting a series of terrorist incidents. The National Grid denied any power surges. London Underground had suspended its services. Government reports were suggesting twenty dead in a series of bombings. There were ninety casualties at one Tube station alone.

Aisha spoke for everyone. 'This is terrible. It's mass murder.'

They watched mesmerised as the drama unfolded on a large screen. A crowd had gathered, struggling to take it in. There were headlines against a red background. *London Blasts*. Several people had their hands over their mouths in shock. The reports came in snatches.

'I can confirm that all London hospitals are on major incident alert.'

'The London Underground system has been suspended.'

Wailing sirens formed the soundtrack to the reports. The imagery of horror formed. A bus lay crumpled in the middle of the road. It had been ripped apart by a bomb. Footage followed from two Tube stations. People staggered dazed from the entrances. One victim had bandages covering her whole face, making her look like a mummy.

'Look at that poor woman,' Aisha said. 'She must have terrible burns.'

Stony silence met her words. Imran wondered what she'd done wrong. His gaze swept across the concourse. It was unnaturally quiet. Golden sunlight streamed through the huge windows and fell on dozens of upturned faces. Everybody was watching the breaking news.

The news anchor added some new information: 'Middle Eastern sources say that the bombings are almost certainly the work of Al-Qaeda.'

Imran realised that the woman behind him was staring at him. He turned round and discovered she wasn't the only one with her eye on him. Most of the people around them were watching him, Dad and Aisha. One of them, a shaven-headed man in T-shirt, shorts and flip flops, finally said something. 'When are you people going to take responsibility for the extremists in your midst?'

'What do you mean these people are our responsibility?' Dad snapped. 'How are they? Are the BNP your responsibility?'

'Don't talk to me like that,' the man retorted. 'I haven't done anything wrong.'

Dad was furious. 'Neither have I!'

The man didn't back down. 'You might not have done, but your kind have.'

'My kind!' Dad's eyes were hard with anger. 'You had better explain what you mean by that.'

The man turned away. 'Oh, go back to Islam.'

Dad stared for a moment, then he burst out laughing at the sheer stupidity of the comment. He was the only one laughing. It sounded strange in the echoing building.

Aisha tried to get him to move. 'He's not worth talking to. He's an idiot. He must be if he thinks Islam is a country.'

Dad nodded vaguely as if he hadn't heard her properly. 'Use the toilet if you need it,' he said, still angry. 'Why do they want every Muslim to apologise? Does every Jew have to apologise for the things Israel does? Do Christians have to apologise for Bush and Blair?' He took out his car keys. 'We're getting out of here. We will eat when we get home.'

The Political Soldier

Quade walked up to the hotel reception. His laptop was hanging from his left shoulder in a black zip-up case. He lugged his suitcase in the right. As usual there was a queue. He shifted his feet, darted his eyes to left and right, huffed loudly and checked his watch as he waited. Did anything work in this country? Finally he got served. 'I'd like to pay my bill please.'

The slim blonde across the desk gave the standard sweet, plastic smile. 'Of course, sir. Sorry for your wait. What name is it?'

He detested the singsong delivery. She could at least *try* to sound sincere. 'It's Quade. Derek Quade. Room 248.'

'Was everything all right with your stay, sir?'

He remembered the featureless room, the window that wouldn't open, giving him a thumping headache, the whiff of chemicals that impregnated the towels and sheets. He couldn't be bothered to complain. At least it was clean.

That was more than could be said for some of the places he had stayed.

'Yes, fine.'

Insincerity was contagious.

She consulted the screen. 'There is the room charge, a film, an evening meal. That's £114.50, sir. Are you paying with the same card?'

'That's right.'

'May I have your card, sir?'

She'd said sir three times in less than a minute. That must be a record for obsequiousness. The two Ibuprofen he had swallowed had still not kicked in. He was in a foul mood but he didn't even have the energy to take it out on the receptionist. She swiped the card and returned it, delivering part two of the plastic smile.

'Shall I staple the receipt to the bill, sir?'

There it was again. Sir. Irritation thrummed in his voice. 'Sure, whatever.'

Just get on with it.

He crossed the car park and dropped into the driver's seat of the four-year-old Volvo estate. He sighed and leaned his head back against the rest.

Another suitcase.

Another hotel.

Another evening meal alone.

Another inedible breakfast of stiff bacon and flaccid eggs. The toast was rubbery and the service was weary.

He drove out of the main gate, tapping in the barrier code. It was 4445. It should be 666, the Name of the Beast. Leaving the hotel behind, he accelerated onto the busy dual carriageway to join the M1. His appointment was just off the next junction going south.

He was driving too slowly for the white van man behind him. White van man hit the horn and Quade flashed a two-finger salute. Moron. The radio was tuned to some cheesy commercial station. The hyperactive DJ, some twenty-something who was way too pleased with himself, babbled inanities. The endless prattle drove Quade's finger to the tuning button.

As he roamed the airwaves, looking for anything remotely inoffensive to the ear, something strange happened. The overhead motorway signs ahead of him lit up. Amber flashes flickered all the way down the road. He read the message and his throat tightened.

AVOID LONDON.

AREA CLOSED.

TURN ON RADIO.

What the hell was this? How could London be closed? It was as if he was in the middle of *War of the Worlds* or *The Day After Tomorrow*. He expected walking tripods or vast walls of water. It felt like the end of the world. London closed? What in God's name did that mean?

His heart thudded as he searched the radio channels. He finally found a news bulletin. He listened as the horror unfolded. Knuckles turning white on the steering wheel, he committed every detail to memory. Bombers had hit the city's Tube stations. They had also targeted a bus.

On a bright summer's day they had struck the heart of London. Scum. What was it old Enoch said? Rivers of blood. Congratulations politicians, that's exactly what they'd got: the greatest city of the nation foaming with blood. You fools, you self-destructive fools. That's the outcome of your obsession with a multicultural society.

Quade remembered a recent visit to the city centre. There used to be a beautiful Saturday market. Now it was more like a bazaar. He had come across a vendor with a huge bushy beard, dressed in shalwar kameez. Quade had stood observing the scene while Qur'anic verses rang out from a stereo on a market stall.

He voiced his thoughts in the privacy of the car. 'So it's begun. The ragheads have started their jihad.'

They had got their holy war. It was time somebody hit back. Britain needed a political soldier.

Chris

7 JULY 2005.

Joe and Kelly were at my house when the news broke.

Kelly saw the roundup and swallowed hard. 'Those poor people.'

Joe reacted with fury. 'I hope the police hunt down whoever did this. They ought to hang the lot of them.'

Kelly gave him a pitying look. 'You've been listening to Dad again.' She explained for Chris's benefit. 'He's a bit hang 'em, flog 'em, my dad. Joe, they don't hang people any more.'

'That's right,' Joe said, 'they don't hang them, but they should.'

I remember watching as one of the emergency workers guided a woman in a foil cape to a waiting ambulance. I will never forget her unsteady progress. The image seemed to sum up a city in shock. 'How could they do that to innocent people? I mean, the people who planted those bombs don't even know who they're killing. It's completely indiscriminate. Why do they do it?'

Joe had an answer. 'They're fanatics, that's why. First it was New York. Now it's London.'

Kelly wondered out loud who did it.

'Who do you think?' Joe answered. 'Arab terrorists, Al-Qaeda. It's got to be. We should bomb them where *they* live.'

Kelly pulled a face. 'I think we already did.'

Joe frowned. 'What are you on about?'

'Iraq. Afghanistan. You know, Blair, Bush, the war on terror. We bomb them. They bomb us. Or don't you listen to the news?'

Joe scowled.

Just then tyres crunched on the gravel drive. 'Mum and Dad are back,' I observed needlessly.

Joe drained his Coke and dropped the can in the swing bin. 'We'd better go. Come on, sis.' As he left he shouted a reminder. 'We're fighting tomorrow, Hooky. Get a good sleep.'

Joe and Kelly exchanged a few words with my parents. Dad's gaze flitted to the screen. 'They should bring back hanging.'

'That's what Joe said.'

Mum started putting the shopping away. I left Dad grumbling in front of the TV and helped her.

'I just keep thinking about the families of the victims,' she said as she stocked the freezer. 'It's hard to imagine. All those people – they're mothers, fathers, sons, daughters, sisters, brothers. Just imagine the heartache this has caused. Think of the consequences.'

She tugged my sleeve. 'Guess who I bumped into today?'

'I don't know, the Queen?'

'Sarcasm is the lowest form of wit, Chris. It was Imran's mum.'

I felt guilty. It was weeks since I'd been in touch with Imran. Even now I can't explain how we drifted apart. I suppose I just had so much going on in my life. I somehow forgot to make room for Imran. I was too busy with my boxing and Joe and thinking about Kelly. 'How is she?'

'She seems fine. Rafiq should be getting out of prison early next year.' She lowered her eyes.

I didn't like the sudden silence. 'Is something wrong? Mum?'

She gave a sad smile. 'No, there's nothing wrong as such. It's just . . . Oh, you know, you live next to somebody all those years. One day you meet them again and you've got so little to say. You feel like strangers.'

She was right. Whenever I spoke to Imran now, which wasn't often, there were long pauses. Neither of us knew what to say. The ease we once felt in one another's company had gone. Why had we let that happen? It was a betrayal of our entire childhood. We weren't blood brothers anymore. We were becoming strangers.

Thirteen

Imran

They're almost there. Imran has just seen the second sign for the barracks. As they accelerate away from lights there is a police motorcyclist on the next street corner. Moments later there is the chatter of helicopter rotor blades overhead. There was a helicopter that night of the riots. Imran heard its roar late into the night. He cranes his neck to catch sight of this one. The word *police* is painted on the underbelly. These are the first signs of the security surrounding the prince's visit. Rafiq watches the slowing traffic.

The past is a burden. Imran can never go back, but maybe he can make up for his mistakes.

Inshallah.

Imran

Rafiq walked out of the prison gates one showery spring afternoon. He paused for a moment and gazed at the rainbow arching over the busy dual carriageway. The moment of reflection lasted a matter of seconds then Imran and Aisha raced forward to embrace him. The first drops of rain fell, thudding on Imran's shoulders. Mum joined her children. She was stroking Rafiq's face as if unable to believe he had returned from that terrible place.

Dad stood back from the show of affection. He was a man apart. He had aged more than two years while Rafiq was inside. Imran hated his father for his lack of feeling. He wished he had the courage to shake him out of his blind, stupid attachment to appearances. Oblivious, Dad took Rafiq's bag and tossed it in the boot. There was no embrace. There was no handshake. Not a single word passed between them. Rafiq came home. As far as Dad was concerned his son carried the smell of prison on his clothes.

Maybe he always would.

Rafiq had only been home a few days when the trouble began. Dad asked him when he was going to give some thought to his future.

'What future?' Rafiq demanded. 'Didn't you notice? I just did a prison sentence. I've got no references, no CV. Who's going to give me a job?'

Dad didn't like Rafiq's attitude. He detested the reek of defeat that hung around him. 'You have served your sentence. It is time to rebuild your life.'

'So how am I supposed to do that?'

'Find a job. Better still, return to your studies. Stop feeling sorry for yourself.'

'You think I am wallowing in self pity?' There was no answer. 'I threw a bottle and they treated me like a criminal. They locked me up for two years – two years! For standing up to fascists. There is no justice in this country.'

Imran wanted them to stop. He gazed imploringly at Dad. But he was in no mood to compromise.

'Do not shout at me! How many times must we go over this argument? The sentence was too harsh. But do not turn what has happened into an excuse. Many people have suffered worse examples of injustice than you and made something of themselves.'

Imran loved both of them. Why did they seem so determined to destroy each other?

Rafiq snorted his impatience. 'Are you comparing me to Nelson Mandela now? I'm no hero. I did my time. It nearly drove me crazy. What's the point of talking about past heroes, Abbu? Do you really think any of this is going to help?'

Imran wanted to scream. That day when Rafiq walked free he thought life was going to get back to normal. He wanted things to be the way they always used to be, but, with Aisha back in Manchester and Rafiq so unhappy, things were even worse than before. The furious quarrel did not stop. Recriminations flew. 'I did not raise you to give up at the first setback.'

'No, you didn't. You raised me to be British and to believe in British laws.' Rafiq threw up his arms. 'Say your prayers, Rafiq. Study hard, Rafiq. Make a contribution to the country that has given your family a home. Pass the cricket test. Support England.' He crashed his fist into the cupboard next to him. 'That's it, isn't it?'

Dad glared across the room. He heard Rafiq out then gave his answer. 'Why do you mock me this way? This is the right thing to do. What is your solution? Do you want to take from this country and spit on its values?'

Rafiq threw the question back. 'What values, Abbu? They allow thugs to walk into our town and taunt us. They send me to prison for throwing a bottle. I am responsible for one lousy mistake and they make an example of me. That solicitor virtually promised me my freedom if I cooperated. Your stinking British justice hung me out to dry. Tell me they don't hate Muslims. They bomb Afghanistan. They bomb Iraq. They support Israel against the Palestinians. I'm not the one who spits on Britain. This country spat on me.'

This enraged Dad. 'Do not preach to me, Rafiq!'

'Maybe that is exactly what I have to do. Why do you still cling to your precious Labour Party? Go on, tell me that.'

Mum came in from the shops. She could hear the raised voices from the street. She set down her bags and listened. She caught Imran's eye.

'When your grandfather came to this country from Pakistan,' Dad was saying, 'he went through difficult times. He had to live in lodgings with four other men. In those days there was a lot of hostility towards immigrants. He looked for somebody to represent him. He joined the Labour Party because he thought it stood up for the working man, regardless of colour or religion. I can't forget what he went through to make a home for us. I can't walk away from the things he stood for.'

Rafiq retorted fiercely. 'So you walk away from Islam instead.'

Silence followed. Imran looked across the room. Dad had his fists clenched. He was like a coiled spring waiting for Rafiq to take his goading too far.

Mum tried to stop the quarrel. '*Buss Rafiq ub choop karo!* How dare you speak to your father in this way? You must show him more respect.'

Rafiq refused to be reined in. 'Like the respect he showed me?' He turned on Dad. There was a wretched sob in his voice. He felt betrayed and Imran felt betrayed with him. 'You could hardly look at me when you visited me in prison, Abbu. You carried your shame for all to see, as if I was a burden.'

Dad flinched at the accusation. 'You are my son. I am not ashamed of you.'

Rafiq spoke more quietly. 'Are you so sure about that?' He walked towards the door. 'You had your chance to be a father and you blew it.'

Imran tried to go after Rafiq but Dad grabbed his arm. 'No, let him go, Imran. He is a man. You must give him time to make his own decisions. It will take time for him to adjust to life outside prison.'

With Rafiq gone, the house felt empty. There was a time when Imran could have confided in Chris, but he hardly saw him anymore. Somehow he didn't want to see him either. He wasn't sure why not.

Suddenly he was afraid for the future.

Imran got home from school at the usual time, about four o'clock. He entered through the back door as usual past the shooting basket that nobody used any more. It was rusty and the backboard was rotten. The top right-hand corner had broken away. The moment he stepped inside the house he knew something was wrong. Mum should have been in the kitchen cooking but she wasn't there. Imran called her.

He walked through to the living room. There was nobody there. The TV was off. He didn't remember the house ever being this quiet. He felt the tug of anxiety. He called her again.

'I am upstairs.'

Imran climbed the stairs two at a time.

'What's wrong?'

He found her in Rafiq's room. She was sitting on the edge of the bed. Her face was turned away. Strangely, she didn't look up from what she was doing. She had a piece of paper in her hand and she seemed to be reading it over and over again.

'Ammi?'

Still she didn't look at Imran directly. Instead she glanced at the wardrobe. Imran followed the direction of her gaze. The doors were open. It was empty.

'Where are Rafiq's clothes? What's going on?'

She handed him the letter she had been holding. Imran started reading:

Don't be angry with me.

Since I got home I have been impossible to live with. I didn't mean to shout at Abbu-ji. I didn't mean to say those things. All those months I was inside, I dreamed of getting out and coming home. I thought I could pick up where I left off. It was never going to be that easy. Nothing's the same. It doesn't feel like home anymore. I

*don't blame it on anyone but myself. This is what prison
has done to me.*

*I need to sort myself out. That's why I'm going away.
I will be in touch when I've found somewhere to stay.*

This is something I have to do. Don't worry about me.

Rafiq.

Imran stared at the words. They began to blur. He
realised that he was weeping. He stumbled down the stairs
and out into the street. He rubbed at his face with his
sleeve as if he was a little kid again. He ran until he
could barely breathe. He was cold. Why did people keep
vanishing from his life? The years were rushing by like
shadows over the face of the sun and he was lost in the
darkness.

Lost, friendless. Sure, Imran hung out. But he never got
that close to anyone else. He only had friends the way
people have friends on MySpace. They were group friends,
pack friends, friends he numbered, labelled, weighed. But
could he pick a single one of them who was really close?
Would anyone text in the early hours of the morning to
share his thoughts? Would anyone take a beating the way
Chris had when Link and his mates ambushed them? Was
there a blood brother among them?

He had coped with Chris leaving. He'd had to. He'd
had his football. He'd had the routines of family life.
He'd even had school. But he'd never found anyone to
take Chris's place. It was hard to say why. Maybe all the
friendship groups were formed by then. Maybe he didn't
try hard enough. But he was safe when he got home. He
lived so much of his life inside his family. There was
always that.

So long as Rafiq was around he was OK. He was Imran's rock, the pillar of strength he had always been. Now even he had gone, without a word of explanation. Imran felt betrayed. He had fought to be included in every prison visit. So how did Rafiq repay his loyalty? The first chance he got he just walked away. In that moment Imran realised that heartbreak isn't a saying. It is an accurate description of what happens when people hurt you. Something breaks inside.

Fourteen

Chris

April 2008.

The gym echoed with a yelp of pain. Joe's face creased with agony and he hopped away holding his ribs. He sagged against the ropes and gasped for breath.

'What was that about, Hooky?' he wheezed. 'We're only supposed to be sparring.'

Our coach Charlie Falconer called time out. 'Go easy, Hooky lad. I want Joe fighting next month, not nursing broken ribs.'

I looped an arm round Joe's shoulders. 'You all right?' I asked.

Joe straightened slowly. 'Yes, it only hurts when I breathe.' He grinned ruefully. 'So what lit your fire?'

'My dad,' I told him.

'What is it this time?' Joe said, getting his breath back.

'He's been giving me grief about school. He doesn't know when to stop.'

137

'Why doesn't he chill?' Joe said. 'We can't all be Einstein.'

Charlie climbed into the ring and examined Joe's ribs. 'You'll live.' He glanced at me. 'There's always the Army, Hooky.'

'That's what I keep telling him,' Joe said. 'I can start initial training straight after GCSEs. I'm going into my dad's regiment.'

Charlie shoved his hands in his pockets. 'I followed my old man into the Marines. It was a great life. I was a right tearaway when I was a lad but the Army made a man of me. Invent the elixir of youth and I'd do it all over again.' He pointed at some of the photos on the wall. 'I learned my ring craft in the regiment. You could do a lot worse, Chris.'

I told them I'd think about it.

I broached the idea the moment I got home. I don't think I was serious about it at that point. Not that it made much difference what I thought. I saw the exchange of glances between my parents. Dad didn't say much, but Mum was horrified.

'Please tell me you don't mean it,' she said. 'Boys are getting killed out there, Chris.'

I held out my arms and gave her a hug. 'Don't worry, Mum,' I told her. 'It was just a thought.'

The Political Soldier

Quade had seen 7 July 2005 as a call to arms. He'd imagined an imminent race war carried out against the background of rippling Union flags. He'd imagined a white power revolution that would sweep away the corrupt power structure. The reality had been mundane. In the three years since the London bombings, the nationalist parties had been a disappointment.

He had had a spell with the National Front in the seventies. He was a young man then, eager to trade punches with the red hecklers. The organisation descended into infighting and ultimately farce. The whole project had ended in tears. He'd fared no better in the BNP. Quade wanted a righteous storm and all they offered was talk. He imagined laying siege to the Muslim ghettos, but they were keen to wear a mask of respectability.

He'd spent most of his time sitting in meetings listening to men in suits talking about electoral advances and the need for moderation. He'd heard them discuss necessary compromises. There'd been nods and winks about a true agenda that would be unveiled when the time came. Quade knew the time would never be right. He had tried their mainstream route to victory and found it wanting.

He'd canvassed. He'd handed out leaflets. He'd gone down to Barking to support Nick Griffin's campaign to be elected as an MP. What a fiasco! They were beaten out of sight. He'd written letters to websites and the press. He'd warned about sharia law and an Islamic state. There'd been enough talk to float a hot air balloon, but there was no action.

The votes had piled up but they were never enough to make the predicted electoral breakthrough. What effect did it have? Quade still saw the women in their full-face niqab veils. He saw the men with their unkempt beards.

He heard the call of the muezzin. There it was, the sound of the East floating over the roofs of an English city.

Week after week, month after month, the march of the Islamists continued and the snivelling leftist establishment had sat back and let it happen. The enemy had been fighting World War Three by stealth and Quade had known he was on the losing side. He'd burned with shame at the dilution of the race. He'd dreamed of the day Britannia would rule the waves once more. He'd raged against the slow, grinding death of the England he loved. He'd raised his concerns with the party leaders. They'd nodded. They'd tapped their noses and hinted at great things. Still they'd done nothing.

Quade made his decision. He would give the party a few months to prove they were capable of more than talk. If there was no progress he would abandon an organisation of thousands and trust in the power of one.

One just man.

A man in arms.

A Christian soldier.

Chris

10 June 2008.

Charlie was doing his best to gee me up. 'You're stronger than this lad, Hooky. You've just got to believe in yourself.'

I glanced at him. 'He's way ahead on points.'

'Has he hurt you once?'

'Well, no.'

140

'You've got to influence the judges. Go on the offensive. It's clean punches you need and lots of them. Hit hard. Hit fast. Combination work. You've nothing to lose.'

I nodded and walked to the middle of the ring. I glanced back and Charlie nodded. In spite of his encouragement from the ringside, I wasn't confident. I'd taken too long to impose myself. Two minutes to impress. I forced my opponent back right from the bell. I was starting to enjoy myself. Why didn't I do this earlier? Suddenly the momentum was with me. My opponent was tiring, but had I left it too late?

'Force the pace, Hooky!'

That was Charlie shouting instructions. I came forward. My opponent didn't have any answer to the late show of raw power. All the craft and guile he'd shown in the opening rounds vanished as I pressed him. He was hanging on, wilting under my attacks. I could hear him breathing hard. I hit him with a combination, bouncing him back against the ropes, watching the strength drain from him. I could see panic in his eyes.

I glimpsed Charlie and Joe urging me on. Dad had promised to come, but he had had to pull out. He said it was something to do with work. I remembered all those heart to hearts about my school reports. This was the one place I wasn't a failure. He should have been here. I jabbed.

Right.

Left.

Right.

Fast.

Scoring punches.

I watched my man bob and weave, trying to deflect

their power. He tried to move but there was nowhere he could go that I didn't follow. The punches thudded into his tiring frame but he wriggled and squirmed, taking most of them on his arms and gloves. He was good. Even though he was out on his feet, I had an ominous feeling that I wasn't closing the gap fast enough.

I moved in one last time. If I could stand him up I might just score enough points to square the bout. My opponent tried the same manoeuvre once too often and I caught him with the right. He gasped with pain. I hit him with a body shot. I felt my man go slack. Only the bell stopped him sinking to the floor.

We touched gloves and waited for the verdict. I squeezed my eyes shut and waited. The ref gripped my wrist and raised my arm. In that moment elation surged through me. I'd won. After a feeble first round, I had come back and won. I bumped gloves with my defeated opponent and climbed out of the ring. If only Dad could have seen that I wasn't the loser he thought.

Joe gave me a bear hug. 'That was awesome, Chris. You took the fight to a more experienced opponent and you made him look ordinary. You're a warrior.' Joe had lost his bout and he was sporting a cut over his left eye. There was identical damage to my right. 'Look at that, matching cuts. That makes us blood brothers.'

Suddenly I thought of Imran. I remembered the time we were ambushed on the way home from football.

Joe must have seen my expression change. 'Something wrong?'

'No, of course not. Look, I'm getting a shower then we're good to go. What time's your dad coming to pick us up?'

Joe told me he was probably outside waiting. I showered quickly and got dressed. There was a surprise when I got into the back of the car.

'Oh hi, Kelly.' I got a lump in my throat every time she was near. My eyes followed her about. Sometimes she caught me looking. Every time she smiled.

There it was again, the dazzling smile that illuminated the vehicle. I watched the full lips parting to reveal even white teeth. It was a moment before I realised that she was talking to me. 'I'm guessing you lost?'

I was confused for a moment then I remembered the cut over my eye. 'This? No, you should see the other guy. I won.'

Kelly ran a finger over my eyebrow. I felt an electric charge run through me. I liked her touch on my skin. It was soft and cooling, the gentlest of caresses. What I'd have given to have her touching me for the rest of my life.

'They should have put a stitch in this for you,' she said. 'It's quite deep.'

My eyes travelled down the line of her arm to the neckline of her top. She saw the way I was looking at her. Her eyelids fluttered for a second. A flush rose in her cheeks and she withdrew her hand. I wanted her to touch me again. There was a moment when her gaze wandered over my face, then she pulled away and leaned forward to talk to her dad.

'Do you want to get a Mackies on the way home? There's a Drive-Thru just up the road.'

Mr Latham laughed. 'McDonald's isn't the right diet for a couple of sportsmen. Or soldiers.'

'Oh, go on,' Kelly said. 'It's a one-off. This is Chris's best win yet. That's right, isn't it Joe?'

'I can't argue with that,' Joe replied. 'He surpassed me years ago.'

All the way back I was aware of Kelly next to me, the mane of blonde hair, the soft press of her leg against mine. I felt her warmth and smelled her perfume. A long time ago Joe had teased me about my feelings for Kelly. He said I loved her. It wasn't true when he said it.

It was that June night.

The White Leopard

Nabeel wants to know if I am ready to serve.

'I am.'

I have done my apprenticeship. Nabeel rented a cottage on the North Yorkshire moors. This was where he started to pass on the skills he had gained in training camps abroad. He hardly ever spoke about his own experiences. Just once he had let a few details slip. He had travelled – what did he say? – to Pakistan, through Pakistan? I don't remember. I learned to strip down and reassemble firearms. I learned to mix chemicals. I absorbed the names quickly: triacetone triperoxide, citric acid, hydrogen peroxide. I was a good student. They accept me at last. They trust me. The time for action has come. I want to be told my assignment. I know Nabeel's every argument off by heart.

'While your sisters are abused, your brothers slaughtered in Palestine, Iraq and Afghanistan, US-backed tyrants restrain the Muslim soldiers who could free their lands. If there was an Islamic state, a khilafah, the terror in Bosnia would not have happened; Chechnya would not have happened; Iraq, Afghanistan, Palestine would be free. Those so-called Muslims who disagree are lackeys of the Americans and the British. You owe no loyalty or allegiance to this country. Your only loyalty is to one Muslim community, one Ummah. Your duty is to submit to Allah.'

I submit. I fear Allah. With Allah's help I will have my revenge on all those who have humiliated me, on everyone who has crushed my dreams. I am ready. I stand in front of the mirror and shave off my beard. Tomorrow I will find a barber and have my hair styled.

Nabeel has given me my mission. I am going to be a sleeper, inserted in the belly of the beast. Where I am going I have to fit in. I will wear fashionable clothes. I will talk about the latest TV programmes. I will know who is favourite to win *X Factor*. I will care who is top of the Premier League. I will drink alcohol and smoke cigarettes outside the back door where workplace regulations don't apply. I will tell my workmates that I was baptised into the Church of England. I will be part of the kuffar. I will join them to destroy them.

I have sent in the application form. My qualifications are excellent. I had no life so what else did I have to occupy myself but study? All that remains is the interview.

Arshad asks if I understand what is expected of me. I will not use the Muslim name I adopted. I will no longer be known as Usman. I will not attend the mosque. I will not demonstrate any special knowledge of Islam in front of the kuffar. My job is to infiltrate the enemy. I will tunnel deep inside. When the time comes I will reach up and tear out his heart.

Arshad and Nabeel ask more questions. I answer them

all with the same assurance and conviction. I am not the same impressionable youth who came to them. From now on I will pretend to accept the morals and way of life of this God-forsaken country. Allah is on my side. I will enter the house of the infidel. Then, when the time comes, I will strike. I am a soldier. I am at war.

Fifteen

Chris

I am a soldier.

I am Private Chris Hook.

I have been trained to react in an emergency. But I do nothing. I am paralysed, not with fear, but with the crushing weight of responsibility.

There is no bomb, Dad says.

There is no bomber.

But what if there is? Could Imran really have got in so deep?

There is a picture in my head. A man is waddling on shattered stumps through his own blood slick.

Dare I take the risk?

Because soldiers don't just fight. They take decisions whose consequences are weighed in human lives. I swallow. Where was the fork in the road? When did Imran and I take the turning that led us here?

147

Imran

Omar was one of the lads Imran hung out with. His house was around the corner and down the hill. Imran was perched on the arm of Omar's chair. Faisal was there too, standing with his back against the wall. Imran used to knock round with them from time to time, usually as part of a large group. He was sitting with them watching the latest coverage of Israel's drive into Gaza. Omar's family had Al-Jazeera on cable. The Israeli tanks drove forward. One smashed down a palm tree and bulldozed a wall. Medics rushed a boy to a waiting ambulance. He was nine or ten years old. He lay unconscious, stripped to the waist. An oxygen mask covered his face.

In another image a child screamed and beat her chest as she knelt next to her dead father. The victim of a bombing run lay with his back arched, his face a rictus moan of agony. He was frozen in the moment the shockwave of the explosion hit him. The girl's screams reminded Imran of the cry of a seagull. The sharpness of that child's misery cut him like a knife. He watched the images of death and suffering. He wanted to grow steel claws and rip planes from the flawless, blue sky. This was happening to Muslims. It was happening to people like him. Yet he did nothing. The helplessness made him feel as if he was nothing.

He was nothing.

He had nothing.

His beloved family was crumbling. His friend had abandoned him.

He was nothing.

He had nothing.

All he possessed was an anger he had to vent. There in front of him was a focus for his misery and his hatred.

He sat forward and murmured. 'This is murder.'

Faisal pulled a face. 'Tell us something we don't know. Where have you been, Imran? This has been going on for years.' He assumed an expression of pitying superiority. 'Why are you so shocked all of a sudden?'

'I don't know. This is more graphic than anything I have seen before.'

'That's because Al-Jazeera shows the truth. It's better than British TV.'

Imran found himself blaming his father. He always listened to the BBC news. He provided his own commentary, always reasonable, always moderate. It was always the same mantra. If you are born in this country you should watch the news made in this country.

Omar joined in. 'Al-Jazeera doesn't take orders from George Bush and Tony Blair.'

Imran stared at the screen. He couldn't tear his eyes from the victims. Faisal and Omar didn't pay much attention to the images of tanks and planes and white phosphorus. They didn't like what they saw, but they weren't moved to rage or tears.

'What's got into you, man?' Omar asked. 'This has been happening all our lives. Nothing changes. Nobody does anything to help. Get used to it.'

Imran held his gaze. 'That's just it. I can't.'

'Remember what happened here. You should know,' Faisal said. 'Your own brother took a stand against racists and the courts banged him up.'

Omar frowned. 'You've got to lighten up, Imran. You can't do anything about it. If you think too much you're going to drive yourself mad.'

He didn't like the way Imran was behaving in his house. His mum was hovering, frowning. She wanted to know why their voices were raised. Imran apologised and headed for the door.

Omar followed. 'Where are you going?'

'I don't know. I just need to clear my head.'

Imran stepped out into the whipping wind. He started walking fast. His eyes were stinging. The pictures of Gaza were still racing through his mind, but that was only half of it. He was sorry for those people. He was equally sorry for himself. Rafiq kept in touch. He always remembered birthdays. He phoned occasionally or sent an email. But he had made a break with the family. He was turning into a stranger, just like Chris.

Why did everybody walk away?

Chris

2 FEBRUARY 2009.

The phone rang. I sat up on the sofa and reached for it.

'Yes?' I croaked the word. I was still half asleep.

'How are you doing, Hooky?'

'Joe!' I fumbled for the remote and muted the TV. 'When do you get back? Where are you?'

I heard a knock on the front window and turned round. There was Joe, standing on the lawn, phone in hand, grinning a cheerful hello. It is an image of my friend that will stay with me all my life. I scrambled to my feet, cancelled the call, and opened the door. Before I knew it, Joe had me in a bear hug. Slightly embarrassed at the show of affection, I slapped him on the back.

'Nobody in?' he asked.

'They're at Jess's parents' evening.'

'How's she doing?'

'Soaring like a bird. You know Jess. She's got a brain the size of Yorkshire.' I was more interested in Joe. 'How long have you been home?'

'Only an hour. I caught up with the latest goss round ours. Then I thought I'd come over and annoy you.'

He seemed a lot older than when he went away on initial training. It was a man talking to a boy.

'How are you enjoying Army life?'

Joe laced his fingers behind his head. 'Love it. I've never felt so fit in my life. I'm with a great bunch of lads, dead easy to get on with. What's not to like? I've been on the range, using an SA80 rifle. It's a cracking piece of kit.'

I tried to take the rise out of him. 'Kill any low-flying ducks?'

'You're a bit wide of the mark there, Hooky. I'm a natural. I got the second highest score in the company.'

'Need glasses do they, the rest of them?'

Joe changed the subject. 'Have you got anywhere with our Kelly yet?'

'Got anywhere how?'

'Come off it,' he said. 'You're not fooling me, you know. You fancy her to bits. I think it's mutual. Don't tell me you still haven't asked her out.'

My face was hot with embarrassment. 'Knock it off, will you? She's a friend.'

'Oh, come off it, Hooky. How many guys do you know who stay friends with a good-looking girl when they could be just that bit more?' Joe was enjoying making me squirm. 'I've touched a nerve, haven't I?'

Joe was right. I thought about her all the time. Eyes open. Eyes shut. She was always there. The friendship thing kept getting in the way. I'd known her too long as a mate to make a move. 'Do you want something to drink?'

'Red Bull.'

I stood by the fridge while Joe teased me about Kelly. 'You could end up in Afghanistan, you know. We've got eight thousand troops out there now.'

Joe wasn't fazed. 'Bring it on.'

'Doesn't it bother you? I mean, I've seen it on the news. Remember that idiot of a politician who said we'd get out without firing a shot? It didn't look like that in the film I saw. The film crew was using night vision. They captured the whole thing. The Taliban were attacking a base in one of the villages. The Brits were just pumping out thousands of rounds at these figures in the night. You could see the tracer racing across the sky. It looked mental.'

Joe toyed with the can. 'That's what I want, Hooky: action.' He glanced out of the window. 'Look at this place. You could die of boredom here.'

'It's not that bad.'

'Say that when you've been on the dole for six months.'

'I'm not on the dole!'

'Since when?' he asked. 'Go on, where are you working?'

I wished I had kept my mouth shut. 'You're only going to poke fun.'

'Come on,' he said. 'Cough.'

'I'm stacking shelves in Sainsbury's.'

Joe brayed with laughter. 'Oh, that's priceless, that is. Do you get to wear one of those cute little aprons?' He did a little wiggle.

'They're called tabards and that's the female staff.'

'You'll turn into one of the female staff if you work there much longer. You'll have to change your name to Christine.'

'I'll get something else eventually.'

'Like what? The pits, factories, steel mills – they're ancient history. There aren't any jobs around any more, not without qualifications. You need a degree to work in Starbucks these days.' He pulls a face. 'Women can even have babies without us. We're a redundant breed, Hooky. First it was the dinosaurs. Now it's men. We've got no future. Think about it.'

And that's what I did.

The Political Soldier

Quade had found what he wanted. He was a one-man cell. He had freedom of action. There would be no betrayal. But no man is an island. He needed the logistical support of a committed combat organisation and he had found it. His comrades called themselves Aryan Reformation. The arrangement suited him perfectly.

There were no cowards in the brotherhood, no opportunists. Most had followed the same well-trodden path. They had done their time with the mainstream nationalists, canvassed, gone on radio phone-ins, listened enraptured while the Great Leader promised electoral breakthrough, representation, power. They had watched while the chairman and his cronies betrayed their blood, their honour. They had listened to the weasel words as the leadership promised to let non-whites become members. Is that where their electoral strategy had led them, the musclebound men in suits, to the final betrayal of the race?

He felt reborn. He didn't have to hide his views anymore. He didn't play the National Socialist on a Sunday then put on the mask of moderation on a Monday. He was not afraid to declare his allegiance to the swastika. He did not disown the Führer. It was hard to know how many members there were in the organisation. He communicated by email. He used code names. They were professional. The cell structure was the highest form of political organisation, he realised. There were no traitors here. He was not interested in the dung heap of democracy like those partial nationalists. His politics was action.

He looked in the mirror and finished knotting his tie. Action would have to wait until tomorrow. Today he was going to honour his mother, the only woman who ever truly loved him.

He went to the front door where the hearse was creeping down the street. His eyes travelled along the windows of his neighbours. The curtains were drawn at two of the houses. Two? When he was a boy the whole street would have shown its respect. There was a community then. Nobody talked anymore. They didn't even know one another. They needed a common cause to shake them out of their suburban apathy. He had found it. It was time to unite the nation in a great crusade. Islam was a vampire feeding on the lifeblood of the people. It was time to tear the parasite from the throat of Britain.

There was a knock at the door. 'It is time, sir.'

He thanked the undertaker and walked to the car. He placed his hand on the side of the hearse bearing his mother's coffin. Once she had been laid in the earth, the last obstacle to his freedom would have been removed. While she was alive he held back from the ultimate commitment. Within the hour he would have said his goodbyes. Aryan Reformation had the contacts. It had the expertise. They would train him, then he would be on his own, a lone political soldier for race and nation. He would take up arms.

Chris

8 FEBRUARY 2009.

Joe was going back that night. I suggested we call on Charlie. He was delighted to see us, especially Joe. He saw me twice a week for training so I wasn't much of a novelty.

'How's my boy doing?' Joe asked.

'This big lump?' Charlie said. 'He's good. He could be a champion.'

I told him not to exaggerate.

'Who's exaggerating? You're strong as an ox. If you had a bit more of a killer instinct you'd be unstoppable.' He winked conspiratorially at Joe. 'He's got some sap on the ropes and what does he do? He paws at him.' He mimicked gently patting an imagined opponent. 'You've got to learn to go for the jugular, Hooky boy.'

It wasn't long before Army life started to dominate the evening's conversation. The pair of them exchanged stories. I sat listening, feeling completely left out. We put away a few lagers then it was time to go. Joe was halfway down the path when Charlie grabbed my sleeve.

'Army life's suiting Joe.'

I glanced at him. 'Yes, I know.'

'You could do worse,' Charlie said. 'You're wasting yourself in that supermarket. You need a challenge, son.'

I clenched a fist and pretended to sock him on the jaw. 'What are you, Charlie, a recruitment officer?'

I caught up with Joe and we walked home together. It was cold and our breath misted as we talked. We stopped outside his house glancing at the lighted window.

'When are you off?' I asked.

'About an hour.'

I stuck out my hand. He took it.

'I wonder how a uniform would suit me,' I said.

He gave me a sideways glance. 'What are you on about?'

'I'm going to sign on the dotted line.'

His face lit up. 'Seriously?'

'Yes, seriously.'

Now all I'd got to do was convince Mum and Dad.

Sixteen

Imran

Imran walked past his mother and set off up the stairs.

He heard her say, 'We are going to eat in an hour when your father gets home.'

'OK.'

He heard the concern in her voice. 'Is everything all right, Imran? Why do you never stay downstairs and talk anymore?'

'I've got homework, Ammi-ji.'

'It's not good for a boy your age to spend so much time up in his room. Why don't you go and see your friends?'

'I saw them yesterday.'

'When you have true friends you want to see them every day. That's the way it was with Chris.'

Imran stiffened. He didn't want to be reminded. 'We were little kids. Things change.' He pulled a face. 'Chris changed.'

There were no true friends, were there? Everyone went

157

away. Mum shook her head. He watched her for a moment then retreated to his room. He had not been able to get the images of Gaza out of his mind. He switched on his laptop and started to surf. He glanced at the door and plugged in his earphones. This was for his eyes only, his ears. He started his search.

It wasn't long before he found what he wanted. There was a group of bearded men, dressed in black. They were squatting on a carpet. Kalashnikovs were stacked against the wall behind them. Imran heard their voices thudding out of the earphones. They spoke directly to him.

His God was no longer at home. Imran didn't want the private, personal God of his parents. His God was to be found in the drive, energy and militancy of these fighters. Imran listened to the call to arms.

Do it where you are.

Do it at home.

Do it in your own backyard.

It is your obligation as a Muslim.

He watched masked men in military fatigues crawling through obstacles. The camera cut from pictures of war and resistance to others that showed small Palestinian children. Their faces were peppered with shrapnel scars. He witnessed crowds of young men bearing their dead on biers. He witnessed the anguish and the cries for resistance. The screen switched to a roadside bombing. Then the voices roared through his earphones.

Allahu Akbar.

Jihad.

His heart pounded. He turned up the sound and let it pulse in his head. He shook his head and slammed the lid shut. No, this was not the Islam of his childhood. This was hatred, fanaticism. He would shut it out. He had to. Otherwise he would lose his soul.

Chris

It was a stormy night when my life jumped tracks. I got off the bus and jogged through the rain-washed streets of the estate. Strands of mist dangled from street lamps and rippled away into the darkness. I relived my points win. There was nobody to see it. Dad was working a late shift and Mum had had to pick Jess up from school to drive her to a dance show in Leeds. I pounded across the estate, blinking the raindrops from my eyes.

Joe had phoned. He talked about doing something called FIBUA – fighting in a built up area. 'The lads call it FISH, fighting in someone else's house.' His voice had buzzed with excitement as he described the smoke, the shouting, the gunfire. But that was Joe. His dad said proudly that if you cut him he would bleed green. Soldiering was in his DNA.

I turned the corner into the close. I happened to look up and there was Kelly. The bedside lamp lit her face. This was how she worked, sitting on the bed with her back against the banked pillows and cushions. She didn't notice me. She was leaning forwards, her blonde hair tumbling across her cheeks as she read from her laptop screen. She was taking English, French and History at A-level, thinking about becoming a teacher. Or something. Joe always joked that when they were born she got all the brains. I asked him once what he got. He thought for a moment or two then he winked.

'Me? Hooky, I got a devil inside me.'

I watched Kelly for a moment, aching with longing, then I let myself into the empty house. I switched on the light and shook the damp from my coat. I wondered what it would be like to come home to her. The thought made me warm inside. There was a bundle of mail on the mat. For once I was the first home. I leafed through it and my heart stuttered. I ran my eyes over the letter and smiled. I was sitting with the letter in my lap when Mum and Jess arrived home. Jess was talking animatedly about the show.

'So it went well?' I asked.

'Yes, we came first. That means we go to the regional finals.'

'Go you.'

'What about your night?' Mum asked. 'Did you win?'

'I did.'

She noticed something in my voice. 'Chris?'

'I've got some news.' I handed her the letter. 'You'd better see for yourself.'

She was subdued for the rest of the evening. Dad noticed the atmosphere as soon as he arrived home just before midnight. He raised a quizzical eyebrow and Mum handed him the letter.

'It's from the Army,' she told him. 'Chris is in.' She swallowed. 'Our son is a soldier.'

Imran

Imran opened his bedroom door and froze. Dad was in his room.

'Abbu?'

He was sitting on the bed. He tossed a notebook in Imran's direction. Imran recognised his own handwriting. 'What is the meaning of this?'

Imran stared at the pad and read the list of websites and chat rooms. He stammered out an explanation. 'I was curious.'

Dad glowered at him. 'Curious. Did I raise my son to be a fool? We brought you up to be a good Muslim. Surely you understand your faith by now. Where does this anger come from? This is not what our religion means. Islam is an act of love.'

Deep inside, this is what Imran wanted. But you stopped showing us love, Abbu. You drove Rafiq away. You command unquestioning obedience.

'This filthy propaganda is not religion,' Dad barked. 'It is the kind of extremism that leads to terrorism. The people who post this rubbish are a fringe. They do not represent Islam. They represent despair. With one click of the mouse you can open the gates of hell.' He was shaking with anger. 'Imran, if you want to study the Qur'an, you should go to your Imam. I will arrange for you to speak to him.'

Imran protested that Imam Nawaz was weak. 'He never answers the questions I ask.'

His words provoked another outburst of rage from his

father. 'How dare you talk about him like that? If you want to remain under my roof you must renounce this nonsense.'

Must. A command.

'You listen to me, Imran. I was raising money for charities before you were born, boy. You know that I have been fundraising for the Gaza Emergency Appeal. You could have helped.'

Imran didn't want to hear about charity. 'It isn't enough, Abbu.'

Dad was struggling to keep his patience. 'You think the world is so simple, don't you? Why do you not read your history? Our story is not one of endless victimhood as these extremists say.' He let out a sigh. 'If you want to change the world, you must get an education first.'

Imran glanced at the laptop. 'I am getting an education.'

Dad shook his head. 'You know that is not what I mean. You were a good student, Imran. What happened? Your teachers are not happy with you. They say you should be getting straight A grades, but you are failing to give work in on time. You are not doing yourself justice.'

'I have a lot on my mind.'

'What kind of things do you have on your mind?' Dad said. 'The only thing you should be thinking about is your studies.'

'But I want to know why Muslims are dying in Iraq, Afghanistan, Palestine. I want to understand.'

His father dismissed him with an impatient wave of the hand. 'What have I done to have such sons?'

Imran accepted the challenge his father had thrown down. 'Do you really want to know what you did wrong, Abbu? You did nothing. Your Tony Blair sent troops to

Iraq and you did nothing. Racists came to this town and you did nothing. When Rafiq went to prison and needed your love and support you did nothing then either.'

Dad looked stunned. Imran's hurt continued to pour out. 'You even permit the goreh to call you Mo at work, don't you? That's right, Rafiq told me once. Your name is Mohammed, the name of the Prophet, peace be upon him, and you allow these people to shorten it to Mo. They mock you. They mock your religion.'

'They mean no harm,' he answered. 'They are not saying it in a hostile way. It does not make me any less of a Muslim.'

Imran sneered. 'Are you sure about that?'

Finally Dad snapped, wagging a finger in front of Imran's face. 'Shut your mouth, boy. I will have no more of this. I will be checking the sites you visit. I will examine this computer every single day. If you dare to defy me I will remove it from your room. I forbid you to look at this material, do you hear me? I forbid it.'

Imran was desperate to hang on to his computer. He pretended to give in. 'I am sorry, Abbu-ji. I will do as you say.'

Dad seemed surprised that Imran had caved in so easily, after such a show of defiance. 'You are accepting my authority in this?'

'Yes.'

He swept from the room. Imran listened to his father's tread on the stairs. That night he would return to the sites. This time he would remember to erase the history and commit things to memory rather than keeping a written record.

*

Twice Imran switched on the laptop. Twice he fought the temptation to return to the sites. The third time, he typed in the html. He had been using a chat room for several weeks, leaving a comment from time to time. He logged in and scrolled through the messages. There was one from a name he recognised from previous visits. The sender was called Abu Yahya. It asked if he wanted to meet. Imran's neck prickled. Every time he had visited these sites he had felt a mixture of excitement and apprehension. It reminded him of the day he stood on the ice with Chris. He remembered how the cracks had started to spread. Staring at the message it was as if they had been spreading ever since.

Imran sat looking at the screen. He wants to meet me, he thought. His every instinct screamed a warning. Ever since he'd got his first computer when he was seven his parents had been telling him about Internet safety. But that was then and this was now. He had had enough of safety and obedience. Dad had had his way and what good had it done? Imran sent a message.

Meet why?

The answer came back immediately.

Have you ever cried over the suffering of your fellow Muslims?

How did you know?

Because I have done it too.

The exchange continued. Imran sensed that Abu Yahya was testing him. Finally he invited Imran to a meeting at the local college. Imran made a note of the details. Once he had done it, he wiped the history then visited Facebook, You Tube, Google Maps and a couple of other innocuous sites so they would show up if Dad checked up on him. Imran shut the laptop down and switched off the light, but it was a long time before he could sleep. Though he knew he was going to go through with the meeting, somewhere inside, he also knew he had just walked into a dark place.

Seventeen

The White Leopard

'Asalaam alaikum.' Peace unto you.

'Walaikum salaam.' Peace unto you too.

'Did you get the job?'

Arshad's eyes were black like diamonds. He sat forward on the edge of his chair, waiting for my answer.

Suddenly I felt like the strong one. I allowed myself a quiet smile. 'I'm in.'

Arshad relaxed. 'That is good.' There was satisfaction in his voice. 'Yes, that is very good. You know what you have to do?'

I have repeated it a hundred times. Lie low. Be punctual. Go on nights out with my work colleagues. Act flattered when their painted whores come to sit on my knee. Become employee of the month. Do as my so-called friends do.

Arshad nodded and told me I had done well.

I told him it was as God willed it.

Mashallah.

Arshad smiled. 'Mashallah.' He held out his hand. 'One day you will do shaheed. You will die a martyr.'

I told him I was a soldier. I was at war. I would prepare. Then I would strike.

Arshad looked at me in a way I had never seen before. There was admiration in his gaze.

'You are not the child who came to us. You are a man now. You have shown loyalty to Islam and the Muslims.'

It has not been easy. I have sustained my studies with a series of degrading, part-time jobs. Soon it will be worth it.

'I submit to Allah. I am ready to make myself a weapon against this godless land.'

Once I was nothing. Now I am part of a community of the faithful, a band of brothers.

The awakening has started. Praise be to God.

Eighteen

Chris

10 APRIL 2010.

I heard Mum calling me. 'Chris, it's Joe for you.'

'Send him up.'

Joe appeared in the doorway. 'I've got a present for you.'

He tossed a plastic card on the bed.

'What's this?'

'Fake ID.'

I inspected the student union card.

'This will never work.'

'It will, you know. Some of the clubs are tightening up a bit. One or two are asking for passports but I know which clubs to go to.'

I pulled a face. 'My mum will crack up if I'm caught underage drinking.'

'You're not going to wimp out on us, are you? You could be fighting the Taliban in a year or so and you're worried about being caught underage drinking! You're priceless. Come on, Hooky. It's all the lads from school. It's Danny's eighteenth birthday.'

'Danny Moncur?'

'That's right,' Joe replied. 'How many other Dannys do you know?'

I gave in. 'OK, if it's his birthday. All I've got to do is come up with an excuse for my mum.'

'Leave it to me,' Joe told me. 'I'm an expert at this stuff.'

The fake ID got me past the bouncers.

'Told you. You look the part. You're big enough and ugly enough to be twenty-odd.'

There were eight of us celebrating Danny's eighteenth. I noticed that Danny was really loud but that was probably because he'd had a few before we met up. Soon we were swigging from bottles. Joe led the way approaching girls. I stayed put, nursing my drink. I watched as the other lads got to work. Before long, Joe wandered over.

'What's the matter, Hooky, pining for our Kelly?'

I watched the flirting game and told Joe I wasn't in the mood. 'Can't we just have a lads' night out?'

Danny overheard. 'What's up with Hooky? Turning gay, are you, mate?'

I told him not to be stupid.

'So lighten up,' he told me. 'It's Christmas in a few months. Pull a cracker.'

I shook my head. 'Just leave it, yeah? I'm not in the mood.'

Danny started to camp it up. 'Oh, you're definitely on the turn, lad. Are you really telling me you're not up for it? There's some talent in here tonight or haven't you noticed?'

I held his gaze. 'I told you to knock it off, Danny. Which bit of stop don't you understand?'

At this point Joe intervened. He knew my limits. 'Leave it, Dan.'

Danny got the message. For the time being. I was starting to remember a few incidents at school. Danny Moncur was like a magnet. He attracted trouble. From that moment on I kept an eye on him. Most of the time he was trying it on with some girl or other. One time he nearly provoked a fight by trying to pull one who was clearly attached. Her boyfriend looked like a rugby player. He was as broad as he was tall. Even his muscles had muscles. That didn't mean Danny was going to back off. It took Joe and another lad to pull him away. I dragged Joe to one side.

'I didn't know he was like this,' I hissed.

'Like what?'

'A maniac, that's what.'

Joe laughed and took a swig from his bottle.

'Danny's all right.'

I grimaced. 'That's what I thought until tonight, but I've never seen him outside school before. We should get out of here before something kicks off.'

Joe told me to lighten up. 'He's not that bad. Besides, we'll be getting a taxi back in half an hour.'

By the time we left the bar Danny was definitely the worse for wear.

'Come on, birthday boy,' Joe said. 'Let's get you home.'

I wasn't happy. 'Why do we have to take responsibility for him?'

'His house is on the way to our estate,' he replied. 'It makes sense for him to get a cab with us.'

I was on edge throughout our twenty-minute wait at the taxi rank but it wasn't as bad as I'd feared. Danny was happy drunk. He bantered with the couple in front of us in the queue, mostly about football. Joe met my eye. I managed a thin smile in return. OK, maybe I'd over-reacted. Finally we got our cab. The city raced by. I noticed the taxi driver's name on his plate. It was Hussain. I asked if he knew Mohammed Hussain.

'It's a common name,' the driver answered. He didn't want to talk. I carried on anyway.

'He used to be a councillor.'

'Yes, I know him. Why?'

'Oh, I thought you might be related to him or some-thing.'

The driver clocked me in his mirror. 'No, we're not related.'

I felt stupid. I wouldn't ask somebody called Smith if they knew John Smith. 'Oh, I just wondered. I know his son.'

That's when Danny made his presence felt.

'I didn't know you were mates with the local branch of the Taliban,' he said. He burst out laughing, as if he'd made the best joke in the world.

My neck burned. 'Shut it, Danny.'

The driver's eyes stared back from the mirror.

Danny wasn't finished. 'Pakis,' he slurred. 'They're everywhere.'

The driver glared.

'It's all right,' Joe said, trying to placate him. 'He doesn't mean anything. It's the drink talking.'

'He insulted me,' the driver said. 'One more word and you will have to get out.'

That lit the touch paper. Danny reared out of his seat, jabbing a finger at the driver. 'Did you threaten us?' he snarled. 'Who are you to give us orders? This is our country. Do as you're told or go back where you belong.'

Joe told him to be quiet.

The driver had had enough. 'You will have to get out.'

Danny started to pound on the partition glass. 'I'm not getting out till you drop me outside my front door.'

The driver pulled in at the side of the road. He shifted in the seat so he could look at us. His eyes roved along the back seat as he assessed the situation.

'I am asking you politely to get out of my cab.'

Danny wasn't giving in. 'Make me.'

'Just go.'

'Why should I?' Danny's face twisted. 'Take me home ... Paki!'

The driver stood his ground. 'Get him out of my cab right now.'

Danny folded his arms. 'We're not getting out until we get our ride home, are we lads?'

I'd had enough. 'Oh, we're getting out. You're a disgrace, Moncur.' I looked at the driver. 'Sorry about that idiot. How much do we owe you?'

Danny shrieked a protest. 'You're not paying him? Hooky, he's robbing us blind here. He's supposed to take us all the way.'

I told Joe to shut him up. 'If you don't I'm going to swing for him.'

With Joe's help I finally got Danny out of the cab. I set off down the street. Joe wanted to know where I was going.

'Home,' I told him.

Joe was holding Danny up. 'Aren't you going to give me a hand with him?'

I told Joe to leave him in the gutter where he belonged.

Danny lifted his head. 'What did you say?'

'I said you belong in the gutter, you lousy racist. I couldn't look that man in the eye.' I stabbed a finger at him. 'That's because of you, Moncur.'

Danny was still yelling as I turned the next corner. 'Clear off then, Paki-lover.'

I stiffened but I didn't go back.

Imran
10 APRIL 2010.

Imran found the community centre at the end of a shabby parade of shops. Dusk was gathering as he entered the meeting room. He glanced at the score of people taking their seats and asked for Abu Yahya.

'Arshad,' the man vetting new arrivals said. 'There is somebody here for you.'

Imran protested that he had come to see Abu Yahya.

'That's me,' said Arshad. 'Abu Yahya is the name I use online.'

One day Imran would discover that Arshad wasn't his real name either.

Imran shifted his feet self-consciously. What was he getting himself into? Most of the audience was male. There were three women. Two were wearing hijab. One wore the niqab. Imran took his place and listened to Arshad's speech. He was using a microphone even though his voice would carry perfectly well without it. At one point Arshad asked the audience if Al-Qaeda was a terrorist organisation. The word *no* rumbled round the room. Imran's heart thumped. What would Abbu think?

Arshad spoke quickly. 'The Prophet – peace be upon him – engaged in jihad. The Americans and their British lap dogs have been killing Muslims all over the world. What is wrong with fighting back?'

The audience was with him. Imran darted glances to his left and right, trying to take his cue from those around him. These weren't the kind of ideas he heard at home or from Imam Nawaz.

Arshad sensed Imran's hesitation. 'I think you want to ask me something.' Imran felt like a specimen on a petri dish. 'What is it?'

'My father says jihad is not about holy war. That is a small part of its meaning.' People were looking at him. His voice faltered.

'Go on.'

'It means lots of things. The word is used in the name of some charities.'

Arshad's face was a mask. 'Go on.'

Imran stumbled on for a few moments then he fell silent.

'Do you trust your father?'

'I don't know.' Imran's throat was tight. 'We argue a lot. His ways don't work. I'm looking for something different.'

'You thought you would find it here?'

'Yes.'

'What do you quarrel about?'

Imran talked about the riots. He talked about the persecution of Muslims overseas.

Arshad nodded. 'You are not being disloyal to your father. You are being loyal to your faith.' He explained what he meant by jihad. He quoted from the Qur'an by memory. He challenged Imran to disprove anything he had said. 'You must fear Allah, brother. Fear Allah. Your father is feeding you half-truths. He will be an obstacle to your commitment to God's work.' He looked around the audience. 'It is not the Muslims who choose this fight. The West is at war with Islam. Can you deny this? Britain and America arm Israel. Against whom? Against the Muslims. Their army's boots tread the lands of Iraq and Afghanistan. Whose lands are they? They are Muslim lands. The kuffar will not let people be at peace. That is why a new generation of Muslims has woken up.'

Arshad asked Imran what else his father had told him. Some of the audience laughed.

'Maybe he has told you to be a good British boy. Does he tell you to support the English football team?' He shook his head. 'Does he want you to have Christian friends?' He got a reaction from Imran. 'Maybe he wants you to integrate. What are we supposed to integrate into, tell me that? Binge drinking? Gambling?'

Imran was making his way out of the room at the end of the meeting when he felt a hand on his shoulder. It was Arshad.

'You think I was hard on you, don't you?'

'I don't know. Maybe.'

For the first time a smile crossed Arshad's face. 'I did it for your own good, my friend. You must strip the scales from your eyes. You must be reborn as a true Muslim. Now, do you want to know more?'

Imran hesitated.

'Do you?'

An internal voice screamed no. He said, 'Yes.'

Arshad smiled. 'You have made the right choice my friend.' He scribbled his mobile number on a scrap of paper. 'Give me a call.' He thought for a moment and added his address. 'You can come round to my flat. We have a study circle. But you must always call first. Always. You got that?'

'Sure,' Imran said. 'I've got to call first.'

Chris

10 APRIL 2010.

My mobile rang. The caller ID told me it was Joe.

'Yes, what's up?'

'What are you doing, Hooky?

'I'm in town shopping.'

'You with anybody?'

'No,' I told him. 'I'm on my own.'

'What do you say we meet up?'

I was still angry with him over the night out. 'I don't know. I've got things to do at home. I'm on my way to the bus station.'

Joe wouldn't take no for an answer. 'Come on, mate. I've got to go back tonight. I'll be shipping out to Afghanistan in a few months. What do you say we go for something to eat?'

I gave in. 'Nando's? Half twelve?'

'See you there.'

Half twelve approached and there was a nasty surprise.

Joe walked in with Danny Moncur in tow. I felt like walking out.

'What's he doing here?'

Danny spoke for himself. 'I came to apologise. I was out of order.'

'You don't say.'

Danny and Joe slid into the bench seats opposite. 'Look, I'd had a few over the odds. I got a bit mouthy.'

'A bit!'

'Come on, mate,' Danny said. 'Just accept my apology. I was an embarrassing drunk.'

The waiter came to take our order.

Joe played peacemaker. 'Come on, Hooky. He's said sorry.'

We ordered, made small talk, ate. It didn't take long but Joe seemed satisfied with the way things had gone. We paid and left.

'Look,' I said. 'I've got to get back.'

'Fine,' Joe said, 'I might as well come back with you.'

Danny looked disappointed. 'Isn't anybody coming for a pint?'

Joe and I killed the idea with synchronised stares.

Danny raised his hands. 'OK, I get the message.'

We were crossing the main square towards the bus stop when I noticed the big TV screen that dominated the square. It showed angry scenes at an Army parade somewhere.

'Oh, not that again!'

It was a repeat of what had happened in Luton the year before. About a dozen Asian men were heckling the soldiers. They were shouting 'terrorists' and holding up placards. I read them and winced:

British soldiers go to hell.
Crusader armies out of Afghanistan.
British government. Terrorist government.

Joe was furious. 'Cheeky bastards,' he snarled.

A crowd of white men moved in waving a Union flag. They were shouting 'Scum!' and 'No surrender to the Taliban!' The protestors were mirror images of each other, mouthing insults. They were feeding off one another's rage.

Instinctively I glanced at Danny.

He grinned. 'I'm saying nothing.'

We were about to go when a furious quarrel broke out on the other side of the crowd watching the screen. There was a stand off between two gangs of lads, one white, one Asian.

'They're right,' one of the Asian lads was saying. 'The British Army is a terrorist organisation. Your "heroes" kill women and children.'

Danny made a joke of it. 'Go and give that mouthy one a smack, Joe. He's calling you a terrorist.'

'Hooky's the boxer,' Joe said.

Danny laughed. 'Oh yes, I'm with *two* Army boys. I forgot you were joining up too.'

That's when I saw Imran, there in the middle of it all. His expression made my blood run cold.

'Imran, what are you doing here?'

The familiar face resolved itself into a mask of incomprehension and disgust. 'Is it true? You're joining up?'

'Look . . .'

His eyes were blazing.

'Is it true?'

A moment's hesitation. Then the answer. 'Yes,' I told him. 'Don't go off on one.'

'You joined the Crusader army.'

I shook my head. 'Don't mouth slogans at me, Imran. I'm your mate. Talk to me.'

Danny looked on amused. 'Do you know him, Hooky? Oh, that's classic. You're going to fight the Taliban and your mate's with the local branch. Hooky's got a pet Paki.'

The final word acted as a trigger. Imran threw a punch. It snapped Danny's head back and spun him sideways. Blood was gouting from his nose.

'You're going to pay for that.'

Danny went for Imran and they tussled for a moment or two. Within seconds both of them were smeared with Danny's blood. After that, all hell broke loose. Danny lashed out at Imran, but Imran caught him again, knocking him to the ground. Both sides had been squaring off. Now they flew at each other. I watched Joe trying to staunch the blood, then I spotted Imran heading for the market hall on the far side of the square. I caught up with him.

'Imran, wait.'

He turned. He had Danny's blood on his face and hands. He was so agitated he was trembling. 'What do you want?'

'I told you, I want to talk.'

'Why now? How long's it been, Chris? Maybe you forgot where to find me. Oh no, you used to live right next door. You had my address. You had my phone number.'

'You had mine too,' I reminded him.

He wasn't interested in anything I had to say. 'Now I know why I never heard from you, *soldier boy*. Looking forward to your first kill?' He held out his arms. 'I'm a Muslim. Do you want to kill me?'

'I don't want to kill anybody, Imran,' I protested. I searched for something to say. 'We're over there to protect the people from the Taliban.'

'Is that right?' Imran demanded. 'Do you know how the Crusaders do that? They bomb weddings.'

I recognised the incident from an old news broadcast. 'You don't think anybody did that on purpose, do you? In war the innocent get caught in the crossfire.'

Imran's eyes glittered. 'They wouldn't if there was no crossfire.'

'Oh, come on,' I said. 'We can't just surrender. There are two sides in this war.'

'Yes, one raised from the soil of Afghanistan and one a foreign invader.'

I shook my head. 'Most Afghans want us there. They've done polls.'

'Polls! You're unreal.' Imran started to walk away.

I grabbed his sleeve. 'Just talk to me, Imran. We grew up together.'

'That's right. We did. But it didn't mean anything to you, did it?'

'You're still my mate. We shouldn't be enemies. Look, I joined up to do something with my life ... serve my country.' I hesitated. Was that really why, or was it really because I didn't want to be Christine from Sainsbury's? 'I don't even want to be over there. I just—'

Imran turned. 'You just do your job, that it? I bet that's what the Nazis said.' He became aware of the blood on his hands. To my horror he reached out and smeared it on my face. It was a cold, deliberate act. I was so shocked I just stood there and let him do it.

'Is this what you want, Chris? You want to be blood

brothers again?' He formed his thumb and fingers into the shape of a revolver and pressed it to my forehead. 'Yet you'll go over there and kill my fellow Muslims. Go to hell, man. Yes, just go to hell.'

I tried to catch up with him but he was always faster than me. I lost him in the crowded market. But I'd lost him a long time before that.

'Imran!'

Imran

10 APRIL 2010.

Imran found himself in a run-down part of town, a street of cheap fried chicken joints and boarded-up shops. He walked fast, reliving so many memories. He regretted drifting apart from Chris. Their friendship stood out as one of the happiest times in his life. The passage of time had given it a kind of aura, a mythic feel. Now even that seemed like a lie. It was as if everything they had ever done belonged to a photo album that had been tossed on a fire. One by one the pages curled, blackened and burned. Soon there was only ash swirling in the air.

Everything was lost.

Chris phoned. Imran stared at his name on the caller ID. He didn't answer. Eventually his phone stopped ringing. For a long time he walked aimlessly, senses swimming. The memories spiralled and eddied through his consciousness like wind-blown snow. That thing with the blood, he thought, where did that come from? What's wrong with me? His mind was restless, his feelings chaotic and unformed. There had to be somebody he could talk to. He buried his hands in his pockets and his fingers closed round the scrap of paper on which he had written Arshad's address. Imran remembered he was supposed to call first, but it was only five minutes' walk. He took the next left and strode briskly towards the flat.

Arshad answered the door and frowned. 'You were supposed to phone me before you came round.' He saw the blood. 'What happened to you?'

Imran explained about the confrontation in the square.

Arshad checked the street and ushered him inside. The moment the door closed he grabbed Imran's arm and wrestled him against the wall. His face was taut with hostility.

'Next time you do what I say. There must be no exceptions. We're not playing games here, Imran. This is important.'

Imran stammered an apology.

'Get yourself cleaned up,' Arshad ordered.

Imran was returning from the bathroom when he heard a noise from an adjoining room. There was someone else in the house.

'Who's that?'

Arshad was on edge. He bundled Imran out of the door. 'You should go.'

'But I need to talk,' Imran protested.

Arshad shook his head. 'This isn't a good time.' Then he slammed the door.

Imran set off down the street, wounded and puzzled by Arshad's behaviour.

*

Imran arrived home, coming in the back way and glancing at Lucky's kennel. The little dog had died a few weeks earlier and was buried in The Wilderness where Imran had found him. Imran was tired. He wanted to sleep and shut the world out. Maybe he could make himself nothing. Maybe he could shrink into a dark space where there were no memories, no worries, no terrors. It didn't work out like that. Dad met him at the door.

He demanded to know where Imran had been.

'Walking.'

'Until this hour? Don't lie to me, boy.'

'I am not a boy. I'm almost eighteen.'

'It is a boy who starts fighting in the town centre.'

Imran stared at him. 'How do you know about that?'

'Chris called round. He tried phoning you, but you didn't answer. He was very upset.'

'There is no point him contacting me. I won't talk to him.'

'Why not?'

'He has joined the Army.'

'What is wrong with that? Many Muslims have served in the British military over the years. The Council of Mosques is advising young men to think about it as a career.'

'Then they are as bad as Chris.'

Dad was trying not to lose his temper. 'Chris is your friend.'

'That's a laugh. We haven't been friends for years. It was his choice, not mine. He's chosen his side. I've picked mine.'

Dad clenched his fists. 'Sides? What does that mean?'

'He has joined the kuffar army. He is my enemy.'

Horror flooded Dad's face. 'Where did you hear this filthy word? You are meeting those extremists. They are not Muslims. Islam is peace, love, compassion. Imran, you don't understand what you're dealing with. You can't fight violence with more violence.'

'Don't treat me like a child, Abbu. I listen to what they have to say. They make more sense than you.'

'Don't you dare talk to me like that!' Dad fought to control his anger. 'You want to be a good Muslim and you believe choosing the militant path will help? Imran, you are conflicted. Start by carrying out your first fundamental duty to God, your daily prayers. Pray to Him alone to put you on the correct path, the path of our beloved prophet – not of those who deface Islam with their sermons of hate. I insist you stop seeing these people!'

'What are you going to do, Abbu, send me to sit on the naughty step? Ground me?' Imran tried to shove past. Dad blocked his progress.

'Go to your room, Imran. We will talk tomorrow.'

Imran answered wearily. 'That is what I was trying to do.'

He was about to climb the stairs when Dad threw his parting shot.

'This nonsense will stop.'

Imran spun round. 'You couldn't let it go, could you? You couldn't let me sleep on it. Get out of my way.'

He pushed past, knocking his father off balance.

Mum rushed from the living room. 'Don't go, Imran. Please.'

It was too late. Imran swept out into the night. He walked for an hour in the rain before making the call. This time Arshad said he could come round.

Chris

10 APRIL 2010.

I received a call at home. I pulled out my phone, hoping it was Imran. It was Joe.

'What's up?'

'Where are you?'

'I'm home.'

'Are you alone?'

'No, Mum and Jess are in.'

I heard a sigh of disappointment.

'What are you after, Joe?'

'I need to talk, just you and me.' He thought for a moment. 'Have you eaten?'

'Not since Nando's.'

'I'll see you at the chippy.'

I arrived five minutes later. 'What's up?'

'Once we've had something to eat, I'll tell you.' We both bought chips and gravy. We sat on a bench by the adventure playground and ate them with wooden forks out of Styrofoam trays.

'So how did things turn out in the square?' I asked. 'Sorry I bailed out like that.'

Joe shrugged. 'You had your reasons. The police came. Everybody drifted away. There isn't much to tell.'

I was confused. 'But you said you wanted to talk.'

'I do, but not about that.'

I waited.

'This is it, Hooky. I'm off to Afghanistan.'

'When did you hear?'

185

'When I got home. The last few hours I've been like a cat on hot bricks.'

I heard something in his voice. 'Are you OK?'

Joe dropped his chips in the litterbin. He had only eaten half. 'Not really.'

'But this is what you wanted.'

A scarlet, bloated sun was sinking towards the horizon.

'Yes, I was full of it, wasn't I?'

I looked at him. 'Are you scared?'

He nodded.

'But you kept telling me how much you loved the Army.'

'I do love it.'

I finished my chips. 'I don't get it.'

'Chris, it's like this.'

That's when I knew he was serious. He never called me Chris, always Hooky.

'I love the job. I'm going to do my duty. Anything they ask me to do, I'll carry it out to the best of my ability.'

'So what's wrong?'

'I'm good at what I do. Stick me in front of one of those Taliban, one on one, I'm the man.'

'But ... ?'

'But that isn't what this war's about, is it? You catch a stray bullet, you stand on an IED, you're gone like that.' He snapped his fingers. 'I just get this feeling I might not be coming home.'

Nineteen

Chris

I start to make my way around the perimeter of the parade
ground towards the rest of the company. Nugget and Cent
are by my side. As we walk, the day is beginning to feel
unreal. I hear the pad of my desert-issue boots, rhythmic,
regular like a heartbeat now that I am getting used to my
prosthetic limb. The sound beats out a warning. There's a
bomber. It beats out a threat. The word came from Imran.
I hear Nugget's voice.

'Ready to get that medal?'

I nod, but my mind isn't on the ceremony. Have I made
a mistake following Dad's advice? If this is a ruse to disrupt
the ceremony then it is a sophisticated one. Imran didn't
dream this up. It isn't his style. Whatever I think of the
direction he has taken in life, he has never been sly. That's
one thing I know about him: he's as straight as a pencil.
Alarm bells are going off in my head. I should talk to
somebody.

Nugget exchanges glances with Cent.

I stare at them. The words boom in my head. Nugget puts a hand on my shoulder. 'Come on, Hooky lad. Do it for yourself and do it for your fallen comrades too. Do it for Sean.'

He's talking about Sean McEvoy. I got the news of Mac's death when I was in Headley Court, learning to use my leg. He died in a friendly fire incident. Captain Forrester called in air support. There was a cock-up. The inquiry into the incident has yet to report. They dropped a 500lb bomb right on top of the compound Sean was using for cover. I felt numb when I heard. Then I remember another dead soldier.

Joe.

Chris

18 JUNE 2010.

It was towards the end of my training when I got the news. I'd been on an exercise clearing houses. The officers had this thing about staying within the rules of engagement. We'd had an afternoon of diving through windows. There had been smoke, shouting, gunfire. We weren't using live rounds but it was real enough to set my heart pounding, a taste of things to come. As I left the area I saw Captain Forrester walking towards me. My heart stuttered.

'Are you looking for me, sir?'

He handed me a phone message.

'I'm sorry, Chris,' he said. 'Life's a bastard sometimes.'

I unfolded the notepaper and my senses reeled. 'Oh no. Oh Christ, no.'

'Are you all right?'

I stared at the paper. Kelly had made the call. It was Joe. His instincts had been right. A stray bullet had his name on it. He was killed in a firefight, dead by the time he hit the ground. It was a single shot to the head.

'Chris?'

'Sir?'

'Are you OK?'

I nodded dumbly. But I wasn't OK. I was in shock. I was a ghost, floating through an alien landscape. None of this was real. It was like some kind of film. The colours were too bright. The noises were too loud, too distinct, too sharp. The world around me was a fantasy. At that moment only Joe was real.

And he was dead.

I wanted to spin the world back on its axis and undo the events that had taken Joe. I wanted to unmake the bitter, brutal fact of his death. He had had a premonition. But he did his duty anyway. I just couldn't understand how somebody who was so alive could be dead. How could somebody I had talked to nearly every day of my life for seven years be gone? All of a sudden it felt as if I were standing on quicksand.

'Where do they go?' I murmured.

'Chris?'

'The dead, sir – where do they go?'

'I don't know, son. I'm not religious.'

I found myself saying the first thing that came into my head. 'We ate chips.'

'What?'

'Me and Joe. We sat on a bench eating chips. He knew he was going to die.'

'Do you want to talk to somebody? The chaplain maybe?'

I shook my head. 'No, I just need to be on my own.' I pinched the bridge of my nose. 'I'm ... fine.'

I don't remember the rest of the walk back. I don't know how I ended up sitting on my bed. It was as if I'd been walking in my sleep. I looked at the note for the longest time then something snapped. Suddenly I was trashing my belongings, pulling the pictures off the wall, crashing my boots, my fists against the door, turning things over, roaring my anger and my despair. I felt somebody's arms round me then a voice saying.

'It's OK, Hooky. It's OK.'

Chris

25 JUNE 2010.

But it wasn't OK. It didn't get better. Joe's death didn't unmake itself. It was worse for Kelly. Joe was her big brother, older by five minutes, and he was gone. For eighteen years they had played, laughed, squabbled, fought.

'I'll never hear his voice again,' she said. 'I'll never see his face. Chris, half of me is dead too.' Tears spilled down her cheeks.

I was standing beside her at the graveside. She was dressed all in black. We all were: Joe's family, my mum and dad. I put my arms round her shoulders and she leaned her head on my shoulder. I had dreamed of this closeness. A thousand times I had pictured myself breathing the scent of her hair the way I was doing at that moment. But it was never meant to happen this way. Not in these circumstances. Not with Joe dead.

That word again. Dead.

That reality. Dead.

'I don't know what to say, Kell.'

She told me I didn't need to say anything. 'Just hold me, Chris. That says more than words.'

So I held her and listened to the words of the priest. My eyes drifted to the horizon where storm clouds were massing. Sheet lightning glimmered on the skyline and thunder rumbled far off over the hills. The wind freshened and Kelly shuddered a little. I folded her in my arms and she turned her face into my chest. I felt her weeping before I heard her. Her whole body was trembling. Without thinking, I pressed my lips against her hair.

It was a moment before I realised that my own cheeks were wet with tears.

I went back to the house. Joe's mum and dad had organised a celebration of his life. They had compiled a film with a soundtrack of his favourite music. Kelly sat in an armchair. I perched on the arm. I just wanted to be close to her. Suddenly it felt so right. I watched the sequence of images: Joe as a baby, as a toddler stumbling through the tide at Blackpool beach and falling headfirst into the waves. Everybody laughed. There was no affectation. They were laughing for Joe, to remind themselves of who he was and what he was worth as a son, brother, friend, grandson, cousin or nephew.

Soon there was the Joe I met that day on the bus. He was wearing his brand new school uniform, looking very self-conscious and uncomfortable.

I whispered to Kelly. 'I can smell the past.'

'What?'

'It's like I'm sitting right next to him. I've got that new uniform smell in my nostrils.' I wasn't making it up. It was as if I had been transported back to that September morning. 'Me and Joe were here. You were a few seats up with your friends.'

'Yes, I remember.'

'It's as real as anything in this room. How does that work?'

'Beats me.' Kelly clung to me. 'I love him so much. We fought like cat and dog. I want him to walk through the door and throw his bag down. I want him to tease me and make me yell at him. How can he be gone, Chris? It doesn't make any sense.' She squeezed my hand. 'I just want him back.'

I returned the squeeze. 'Yes, me too, Kell. Me too.'

From that moment on Joe's story was my story. I saw him with his GCSE certificates. I saw him with his boxing trophies. There was film of Joe and Kelly's eighteenth birthday party. I was in almost every shot with them. The film ended with Joe in his uniform, proud, straight, invincible. But he wasn't. He was flesh and blood. He gave himself up to the war in Afghanistan.

I felt Mum and Dad looking at me. I know what they were thinking. I didn't return their gaze. It would have been too cruel. I kept my eyes on the TV screen, for them as much as for me. When the film ended everyone applauded spontaneously. Some of the men shook hands.

Joe's dad got to his feet. 'Ladies and gentlemen, I would like to invite you into the garden for one last goodbye to my wonderful son.' When everyone was outside, he said a few words. The thunder was still rumbling fitfully in the distance, but the rain held off. It was a fine, warm evening. 'It only seems like yesterday that I held my beautiful Joe in my arms. My wife had Kelly in hers. We were so blessed. There they were, Joe and Kelly, our twins, our gifts from God. Imagine it, even as I am standing here I can smell the talcum powder on their heads. Do you know that newborn baby smell?'

Every parent in the room nodded. Kelly clung to me. Her dad was battling on through his speech.

'I watched him grow into a man and I was so proud. We weren't just father and son. We were best friends.' He started to keen, his grief a seeping wound that wouldn't close. 'I can't believe he's gone. My boy, he was so strong, so ... alive. How can he be gone?'

It was the question I had asked myself. Kelly joined her mum comforting him. Finally he was able to conclude his speech. 'He lives on, you know. He lives on in every star in the night sky. He lives on in every atom of this house, in every memory, in every thought. Most of all, he lives on here, in our hearts.' He rubbed at his eyes. 'Look, at me, sobbing like a baby. I'm not saying any more or I'll make a complete fool of myself. Let's celebrate Joe's life.'

Chris

Dad finished his toast and gulped down the last dregs of his mug of tea. 'What time do you leave?'

'I'll have to go about six o'clock this evening.'

He considered the answer. 'I should be able to get home in time to see you off.' He stuck out a hand. 'Just in case, I'd better say my goodbyes now.' I took his hand. Suddenly, on impulse, he pulled me close and embraced me. He whispered in my ear. 'I love you, son.'

I knew he was remembering Joe's funeral and thinking about my tour of duty. 'I love you too, Dad.'

It's hard to say something like that to your dad. I've never been one for all that emotional stuff. It made me uncomfortable. I must have said it when I was a little kid, but not since. It just never seemed to need saying. That kind of love is a fact, like gravity, yes, like apple blossom falling on a windy day. He released me. 'You make sure you come back in one piece. You hear me?'

I forced a smile. 'I hear you.'

Then he was gone. Mum had left half an hour previously to drop Jess off at school before she went to work herself. Suddenly I was alone in the house. I turned the TV on. The breakfast news programmes were just finishing. I surfed for a moment or two then switched off. I opened the fridge and closed it again without choosing anything to eat or drink. I had a whole day to kill and I didn't know how. I'd never been much of a reader and daytime TV was downright depressing. I returned to the living room and glanced outside.

That's when I saw her. Kelly had just left the house. She was wearing a powder blue summer dress. The storms of the previous day had blown away to the west and the overcast skies had been replaced by bright sunshine and a strong breeze. Her dress rippled in the wind. I watched her and my stomach turned over.

I kept watching for the longest time, marvelling at her beauty, wondering when the girl became a woman. The sight of her walking against the wind brought back memories of the way she held onto me at the cemetery. I grabbed my keys and phone and stumbled to the front door, jarring my knee against the armchair. For once I wasn't going to throw away my chance to say how I felt. I flung the door open and ran after her.

'Hey Kell,' I called. 'Where are you going?'

She turned and a smile lit her face. 'Only up to the postbox.' She showed me the letter. She linked arms. 'Mum asked me to get this in the post. They've gone away for a couple of days. They need a bit of time together.'

'How are they managing?'

Kelly met my gaze. 'Dad's taking it worse than Mum. She does the crying, but he's completely lost. He just can't accept that Joe's gone.'

'What about you?'

'Same thing. I still expect him to walk through the door with that cheeky grin on his face.'

'But you're coping?'

'I don't know yet. Ask me in a few months.'

That was when I should have talked to her. About us. The words stalled in my throat. We reached the postbox. I cursed myself for not saying how I felt. It was Kelly who spoke. She wanted to know if she could ask me something.

'Sure. What?'

'What's it like burying your friend and knowing you're going out there too?'

The question slammed into me like a punch to the stomach.

I shrugged. 'I don't know. I try not to think about it.' I didn't tell her that it preyed on my mind every single day and part of every night before sleep took me.

'You must think about it sometimes.'

'I don't think about getting hurt.' It's true. I didn't. Not much. 'I'm scared that I'll let somebody down. I won't do my job properly. I'm scared that, when push comes to shove, I won't be the soldier I'm meant to be.'

She found that hard to understand. 'I'd be wondering where the next danger was coming from.'

'That's how I thought I would be. I can only tell you how I feel right now.'

We reached her front door. I was aching with frustration at my own shyness. It was Kelly who broke the ice. She invited me in. Once inside, there was an awkward silence. I was leaving that evening. I didn't want to go away without saying something. The things I wanted to share weighed me down like chains.

'You like me, don't you, Chris?'

I fell over myself to tell her yes. 'What kind of question is that? You know I do.'

Then she did something wonderful. She took a step forward and rested her palms on my chest. A shaft of sunlight lanced across the room and fell on her face. I was scared that she would feel my heart pounding.

'How much do you like me?'

She was looking deep into my eyes. That made my flesh

burn. My instinct was to drop my gaze but I forced myself to keep looking. It took me a few moments to find the words. 'More than you can imagine.' My voice was thick with emotion and desire. I was breathing in her perfume. My throat was tight. 'Kell . . .'

Her hands moved up my chest and curled round the back of my neck. 'Chris, just stop talking. I want you to kiss me.'

I inclined my head and felt the soft press of her lips. Her breathing was urgent.

Her arms stayed round my neck. Her lips lingered over mine.

'Is this what you want, for us to be together?'

I told her yes, more than anything. 'You?'

She kissed me again. 'You big dope. Are you that bad at picking up the signals a girl's putting out?'

I couldn't believe I'd been so stupid. Joe told me all this and I didn't do anything about it. 'You've been putting out signals!'

There was mischief in her eyes. 'Short of dragging you down on the bed, there isn't much more I could have done.' She pressed herself against me. 'Losing Joe made me realise how much I need you, Chris. When do you go back?'

'This evening.'

'Then we'd better make the most of today.'

I flew out from RAF Brize Norton. The flight to Kandahar took seven hours. I stared out of the window and saw Kelly's face in every play of light. It would have been so easy to stay in my living room watching the TV that

197

morning. I realised how easy it was to let something precious run through my fingers.

Like love.

Like friendship.

In that moment, as I gazed down at the ochre, mountain-rutted ground far below, I wish I'd gone to see Imran before I left. But there had been no reconciliation. I had allowed my friendship with Imran to die. I closed my eyes. Regret gnawed at me as I recalled those last angry exchanges.

However stumblingly, however ineptly, I'd finally managed to tell Kelly how I felt. But I had unfinished business with Imran. I could have spoken to him. I could have made him understand that I wasn't like the Danny Moncurs of this world. I could have explained that I was still the same lad he ran wild with all those years ago.

My gaze travelled over the guys occupying the blue seats around me. Some were dozing. One or two were reading. Others were staring into space. Few were talking. The good humour had subsided after take-off. Soon we got the order to don helmets and body armour. We were plunged into almost total darkness as we began our descent into Kandahar. Only the exit light illuminated the gloom.

Finally we were on the ground. All that was left was the Hercules transport flight on to Camp Bastion. Soon we would see the camp's grid system stretching over eight square kilometers of desert. We would enter one of its air-conditioned pods and wait for orders.

We were crossing the airfield when Cent nudged me. The word went round. It was the repatriation ceremony for a lance corporal who had died in action during the previous week. I stopped to pay my respects as the last post sounded. I joined the soldiers standing to attention. Wind whipped the desert uniforms. A huge sun hung over the horizon. A death sent me on my way from England. A death greeted me in Kandahar. Nobody moved until the aircraft took off, dipping its wings in a final tribute to the fallen man.

Welcome to Afghanistan.

Twenty

Imran

2 JULY 2010.

Imran had become part of Arshad's group. For the last three months he had slipped into the routine of leafletting and persuading possible new recruits to his cause. Then there had been the confrontations. Strangely, Imran had liked that best of all: arguing with opponents, seeing himself as strong where others were weak. He had found an outlet for his anger and that had made him feel more in control of his life.

Then Arshad had told him that they were going to leaflet the mosque where Imran's family worshipped. He didn't want to be there. His heart had been pounding ever since Arshad told him where they were going. He asked to be excused this one time. Arshad would have none of it. He was testing him. Imran didn't feel like a soldier now. He felt like a child.

Imran handed out his leaflets and searched for Dad in the crowd. He imagined the disappointment in his father's eyes. What am I doing? Imran wondered. I left home because I wanted to hurt you, Abbu. I wanted something to happen. I wanted life to be straightforward, certain. The life he had chosen was an act of defiance against his father, against Dad's weakness. Against his own. Even so, part of Imran still wanted to make Dad proud.

He hated himself for clinging on to such childish loyalties, for still hanging on to them somewhere deep inside. So far it hadn't been that difficult to slip into his new lifestyle, like living in a bubble. He'd existed entirely within the group. They ate together, talked together, watched the same videos, parroted the same slogans. None of them failed to pray five times a day. He manned stalls in the local colleges and enjoyed skirmishing with the enemies of Islam. He attended meetings. The daily routine took up all his time, sustained him, protected him from doubt. Only late at night or first thing in the morning was he alone with his thoughts. That was when he imagined himself back in his own room. In those moments he ached for the past.

If only he was like Arshad. He never had doubts. He never mentioned his family, or his childhood. Imran wasn't even sure where he was from. Arshad was the organiser, the teacher. Ask him a question and he answered immediately, quoting from the Qur'an. Now, as they approached the mosque, Imran saw the familiar faces, the looks of astonishment as they saw him and what he was doing. Imran wanted the ground to open and swallow him up. The first protests started to fly. Fingers tapped at Arshad's leaflets. Accusing eyes darted from his face to Imran's.

'This is wrong,' some of the worshippers were saying.

'You are using the house of God, the house of Allah to put forward a political programme. Why do you have to stir things up? We don't want you here.'

Arshad had an answer. 'Palestine is occupied. Afghanistan is invaded. Iraq is torn to bits. The only solution for the Muslims is khilafah.'

There was an angry response. 'You don't know what you're talking about, you young fool. What do you think you're doing, coming here with your talk of a caliphate? You are playing into the hands of our enemies. Every racist will take comfort from your conduct. They take pictures of you and put them in the newspapers. They say that all Muslims are the same as you.'

'Would that be such a bad thing?' Arshad demanded. 'It is time to turn from ignorance to Islam.'

An elderly man in a brown topi hat challenged Arshad.

'Who are you to say who is and who is not a Muslim?' He pointed to two of his companions. 'I have been to Mecca with these men. We are all hajjis. Who are you to lecture us with your extremist nonsense?'

His closest neighbour, a man with rheumy eyes, stared disapprovingly at Imran. 'You come from a good family. What are you doing with this man? Did your father teach you nothing? You are bringing shame upon us.'

The words wounded Imran, but Arshad was full of contempt. Imran took a step back. Suddenly, he wanted to let the bundle of leaflets slip from his fingers and go fluttering down the street. He wanted to fade into the crowd. What was he doing there? When he was sitting in Arshad's flat, watching DVDs of the West's war on Islam, it seemed so easy. He knew he was right. It was God's will. Here, surrounded by neighbours and family friends, his faith in Arshad was faltering.

'You don't speak for the Muslims,' Arshad snarled. 'A new generation has woken up.'

His words were met with derision. 'Where is this new generation? Look at the young people here. They show respect. There are two of you. That's right, just two. Is this your jihad?'

The question provoked scornful laughter. Imran dropped his head. Not Arshad. He snapped back like a cornered animal. He revelled in adversity. The more he was outnumbered, the more righteous he became. Arshad saw Imam Nawaz watching. He caught sight of Imran and vanished into the mosque. Imran saw the way his face changed. The furious exchanges continued. Arshad was stabbing a finger at those around him.

'They expel us from our homes in Palestine, jail us in Guantanamo and deny us our rights in Britain. Are you prepared to let that pass without protest?'

Heads turned. A police officer was approaching. He took one of Arshad's leaflets and ran his eyes over it. 'There have been complaints from the mosque,' he said. 'I suggest you stop troubling these people. If you move away now then we don't have to take things further.'

Arshad spat his anger at the men around him. 'How dare you call the kuffar police? It is haram to get the police involved in Muslim affairs.'

The police officer wanted to know if Arshad was going to move on. Arshad ignored him and continued to address the crowd milling round the entrance to the mosque. 'The Prophet – peace be upon him – engaged in jihad,' he told them. 'The Americans and their lap dogs here in Britain have been killing Muslims all over the world. Are you going to tell me it is wrong to fight back?'

A member of the mosque committee retorted that he didn't understand. 'The Prophet took up arms against thirteen years of torture, persecution and the killing of his companions by pagans. His jihad was to bring peace, not war. Do you want to bring peace? In a valid jihad the Prophet forbade the killing of priests, women, children and non-combatants. Do you justify the deaths of innocents?'

When Arshad continued to berate the crowd the policeman waved to his waiting colleagues. Arshad noticed the gesture and finally agreed to leave. That was when Imran saw his father.

'Is this the reason you walked out of my house?' Dad demanded. 'You did it to come here and peddle lies?'

Imran felt Arshad's stare. This was the crucial test.

Dad made Imran's mind up for him. He didn't try to talk. He yelled.

'I warned you against these people.' He tore the leaflets from his son's hands and threw them in his face. 'Is this my reward for raising you to respect the country you live in? Why do you want to make a fool of yourself in front of all these people?'

Finally Imran found his voice. His words flew like poisoned darts. 'You ask me to respect British democracy. What is it I am meant to respect? This government is involved in the bombing, torture and imprisonment of your fellow Muslims. When you accept the laws of this godless land you accept their war against us. You go against Islam.'

Arshad was satisfied. He started to go. Imran glimpsed

his father's face. It was taut with pain and humiliation. 'If you go with that man, you are no longer my son.'

The words struck home. They sank deep inside Imran, piercing a hole in his heart. He steeled himself. He turned and followed Arshad. Behind him, his dad shouted, but the words were lost on the wind.

'Where are you going?' Arshad demanded when Imran walked away up the hill.

'I need some time to myself,' Imran replied.

He was angry.

At Arshad.

At Abbu.

At himself.

That most of all. His heart banged in his chest as he climbed the steep gradient. Stupid! His life was crazy. He wanted to be strong but he was weak. He wanted to be hard but he was soft. He stumbled from one crisis to another. He skirted the old neighbourhood.

It was a few moments before he realised where he was going. It was The Wilderness. Memories came rushing back. He was always happy there. It was where he came every time he was hurt, lonely or afraid. Every time he came away revived.

Not this time. Earthmovers were rolling back and forth over the spot where he had buried Lucky. The ground had been levelled. The concrete arteries of a new retail park were spreading across the cleared space. He stared at a huge hoarding. It announced the development of a unique shopping experience.

This time there was no solace to be had in The Wilderness.

The Political Soldier

Quade watched the confrontation outside the mosque from the comfort of his car. He shook his head when the police failed to arrest the loud-mouthed jihadi. Wasn't that just typical? They shouted their poisonous beliefs from the rooftop and the boys in blue didn't do a thing to stop them.

So much for this gutless state with its lunatic Human Rights Act. What about the human rights of the indigenous British? The police were stripped of any real power. They got their orders from the liberal establishment. This was their tolerance. This was their democracy. They were sleepwalking into an Islamic state. Quade used his iPhone to photograph the main players. He couldn't let this pass without taking action.

The quarrel interested him. From what he could hear it was between father and son. It amused him to see civil war breaking out within the ghetto. He imagined them coming to blows but it didn't happen. Well, at least they were feeling some of the pain he felt every day as he saw his country lost, his race drowning in a sea of multiculturalism. When he'd finished taking his photos a thought occurred to him. He didn't have a phone number for his comrades in Aryan Reformation but he did have an email address. He typed a message, glancing up occasionally to watch the worshippers as they filed into the mosque.

Keeping an eye on our friends.
I have an idea for a spectacular.
Do you want to discuss?

He signed it using his codename Der Adler, the eagle, and hit the send button. After a couple of minutes the handset buzzed. He read the reply and smiled. Command was interested.

Imran
3 JULY 2010.

Next morning Imran was manning the group's stall. There were six of them handing out leaflets and arguing with the Saturday crowds. Imran's ears were still ringing. He had had a phone call from his sister Aisha. Their first conversation in months had turned into a furious quarrel.

'What did you do, Imran? Ammi-ji phoned me. She is in tears.'

He answered his sister simply. 'You know what I did.'

He was only able to carry off the show of defiance because they were many miles apart. If they had been face to face she would have seen her little brother hurt, disillusioned. He didn't want to be that boy. He wanted to be a man, a warrior. He wanted to put on armour and protect himself from the feelings that made him soft. Why couldn't he step into the flames of his new life and burn away the past?

Aisha had accused him of disloyalty. 'You humiliated your own father in front of the whole community.'

'I told him the truth.'

'What truth?'

'Abbu-ji's way is a failure, Aisha. What good are elections? Did we get a vote on the Iraq war, on Afghanistan?'

'We did more than vote, Imran,' Aisha protested.

'That's right. You marched. You picketed. You went to meetings. Where did it get you?'

There was a long silence.

'Nowhere,' she admitted. 'We failed. That doesn't mean we were wrong.'

The confession drew her onto his territory. 'What's the point of being right if you are ignored? We will not be ignored.'

'Who is this *we*, Imran? You can stay true to your beliefs without turning to extremism. Go home. Ask for Abbu's forgiveness!'

Imran rejected her plea. 'He is the one who should be asking for forgiveness. He is the one who stayed in the Labour Party even when it waged war against the Muslims. He is the one who drove Rafiq away.'

Aisha seized on the last sentence. 'Is that what this is all about?'

Imran's spine prickled. 'Don't be stupid.'

'I'm not. You've never forgiven him, have you?'

Imran didn't like the way the conversation was going. 'Don't be ridiculous. Aisha, there's nothing more to say.'

She waited a beat before replying. 'No, I don't suppose there is.'

Hours later he was with his brothers, trying to win people to Islam. He put Aisha's call to the back of his mind. Here he was more than just Imran, Mohammed and Fozia's son, exposed before people who had known him all his life.

He became involved in a sharp exchange with two middle-aged men. They were thickset and red-faced. One had the flag of St George tattooed on his bicep.

Imran pointed at it. 'Did you know St George was an Arab, born in Lebanon?'

'Rubbish, he was English.'

Imran raised an eyebrow. 'Look it up on the Internet, my friend.'

The big man came closer. 'I'll look you up, you dirty terrorist-lover. Why don't you go back to your own country?'

Imran didn't flinch. 'I'm in my own country. I was born here.'

'OK, your father's country.'

'He was born here too.'

Imran kept his composure. Arshad had trained him well.

'Your grandfather then. He must have been from Pakistan.'

Imran countered with a question of his own. 'Where is your grandfather from?'

Caught by surprise, his opponent blurted out, 'Ireland.'

'So why don't you go back there?'

The man realised his error. 'That's different.'

'Why?'

'Pakistan breeds terrorism.'

'So did Ireland until recently. Why are you any different from me?'

'I'm white, that's why! I don't go spewing hatred on the street.'

'You're the one who's shouting.'

Infuriated, the man shoved his face in Imran's. 'I'll do more than shout in a minute. I'm telling you to pack up your stall and clear off where you came from.'

'And if I don't?'

'Then I'll give you a good hiding.'

A crowd was gathering. Imran had been afraid the first time this had happened. Now he was used to it. He stood his ground. Some of his brothers joined him. The change in the balance of forces made the men think again. They wandered off, still shouting abuse, but from a safe distance. Imran turned to speak to the others when he glimpsed a pair of familiar faces among the onlookers. It was Chris's parents.

They were carrying shopping bags. Mr Hook browsed the literature and DVDs on the stall. He frowned as he examined the material. He passed one of the DVDs to his wife. She pulled a face and handed it back.

She didn't say much. Just: 'Oh, Imran.'

Mr Hook was more forthright. 'I thought I knew you, son. You and our Chris were as thick as thieves when you were kids. What happened?'

'I grew up.'

'What does your dad say about all this?'

'It's none of his business. I'm not at home anymore.'

Mr Hook waved the DVD. 'What do you call this?'

'It is the truth. It is the word of God.'

Mr Hook read out what one leaflet said about the war in Afghanistan. *The murderous infidel aggressor tortures the peoples of Palestine, Iraq and Afghanistan. We say to you, O Muslims: all your sins are forgiven if you fight the enemies of Islam. We say to the enemies of Islam: we will take the war to your lands. We will infiltrate your security.* 'You can't believe this rubbish. Our Chris is fighting out there.'

'Why is he?' Imran demanded, unfazed.

'What do you mean why? He's a soldier.'

'He should find another career. Britain has no right to be in Afghanistan.'

'We've got every right. The Army is protecting this country against terrorism. What about 7 July? The bombers killed innocent civilians.'

'Islam does not start wars,' Imran said. 'You talk about innocent civilians. What about the innocent civilians in Iraq, Afghanistan and Palestine? George Bush and Tony Blair sent aircraft into Iraq. They killed people. Osama Bin Laden targeted America. What's the difference?'

Arshad's tests came thick and fast. A week later ten of them were speeding down the M1 to Sheffield. Their target was a Yorkshire-wide conference called 'Isolating extremists, engaging communities'. A Home Office minister was going to address community leaders from across the region.

They parked the minibus in a high-rise and walked through to the hotel where the conference was being held. Arshad spotted the minister making his way through the press scrum. He was shaking hands with a group of imams and councillors.

'Crusader armies out of Afghanistan!' Arshad shouted.

The group surged forward. Imran found himself at the front. He punched the air and shouted.

'British government, shame on you!'

'British troops, shame on you!'

The police formed a cordon to block his way. Imran pressed against the human barricade. This was what he wanted: an identifiable enemy, a monster, something he could slay.

'Democracy, go to hell!'

They kept up the chanting for an hour and a half until the meeting finished. The police rushed the minister to his car and the convoy sped away. The group walked down the road satisfied with their work.

'Did you see him?' Arshad mocked. 'He ran like a coward.'

They were heading back to the minibus when Imran heard somebody call his name.

'Imran?'

It was Imam Nawaz.

'I thought it was you,' he said.

Imran bristled. He remembered the scene outside the mosque. 'What do you want? Were you in that traitors' conference?'

'I was there,' Nawaz replied.

'To sell your people down the river?'

'To listen,' Nawaz said. 'You must come home to your parents, Imran. You do not belong with these people. You are young and angry. You want revenge for your brother. You must not allow your heart to be poisoned.'

'This has got nothing to do with Rafiq,' Imran retorted hotly.

Nawaz sighed. 'As you wish.' He met Imran's stare. 'The police have been calling on me.'

'What is a Muslim cleric doing talking to the kuffar police?' Arshad interrupted.

Nawaz ignored him and addressed Imran. 'They say the community should give them more information. They ask me if there are any young people I am concerned about.' He reached out and rested a hand on Imran's shoulder. 'I have not and will not give them names, but I am worried about you, Imran.'

Arshad shoved Nawaz roughly, causing him to stumble. 'Beat it. Imran is with us now.'

Imran stepped between them. 'There's no need for that. He's an old man.'

Arshad sneered. 'He is a puppet. He sits down and talks to a government that sends troops to kill Muslims.' He pointed a finger at Nawaz. 'With our suicide vests we will punish the kuffar.'

Imran heard a voice behind him.

'Boom!'

He saw some of the other conference delegates approaching, disturbed by the turn of events. 'Go with them. You have no business here.'

Nawaz rejoined his companions. He addressed one last plea to Imran. 'Examine your conscience, Imran. Remember your Qur'an: *Whoever kills one human being shall be regarded as having killed all mankind.* You do not belong with the men of violence.'

As they drove north Imran saw his reflection in the window. He remembered the words of his Imam and asked himself: where do I belong?

The Political Soldier

Quade was enjoying the surveillance work. He was the zoologist and the jihadis were his specimens. He watched their every movement, their tussling, their intriguing dance of death. That was the way it would end, in a very English final solution. He watched the one doing most of the talking. It was the same youth he had seen outside the mosque.

The boy intrigued him. He wasn't the same as the others. They were truly blinded, bedazzled by their loud-mouthed, self-appointed leader. Not this one. He went through the motions but there was a strange detachment about him. It would be good to find out more but he didn't have time. Quade wasn't going to examine his specimens. He was going to make them extinct.

He had been keeping surveillance on Friday prayers and the Saturday stall in the city centre for weeks. He had a good idea of their movements. He was looking for a time when they would all be together. That's when the target would be set up. Pretty pins all in a close, tight wedge waiting for him to bowl. Strike. You're all out.

He saw them arguing with his fellow Britons. He wanted to join in. But that would mean giving the game away. There would be no big bang. Quade refused to let his instincts get the better of him. A punch up might make him feel better but it would resolve nothing. His countrymen would do what they always did. They would look on as usual, dispassionate, uninterested. They were like sheep. They didn't have the wit to imagine the wolf entering the field. They needed a shepherd to look after them.

He wouldn't do anything for now. He would wait for the grand finale.

Twenty-One

Chris

MID JULY 2010.

Orders had been issued. I knew what I was meant to do. Even so, I couldn't help glancing round at the more experienced men. I wanted to do it right. I wanted to be a soldier. I wanted to be a man. I felt a slap on the back. It was the black guy from South Wales whom everybody called Cent.

'Watch me and Nugget,' he said.

I smiled. 'I will. You guys know what you're doing.'

Nugget cackled with laughter as he clambered into the Viking troop carrier. 'Don't bet on it.'

The convoy left at 0500, under cover of darkness. The troop carriers roared as they pulled out of the gates. It all seemed so unreal. I made my acquaintance with the rumbling of huge tyres on the stony, dusty earth, the choking smoke, the fifty-degree heat and the acrid stench of fuel. I sat rocking uncomfortably from side to side and imagined Kelly in her powder blue dress, the wind plastering the fabric to her body. She was a world away from all this.

From time to time I snatched glimpses of the strange, almost unworldly landscape, ochre plains and folds that rushed by in a haze. The other guys could tell I was new. I was the only one straining to look. I took on water. Nugget had told me that I would drink nine litres of water a day while out on patrol. I had wondered if it was a wind-up. Until now.

Suddenly a lightning flash of pure azure cut through the landscape. Cent identified it as the Helmand river. Rich, emerald vegetation clung to the banks of the water-way and the irrigation ditches that spread out from it. I remembered what they said about the Nile at school. It gave Egypt life. This was Helmand's Nile.

'Pretty, isn't it?' said Cent.

I nodded.

'Dangerous too. Taliban could be hiding. They might only be a few metres from where we're sitting.'

I looked at the river with respect. And apprehension. Eventually I laid my eyes on my first Afghan town. It was a settlement constructed from mud, low and flat, barely rising out of the surrounding landscape. The houses were pale tan boxes. I saw the old men in their black and white turbans, watching with squinting eyes. There were kids without limbs, women swathed in burkhas. Their robes were the same powder blue as the dress Kelly wore. This fabric didn't cling. It swirled and fluttered in the wind, leaving little impression of the woman within.

There were booths and cafes serving the long-distance lorry drivers. As we tramped past, a scrawny dog stirred and hopped away on three legs. Towards the end of the main street I caught the eye of a little girl, about five years old. Instinctively, I waved. She glanced up at her mother with huge brown eyes. The mother led her inside the house, leaving me feeling stupid.

'Ready to win hearts and minds?' Cent asked. There was a hint of weariness in his voice. We were eight hours out of Camp Bastion. A world away. Before long we entered the Forward Operating Base. Nugget patted my arm.

'You OK?'

I forced a smile. 'I'm cool.'

'Good man.'

The following morning we would push into enemy territory.

The sun was about to rise. It would be my first dawn on the front line. I was sitting round the transport with my mates chatting. Joking. The other guys did most of the talking. I couldn't take my eyes off the beauty of the desert. I'm a city boy, always have been. I didn't remember ever seeing a sky so big, or stars so bright. Back home the streetlights washed away the sense of a fragile planet spinning in a great open space. Here I understood my place in the universe. I felt as small, vulnerable and insignificant as the ants that had left tiny red marks on my back and arms. I was so very far from everything I was used to.

At 0600 we set off. We entered the Green Zone on foot. The news bulletins back home had made me strangely familiar with all this, the compound walls of pressed clay, the courtyards surrounded by high walls, the greenness of the fruit trees, the trenches.

One thing the TV hadn't prepared me for was the smell.

We passed open sewers and drains. Some of the small alleyways were choked with rubbish. Flies were crawling over everything. I glanced down at the irrigation ditches and I remembered what they'd told us in training. Perfect for an ambush. Nugget and another lad were out in front, weaving slow, deliberate, curving movements in the air with their rifles.

Staying alert.

We had been walking for maybe an hour when we got the heads up. All sound and activity had evaporated from the landscape. There was nobody around. There was nobody working. There were no children playing. Even the half-starved dogs I had seen the day before had left. The evidence was there for all to see. The Taliban had told the locals to clear the area. My gut wrenched as the word travelled down the straggling line. Stay alert.

Suddenly we were in the middle of an ambush. Orders barked through the heat. There was the crackle and pop of small arms fire. I tried to make sense of where it was coming from. Maybe that came with experience. All I could see was dust.

Then there was a shout. 'RPG.'

Rocket propelled grenade. There was a rush of air. An explosion. Somebody said it was close. I made sure my rifle's magazine was full and snapped it back in place. I knew I had already checked but I needed something to do to settle my nerves. Cent caught my eye. He knew how I was feeling.

Then we were on the move again. The things they taught us in training ran through my mind. I recalled the fast, urgent runs, the discipline, the teamwork but nothing can prepare you fully for the real thing, especially the fifty-degree heat. Every time I ran my body armour felt like an extra man on my back. I heard the thud of my boots, the raw punch of my breathing from straining lungs. This was the real thing.

There was more fire from the left. Bullets fizzed through the air, slicing the heads off the crops. I squeezed the trigger, puking fire at the unseen enemy. Sweat was running off my eyebrows, stinging my eyes. Around me weapons bucked and jerked, laying down rounds. We got word that the Taliban were retreating. Artillery was called in. There were approving shouts as shells punched into the tree line, tossing up plumes of dust. That's where the Taliban were last seen.

'Yes!'

'Get some!'

We reached the safety of a ditch, gulping down lungfuls of air. The enemy had taken a hit, a big one. They weren't finished. The survivors were maybe one hundred metres away. Cent made sense of the situation for me. He pointed. There was a sniper. We got the word and crossed open ground. My spine tingled. In training you know you'll walk away unscathed. Here I felt as if I had a target painted on my back.

Just for a moment I wondered how the sniper could miss me. I completed the run and tumbled behind a compound wall. Booting down the door, we broke into the compound to use the roof as a firing position. An Apache helicopter fired a Hellfire missile. Dust rose from the Taliban compound.

There were cheers of relief as one of our guys took out the Taliban sniper. The kill relieved the pressure. The remaining Taliban made their escape across a poppy field.

I caught a glimpse of a shalwar kameez as they retreated. It was the only time I saw the enemy. That was all the evidence there was: a piece of flapping white cloth.

After six hours we got to rest in a deserted compound. Nugget poured water down his throat. No chiller cabinets here. It was still warm. He didn't care. Like the rest of us he had a thirst that cut like a razor. It spilled over his chin. He wiped the drops away. 'That's it, Hooky. Your first contact is over.'

I got an hour's rest then there was another four-hour walk back to the Forward Operating Base. There was word of a number of kills. I pictured Joe's face, and told the night I had done it for him.

On the second day some of the villagers brought their children in to be treated by the company doctor. I watched them gathering for a moment then turned my attention to the briefing. Captain Forrester told us to expect sporadic contacts in the next few days.

'You've got to respect your enemy. They know what they're doing. They've got a long history of resistance and they're fighting for what they believe in.'

'Too right,' Nugget whispered under his breath.

I followed him into the harsh sunlight and past the line of people receiving treatment. One old man looked on while a girl of thirteen or fourteen was getting attention. Cent pointed.

'How do you think they're related?'

I ran my eyes over them. 'She's his granddaughter.'

Cent shook his head. 'She's his wife.'

'You've got to be kidding. She's a child.'

'That's the way it is.'

I went down into the village haunted by the girl-wife's face. But for an accident of birth my own sister Jess could be one of these child-brides. We moved in a line down the street through the village. This is what the politicians meant by hearts and minds. I caught the eye of one man and shouted a greeting.

'Salaam alaikum.'

There was a grunted alaikum salaam. I tried greeting a second man. He didn't answer. His face was expressionless. When we got past him Cent told me not to expect too much. 'They don't trust us. These people have seen everything. Russians. Civil War. Us. It must make them pretty cynical.'

I nodded and grumbled about the heat. I already had huge sweat patches on my uniform.

He nodded back. 'Yes, it's a swine. I bet it makes you appreciate the Yorkshire rain.'

I grinned. 'I wouldn't go that far.'

Like the other lads I was chewing sweets to create saliva. Just standing still in this heat was dry, punishing work. I reached the end of the dusty street and became aware of movement. Some of the locals had started to gather. I listened to the translator. They had been promised a school and a clinic. There was one half-built building but the Taliban had trashed most of the fittings a month earlier. The project was back to square one. The villagers were angry about the lack of progress and protection.

'What have you done for us?' their spokesman demanded, once he had located the officer in charge. 'You demolish our homes. We have no schools, no medicine, no hospitals. You come during the day, but you don't stay to protect us. The Taliban arrive at night. They accuse us of helping you. They threaten us. You are supposed to bring us security.'

Captain Forrester tried to explain that it would take time. We needed their help to make these things happen. But these people had been promised help many times. I saw the scepticism written large on every sun-scorched face.

The battle for hearts and minds had barely begun.

I settled into the rhythm of the job. There were long periods of boredom and inactivity, punctuated by short periods of excitement and terror. We hung round. We talked and ran out of things to say. Some of the men sat out in the sun stripped to the waist. They smoked. They wandered round the HESCO walls of the base. These were huge collapsible plastic and wire cubes filled with earth, sand and rock to soak up and deflect attacking fire.

I thought about home all the time, but I didn't say so to the others. I was pretty sure they felt the same as me. They didn't let on. Another day we entered a ghost town. It was that same lead-in to a contact. The streets cleared of people. The women, the young, the elderly vanished. I was starting to get a feel for Helmand. Routine soon fashions itself into instinct. The enemy had identified us. I could feel hidden eyes watching. Suddenly it started. There was the crackle of rifle fire, the rush of an RPG. The fire was coming from a compound on the far side of open ground. There was more small arms fire. A scream. A curse. Somebody had been shot in the calf, a lad called Mitch. I watched as he was given morphine. This was the first wound I'd seen. I couldn't take my eyes off the injured man's face. Mitch wrinkled his nose and grinned.

'Could be worse.'

Would I show that kind of bravery when it was my turn? They patched him up and evacuated him for treatment. It was up to the rest of us to put it to the back of our minds and crack on. We secured one compound and moved on to the next. I was hot under the body armour. Sweat glued my shirt to my skin. I had begun to envy the enemy their loose-fitting clothing and their lack of kit. I wished I could be like them and fight without all this weight on my back. But that's the way it was. You dealt with it. There was a lull in the fighting. I wondered if the Taliban had gone. Cent read my face.

'Dream on, Hooky. They've moved to the south. We haven't seen the last of that lot. Persistent sods, that's what they are.'

It was quiet. The only sound was the wind through the maize. My eyes travelled over the waving crop. Menace rustled through the tall stalks. The crop gave cover to the enemy. I walked. I flicked my gaze to left and right. I sensed that somebody had got their eyes on me. My heart started to thump.

Expectation.

Apprehension.

Soon I was wiping sweat from my brow and tensing as I waited for something to happen. The heat haze shimmered over the open ground. It was coming. Expectation grew. I went forward, eyes following the man in front before switching back to the nodding heads of the maize. Suddenly we were taking incoming fire from three positions. I was running. My boots thumped over the parched ground.

I heard an order behind me. 'Stay on the track!'

It was a warning about IEDs. These improvised explosive devices were the source of eighty per cent of our casualties. The air was thick with the smoky reek of cordite. My mind was working overtime. My training kicked in. Somehow it seemed to come up against my natural instincts. I wanted to take cover, get my head down, but if I jumped into one of these ditches I might just be landing on an IED.

We made a dash across the open ground to gain cover against the mud walls of the compound opposite. The engagement ended with artillery being called in on the enemy positions. Thump. Thump. I watched the smoke. The Taliban refused to give up. We were punching rounds into their positions but they hung on like limpets. It would take fast air to shift them.

An air strike followed. They dropped a five-hundred-pound bomb on the compound. The earth shook.

That was close.

Smoke boiled over the fruit trees. Shrapnel was hitting the walls, tearing out lumps of clay. Orders travelled down the line. I was in danger of running out of ammunition. My throat went dry. Drier. What was I meant to do? Throw my boots at them? Then I heard Captain Forrester's voice.

'We're going to lay on smoke to cover our extraction.'

Artillery fire covered the withdrawal. We crossed open fields back to base. There were reports of enemy dead. I tried to make sense of the news. In all the dust, the running, the confusion of explosions, rushing air, shouting and cursing, that was the result.

Half a dozen men had lost their lives.

Taliban dead.

Not ours.

All the lads grumbled – about the equipment, the accommodation, the pouches of reconstituted food, the heat, the quality of the phone and email connections when we were back in Bastion. Nugget was the world's number one complainer. There were times when I expected him to complain about himself.

That Nugget.

What a noodle.

The last time I contacted home Mum told me about Imran. I remembered our last meeting, the confusion, the anger, the bitterness. So much for our friendship. It felt as if there was a river of blood between us.

I would see Imran in the young men who watched from doorways when I was on patrol in some sun-baked village. I would imagine his finger on the trigger of every AK47 that spluttered fire from the compounds, mulberry trees and maize fields of Helmand. I remembered his eyes the last time we met. It wasn't just anger I saw, it was the pain of betrayal. He'd smeared my face with blood. He'd made the shape of a gun with his fingers and put it to my head. If it had been real, would he have pulled the trigger?

How did we come to this, Imran? How do brothers end up on opposite sides? I resolved to look him up when I got home. I refused to believe our friendship was dead and gone.

I looked around my comrades. Nugget and Cent were playing cards. Mac and Geordie Tweed were tossing a Frisbee back and forth. Cent looked up from the game and winked. He said something to Nugget and they burst out laughing. I demanded to know what that was about. Cent tapped his nose. That was for him to know. I went across and gave him a playful punch, trying to get it out of him. We wrestled a bit. Like I used to with Imran. I went serious.

'Something wrong?' Nugget asked.

'Just thinking about somebody back home.'

'That Kelly of yours?'

I grinned. 'Yes, Kelly.'

Sean McEvoy had been reading. He looked up. 'That's what I miss when I'm here with you ugly beggars. Women.'

There was a bit of banter about wives and girlfriends. Some of the lads produced photographs. I hung back. Mac wanted to see Kelly. Reluctantly I showed him what she looked like. It felt tacky, as if I was letting her down by displaying her picture. Mac liked what he saw. 'She's a belter, Hooky lad. No wonder you're always in a dream.'

Cent wrapped his arm round my neck. 'Look at him blush. It must be love.'

Two days later the Mastiffs dropped us off. These patrol vehicles carried eight men. Captain Forrester warned us about the dickers, locals who kept look-out for the Taliban. I was acutely aware of the radio antennae that made us visible to snipers. It wasn't long before I heard the familiar sound of gunfire. Cent called it Rice Krispies.

Snap.

Crackle.

Pop.

Mac was in front. He turned. 'That was close. Keep low.'

We got more fire from AKs then it was the familiar loud whoosh of another weapon.

Nugget was the first to react. 'RPGs!'

Within seconds we were pinned down. Small arms fire punched holes in the dirt to my left then sputtered along the baked earth.

Captain Forrester made a decision. 'We're sitting ducks here. Let's go forward into that open area.'

By 0830 we had been contacted three times. The game of cat and mouse played out along another cloudy canal. Fire spat through the leaves, making shadows ripple on the ground. At last I made out the muzzle flashes of their weapons. Once we'd identified where the threat was coming from, the Mastiffs supplied extra support. The unit on the hill sighted the enemy with Javelin missiles.

The first explosion rolled across the hills. Smoke rose. The Javelin took out one position. We put down suppressing fire while we waited for air support. It wasn't long before an Apache helicopter came in low and put a stop to the Taliban attack. I remembered the talk of getting out of Afghanistan without a shot being fired. But this was full-scale warfare. I wasn't the only one to make the comparison. Nugget observed ruefully that the enemy was lively that morning.

We regrouped in the nearest compound. I was still amazed to see how the others could unwind so quickly after a contact. Some had a quick smoke or took a leak. We all took on water. In one end, out the other. The temperature was in the mid forties. The respite was short. The sentries had spotted movement. Mac picked up enemy chatter on the radio. Captain Forrester told us to move out. The next communication made my skin crawl. He relayed the uncomfortable news that we were surrounded on three sides.

'They're using the maize as cover.'

There was a line of trees. I ran in its dappled shadow, following Nugget at a decent interval. I was heading north in this fashion when I glimpsed a glint of gunmetal. I skidded to a halt and shouted a warning. I saw the whites of Nugget's eyes. I could almost smell the adrenalin rush coming from him as he realised he had stepped into the enemy's sights. I registered movement. An enemy fighter jumped out right in front of me. I saw the RPG on his shoulder.

My eyes shifted to the right. There was another man. I clocked the warhead pointing straight at Nugget. I saw the loose-fitting cream and brown clothing, the turban with its long swathe of cloth hanging down one side of his neck. For a moment time stood still. Then there was a burst of fire and the figure in the shalwar kameez hit the ground, face first. Cent caught up and raised his SA80 rifle. The second Taliban fighter made his escape. I glimpsed Cent lowering his weapon and we swapped glances.

He tapped my leg with the toe of his boot. 'Nice one, Hooky.'

Nugget stared at the fallen fighter. 'You saved my skin.'

All I could do was nod.

I stared down at the man I had dropped. His skull was shattered. Part of the eye socket had been blasted away. There was a mess of hair, flesh, bone. There was a spray pattern of blood and grey matter in the dirt. This is how a life ends. It was my first kill. I remembered Mac McEvoy talking about his first kill the night before.

How he thought about the man's wife and kids.

For me it was different. My mind didn't work that way. My thoughts were darker, but I didn't confide in anybody. They disturbed me too much.

We cracked on.

Later Captain Forrester asked how I felt. For a moment the question made no sense. I felt nothing. There was a threat. I did a job.

I heard my voice. 'I don't feel guilty about killing a man. He had an RPG pointed at my mate. It was him or us.'

That's what it was: a reflex, something I did as a result of my training. There was no guilt. There was little emotion. There was just a lingering knot of unease. It was the only sensation of any kind in the whole incident, a kind of growing anxiety that would live with me for the rest of the tour, maybe forever. When the enemy stepped from the cornfield I imagined another man's features. When he lay dead I was staring down at somebody I knew. I saw Imran.

Twenty-Two

Imran

1 FEBRUARY 2011. 10.45 A.M.

Imran and Rafiq have driven into a ring of steel. They reach a T-junction. There are police motorcyclists drawn up in a row across one of the exits. A patrol car blocks the other. The barracks stands behind a row of bare horse chestnut trees, but this is as close as they will get. One of the police officers signals for them to pull over. Imran knows the drill. They want them out of the car. Rafiq is already fumbling in his jacket for his driver's licence. The motorcycle cop wants to know their business in the area. There is no easy way to say it.

'We're trying to stop a terrorist incident.'

Glances are exchanged. A lip curls. An eyebrow is raised.

'Stop one? That's a novelty.'

His colleague reprimands him with a stare. He asks for details. Imran tells him he's got intelligence of a terrorist cell.

'And how did you get this intelligence, sir?'

Imran draws breath. 'I thought they just wanted to protest.' There is scepticism in their eyes. One of them has stepped aside. He is speaking into his radio, hand cupped over his mouth. Imran tries to make himself understood. 'Look, I was stupid, OK? I got closer than I should have. I'm not making this up.'

He names names. Arshad. Nabeel. The White Leopard. The first two officers aren't impressed. The third kills the radio communication and the atmosphere changes. Somebody has recognised the names. Another car arrives. A senior policeman appears. He takes the driving license and examines Rafiq's face.

'You are Rafiq Hussain?'

'Yes.'

'You were convicted of riot. You got four years.'

'Yes. I did two and a half.'

He turns to Imran. 'And you are Imran Hussain?'

Imran tells him yes. 'Look, we're wasting time. There's a man trying to blow up the barracks. We've got to stop him.'

There's a cold stare. '*We* have to ascertain that what you are telling us is correct ...' A long pause. 'Sir.'

Imran does his best to answer their questions.

'What is Arshad's second name?'

'I don't know. I think it's an alias anyway.'

'Nabeel's.'

'The same. Sorry.'

'This White Leopard. Do you have a description?'

'I only saw him for a second. He's a white guy.'

White Leopard.

White man.

'So are fifty million other people, sir.'

'Don't you get it? Somebody is going to get killed.'

'That tone of voice isn't going to get you anywhere, sir.'

Imran is screaming inside. Two minutes away by car there is a man in a suicide vest. He is going to do shaheed. Blood will be spilled and all Five-O care about is procedure. And shaking down two Asian men. Muslims. Imran throws his arms up.

'This is madness.'

The senior policeman warns him to control his temper.

'Or what?' Imran demands. 'You'll arrest me? Are you really that stupid?'

Rafiq does his best to calm the situation. He is patient, methodical. He has their attention. Layer by layer, he starts to peel away their suspicions. The longer he speaks, the more Imran appreciates what his brother has done for him.

Chris

1 FEBRUARY 2011. 10.47 A.M.

Before we receive our medals, the regiment remembers its dead. The last strains of Nimrod die away and the traditional words are read out:

They shall grow not old, as we that are left grow old.
Age shall not weary them, nor the years condemn.
At the going down of the sun and in the morning
We will remember them.

Nugget sees the look on my face. He sees the moment the words make everything clear. I do what I should have done the instant I got Imran's message. I show it to him and Cent.

'Christ!'

'When did you get it?'

'A few minutes ago. Dad said ...'

Nugget interrupts. His mind is working overtime. 'We tell somebody. Now.'

Of course we do.

I should have done it the moment I received it.

Please God, don't let it be too late.

Imran

AUGUST, 2010.

The way back started when Rafiq turned up out of the blue. Imran was leaving Friday prayers at his new mosque, four miles from home. He acknowleged the men collecting money for the Pakistan flood victims. Then there was his brother, feet planted apart, arms crossed. He was wearing jeans, a T-shirt, a stylish leather jacket, a decent pair of shades. He was sporting a neat beard. He was looking good, not the haunted man who had left home without warning.

And stayed away.

'Rafiq. You came back.'

Delight turned to dismay in an instant. Rafiq did not return Imran's smile.

'Are you insane?' he demanded.

Arshad emerged from the mosque behind Imran. Arshad wanted to know who he was talking to.

Rafiq beat him to it. 'I'm his brother.'

Arshad held out his hand.

Rafiq kept his arms folded. 'You're one of them, aren't you?'

'One of them?'

'The goons who've got their claws into my brother.'

Arshad was used to fielding hostile comments. 'We have the same convictions, yes.'

Without a word, without any warning, Rafiq seized Arshad by the arm and frog-marched him round the corner, out of sight of the worshippers. By the time he turned the corner, he had Arshad walking on tiptoes to control the stabbing pain in his twisted arm.

Arshad tried to squirm out of Rafiq's grip. 'Get your hands off me!'

Rafiq rammed Arshad's arm up his back even harder, pinning him against the wall.

'Shut your stupid mouth.'

Arshad's cheek scraped against the rough brickwork. He grunted a protest.

'Get this moron off me!'

Imran took a step forward. Rafiq warned him off with a stare and turned his attention to Arshad once more. 'I know your kind.'

'Let me go!'

Imran tried to intervene. 'Rafiq ...'

Rafiq killed his protest. 'Stay out of this, Imran.'

Arshad cried out. 'You're hurting me.'

'I should break you in two.' Rafiq looked at Imran and shook his head. 'What are you doing with this man?'

Imran tried to tell Rafiq he was a soldier. It came out

sounding ridiculous. Rafiq responded with scornful laughter.

'Soldier? I can take that two ways. One, you're playing games. In that case, you're an idiot. Two, you're serious. Which means you're unhinged.'

Imran was speechless. This was the same Rafiq who railed against injustice in Palestine and Iraq, the same Rafiq who walked away in protest at Dad's failure to stand up for his fellow Muslims.

'You said we should resist.'

Rafiq rolled his eyes. 'Yes, resist. March, organise, protest. Don't you get it? It's got to be legal.'

Imran reminded him that two million marched against the war in Iraq. 'All those people did it the way you say. They were legal. The government took no notice.'

Arshad croaked out a Surah of the Qur'an. 'Many a small band has, by God's grace, vanquished a mighty army.'

Rafiq twisted his arm and told him to shut the hell up.

'Don't you dare say another word. I don't want you shaming my religion. You'd say anything to justify the unjustifiable.' He made Arshad squeal with pain. 'You glorify men like Siddique Khan. Bombers aren't heroes. They're not martyrs. Clowns is what they are. The dirt on my shoe is what they are.' He let Arshad go. 'Get out of here. I want to talk to my brother.'

To Imran's surprise, Arshad walked. He went without looking back.

'Don't even think about following him,' Rafiq warned. 'He is a sick, stupid, little man. There's nothing in his life so he fills the hole with hatred.'

Rafiq bundled Imran into his car, a white Lexus.

'Where are we going?'

Rafiq started the engine. 'You'll see.'

Imran looked around the car's interior. 'You must be doing all right for yourself.'

'I'm a community worker in the East End. The management committee doesn't care about my past. I'm working with disaffected youth. It's turned out to be an advantage.'

The drive took about an hour. At first Rafiq waved away any further attempt at conversation. Imran relived the confrontation outside the mosque. He had always seen Arshad as a man of steel, but his abrupt departure had surprised Imran. It wasn't long before Imran started to recognise landmarks. He noticed the motorway services where he'd heard about the events of 7 July 2005.

'Are we going to the prison?'

'That's right.' Rafiq pulled up in a lay-by, overlooking the perimeter walls. 'That place swallowed up two years of my life.'

'I know.'

Rafiq shifted in his seat so he could look at Imran. 'No Imran, you don't know. You don't know because I didn't tell you. I scrubbed up for every visit. I don't just mean making myself look presentable. I put on a mask. I made myself the man you wanted to see. I showed you that I was coping.'

Imran felt stupid. 'So it wasn't true?'

He looked down the hill to the prison and laughed humourlessly. 'What do you think? Every second, every minute, every day in that place was sheer bloody hell. I was climbing the walls.'

'I didn't think. I'm sorry.'

'What are you sorry about, Imran?'

'What happened to you, of course.'

'Don't be. It had nothing to do with you. It's history.'

Imran was confused.

'You don't get it, do you Imran?'

Imran shook his head slowly.

'Abbu-ji called me.'

Imran was amazed. 'He called *you*!'

Rafiq nodded. 'That's right. He got my number from Aisha. It must have taken some doing. He had a lot of pride to swallow. He told me he had failed me. All those months, he stayed distant. That's what he said. Distant.' Rafiq scratched his beard. 'He asked for my forgiveness.'

'What did you say?'

'I heard him out. I said nothing. Not then. I hung up on him.' He closed his eyes, remembering. 'Then I did some thinking. You've only got one life. You get one try at it. This isn't a practice.' He fidgeted with the gear stick. 'I'm no angel. It took me time to come round, but I called him back later. I told him we both had things to be sorry for. We didn't exactly fall into each other's arms. Life's not like that. Anyway, he had other things on his mind.'

'What things?'

Rafiq made his point with a single word. 'You.'

'Oh.'

Rafiq lowered the window to let some fresh air in. 'Tell me what you do with Arshad and his mates.'

Imran went through the group's activities: the leafleting, the meetings, the marches.

Rafiq shook his head. 'I bet you feel really r-r-radical.'

Imran reminded him he felt the same way once.

'Meaning?'

'You opposed the wars in Iraq and Afghanistan. You wanted a free Palestine.'

'Why are you using the past tense? I still do.'

'So why are you criticising me?'

Rafiq looked at Imran as if he was mad. 'Arshad's dangerous. Just think, Imran. He's the leader of the group. Do you think he's going to stop at meetings and demos? He is using you and when he doesn't need you anymore, you'll be destroyed. This is terrorism.'

'He's not a bomber.'

Rafiq held his gaze. '*He* isn't. He grooms others.'

Imran's expression betrayed him. He remembered what Arshad had said to Imam Nawaz. He remembered the shout of '*boom*' behind him.

He didn't fool Rafiq. 'Do they show DVDs of attacks on British troops?' he asked. 'Do they talk about jihad? Do they say you need to strike in your own back yard? Do they point at Israeli troops on TV and talk about driving the Jews into the sea? Have they ever justified the actions of Al-Qaeda or gloated about 9/11?'

Imran looked away. He remembered Sheffield. He heard the word again. *Boom.* His silence spoke volumes.

'What do they do, watch clips of the planes smashing into the twin towers? Do they tell you it was all down to George Bush, the CIA, Mossad? What's the latest conspiracy theory?'

Imran sat tight, avoiding his stare.

Boom.

'Look down there, Imran. Look at HM Prison. That's your future if you hang around with him. That or worse.' He ran his hand through his hair in a gesture of frustration. 'There I am, trying to keep kids out of the hands of the radicals and I discover my own brother has fallen for their lies.' He put his hand round the back of Imran's neck and leaned his forehead against his brother's. 'Listen to me, man. I love you. I've stood eyeball to eyeball with these characters. I've had them calling me filthy names. I've had their spit on my face. I know what they want and it isn't pretty.'

Imran argued back. 'I'm not going to put on a suicide belt. I'm not stupid.' He held Rafiq's gaze. 'I swear, it never entered my mind.'

'Does Arshad know that?'

The question ran through Imran's mind. Was Rafiq right? Arshad had given him a home, a reason to exist. Imran had never asked what he wanted in return.

He looked at Rafiq. 'You think I've made a pact with Shaitan.'

'Haven't you? Let's ask the big question. What you do want from your life, Imran?'

Imran searched for an answer. He looked inside himself and there was nothing but a void. He searched his soul and found emptiness.

Rafiq seized on his silence. 'I've been where you are. I've been lost and angry and drowning in despair. It wasn't easy but I put myself back together. Nobody can pull you out of this but you.'

Imran gave an involuntary shake of the head.

Rafiq interpreted the gesture wrongly and tried another tack. 'Fine. Let me tell you about my life. London was a disaster to begin with. A friend of a friend offered me a couch to sleep on for a couple of weeks. It wasn't long before he wanted me out. A couple of people put me up for a few days, a week. That's when I struck lucky. I got talking to this guy after Friday prayers. He ran a community centre. He asked if I wanted to do some voluntary work.'

'So you said yes?'

'I helped out three days a week. One of the other volunteers had a spare room. Then I met Sayeeda.'

'You've got a lady?'

Rafiq laughed out loud. 'Yes Imran, I've got a lady. She's training to be a solicitor. She's bright, funny, beautiful. Better still, she cares about people. She's the reason I can run this car. It's eighty per cent hers, twenty per cent mine.'

Imran smiled. 'You're a kept man.'

'Watch it. She's amazing, man. I never thought an idiot like me would meet somebody like her.'

'You're not an idiot. You had a place at Newcastle University.'

A shadow crossed Rafiq's face. 'There is more than one way to be an idiot. I found one. You found another.'

Imran compared himself to Rafiq. He didn't have a job. There had been girls, but there was nobody special. So what did he have?

Himself.

And Rafiq.

'I've messed up, bro. I think it's time I got my life together.'

The Lexus coasted past the bollards. Imran looked at the street where he had played as a kid.

'You're kidding. I can't talk to Dad. Not yet.'

Rafiq pulled up. The engine idled while they both gazed at the familiar façade.

'Go in or stay out,' Rafiq said. 'It's your choice.'

'Will you come in with me?'

Rafiq shook his head.

'I've got people to visit. I'll be back in an hour. This you must do alone, little brother.'

'But he disowned me.'

'Come off it, Imran. Parents never disown their kids, not really. Do you think he meant it?'

Imran stared at the door. 'I don't know if I can.'

'You have to. You're not a kid any more, Imran. Stop acting like one. A man finds a way to redeem himself. Only a coward stays where he is and chucks his life away.' He rested his hands on the steering wheel. 'Do you know the easiest way men fall into evil? They just don't get round to saying no to the devil.'

'When did you get so wise, Rafiq?'

Rafiq laughed. 'I didn't. I got hurt. Then I decided to stop the pain.'

Imran walked to the door and rang the doorbell. Mum answered. His heart slammed. What would she say to a son who had shamed her?

'I'm sorry, Ammi-ji. For everything.'

In the event she didn't say a word. She embraced him and kissed his face. Her hands travelled over his hair. He could feel her tears on his cheeks. Then there were footsteps. She moved aside. It was Dad. Imran knew this would be difficult. He dredged up the only words that mattered.

'Can you forgive me, Abbu-ji?'

Abbu answered with a stiff yes. Then there was a long, tense pause. For a moment Imran thought that nothing had changed. But Dad was weeping. Imran wondered what to do next. Dad reached out and there was a clumsy handshake.

He forced out words Imran did not expect to hear. 'I too have things to regret.'

That was it. He continued to grip Imran's hand, then he put his arms round his boy.

'We must all learn from our mistakes, Imran my son.'

Imran dared to voice a concern. 'I was wrong to go with Arshad, but I am still angry with the way this country is treating us.'

'I always expected you to obey me without question,' Dad said. 'But you are a grown man. If we are a good family we should be able to disagree without falling out. There has been too much anger.'

Imran heard his mother's voice. 'Will you stay?'

'Yes, if that's what you want.'

Her face lit with joy. Dad's too. Imran realised they had both been dead inside since he left.

'Are you finished with those people?'

'I will go and see Arshad. I will break with him.'

Dad looked anxious. 'Do you want me to come with you?'

Imran shook his head. 'Rafiq said I had to do this myself. If I am to be a man I must face Arshad alone.' He forced a smile. 'He isn't half as scary as you, Abbu-ji.'

Silently, Imran let himself into the flat. He was instantly aware of Arshad talking to somebody. He listened.

'Do you think he's going to cause problems?'

'Imran?' Arshad laughed. 'He wouldn't know how. He's a weakling, Nabeel. I thought I could make use of him. But he's not important. There'll be others.'

Imran clenched his fists. So that's what you think of me. Still he did not announce his presence. The door was open. He edged noiselessly forward.

He heard Nabeel's reply. 'I had a feeling he would run screaming from the real thing. I don't think he's worth the trouble.'

Imran was about to storm into the room and confront them when he heard a third voice.

'I think we have more important things to discuss, don't you?'

Arshad clapped his hands. 'The date is set. It is scheduled for 1 February.'

Nabeel spoke. 'It's a shame it couldn't be September. We could commemorate the New York martyrs.'

Imran's flesh crawled. He edged forward until he could just make out the third man's profile. He was wearing a short-sleeved shirt and a patterned tie, dark grey trousers and immaculately polished brogue shoes. He was white.

'When the date is confirmed, send me a text. Stay away from the flat. We're too close to the big day.'

The third man rose to his feet. Imran thought quickly. He turned and slammed the front door as if he had just come in. He heard Arshad's voice. He was ushering the third man to the back door. After a few moments Arshad appeared.

'So you're back,' he said. 'I thought you might have fallen for the nonsense that brother of yours was spouting.'

Imran scowled. 'I'm going. I've only come to pick my stuff up.' He tossed his key on the table in the hall.

'You don't leave without my permission,' Arshad said.

Imran pushed past. 'I do as I like.'

Arshad grabbed his sleeve.

Imran shrugged him off. 'Don't touch me,' he warned. 'Rafiq isn't the only one who can show you up for the coward you really are.'

Arshad bristled. 'Try it.'

Imran shook his head. 'You're not worth it.' He went to his room and packed a bag. He jogged down the stairs.

Arshad was waiting. 'If you turn your back on Islam, you will make yourself an apostate.'

'I'm not turning my back on Islam,' Imran told him. 'I'm turning my back on *you*.'

'Jihad is not just a fight against injustice,' Arshad retorted. 'It is a fight against anyone who opposes the Muslim call.' He carried on shouting as Imran walked out of the front door. 'None of your brothers will talk to you.'

Imran carried on going.

'Walk away now and we will cast you out.'

Imran turned and saluted sarcastically. 'Fine by me.'

Arshad stepped aside. 'Go. Leave, you weakling. You're not man enough to be one of us.'

Imran gave his parting shot as he set off down the street. 'I'm man enough to know I don't want to be.'

On the way home Imran wondered about the gora he had seen. He was keenly aware of what Rafiq had said. 'He grooms others.' What could they be planning? He let himself in, embraced Mum as she appeared from the living room and climbed the stairs to his room. He put his bag down and looked around. At his childhood belongings. His books. Photographs. It was a few moments before he noticed what was missing. He heard Abbu's footsteps behind him.

'What happened to my computer?'

'I was worried that there might be something incriminating in the memory,' he said. 'I took it to the dump and smashed the hard drive with a hammer. The police entered my house once before. I had to visit one of my sons in prison. I couldn't do it again, Imran. It would destroy me.'

Imran rested his hand on his father's arm. 'It's all right, Abbu-ji. You did the right thing.'

Imran opened the window and looked out into the street. There were boys standing by the bollards where he used to play with Chris. He smiled. He had come to an end and a beginning.

Twenty-Three

Chris

OCTOBER 2010.

I had seen poverty on my tour. I had seen the dirt, degradation and drug addiction that decades of war had inflicted on this wild, beautiful country. But I had seen nothing to compare with this. Every atom of the place ached with need. There were ragged children, withered old men with cataract-clouded eyes, desperate, emaciated dogs. The furnace heat sat heavily on the flat-roofed shops and houses.

Some of the local village leaders had just had a meal with our senior officers and members of the Afghan security forces. The Afghans call this kind of meeting a shura. The participants were squatting on a faded carpet eating from a communal pot of rice and goat meat. The guys fanned out across the main street – pretty much the only street. Mac gestured to me, tapping the top of his cheekbone. Keep your eyes peeled.

I picked up movement. A child knelt in the dust in the

heat of the day, playing with a wooden toy. A woman peered out from the murk of a shop's interior. I wondered whether it was the child's mother. She saw me watching and retreated inside. There were the usual turbaned men squinting against the sun, their weathered faces as ribbed as the surrounding hills.

Two members of the Afghan National Police leaned against their Ford Ranger. They stood smoking for a few moments. I looked away and scanned the street, watching for any kind of suspicious movement. Soon my attention drifted back to the ANP guys.

One of them removed his peaked blue cap to wipe the sweat from his brow then he nudged his colleague. Instantly my spine tingled. I followed the direction of his stare. Two men had just risen from where they were squatting. A woman swathed in black from head to foot lifted her child from the dirt outside the door. I signalled to Cent. The heads up swept round the platoon. The sight of the locals vanishing from the street was a signal that trouble was brewing. The word went inside.

Something's up.

Clear the house.

That's when I saw the moped approaching. The rider skidded to a halt and a young man spilled from the pillion. He said something in the local Pashtu tongue. The moped took off. The ANP were yelling for the rider to stop. For a moment I was transfixed by the white-garbed figure striding through the dust. The haze started to clear and I saw the dangling wire, the switch in his hand. Suicide bomber. Weapons pointed. Warning shouts cracked through the heat.

Then I saw the child. She was right in the path of the

bomber. Before I knew it I was on my toes, pounding towards the little girl. All the while I was aware of the bomber, a phantom presence in the sand rush. I scooped the child up, feeling her rib cage under my palm. She screamed, kicked. I felt the jerk of her heart, the scratch of her fingers.

Then there was the roll of thunder, the hammer blast of the explosion. My last thought was to fold the child in my arms, then I slammed into a wall. There was dirt, debris, chaos. The woman in the shop scurried out to retrieve her child. No words were exchanged. I didn't even see her face. By the time I was able to sit up blinking against the aftermath of the blast they were both gone. As the dust plume cleared I saw the horrific scene unfold.

One of the ANP was already dead. The blast had torn away half his face. If I had any doubts before, I didn't have any now. War is inhuman, implacable, mischievous in its random choice of victim. Ears ringing, I looked for the second ANP man. I discovered him face down in the dust, most of the flesh ripped from his torso, one arm torn from its socket, blood soaking the ground around him. The worst was still to come. A high-pitched scream drew my attention. One of the old men was writhing in a congealed, scarlet puddle. His legs had gone. His left arm was a mangled, sticky mess. He was shrieking something, probably a plea to be put out of his misery. It was only a matter of time before the shock and massive blood loss ended his torment.

There was something even worse than the stomach-churning spectacle before me. It was the stench. There was the nauseating sweetness of roasted flesh, the reek of petrol and scorched clothing. I heard a loud crack and turned slowly. Everything felt like a dream. Things were moving in slow motion. I looked down the street just in time to see the moped rider tumble to the ground. The platoon sniper had taken him down as he sped away. My senses were still reeling when Mac's face appeared through the subsiding murk.

'You all right, Hooky?'

I managed a nod.

Back in the base Captain Forrester led the debriefing. The guys were gathered round listening.

'Yesterday was unexpected,' he said. 'The enemy fell down on their communications. They didn't give the locals enough time to clear the street. The friendly neighbourhood Taliban are usually smart enough to make sure the locals don't become victims. It looks like they're getting more daring . . . or desperate.' He asked if anybody needed to talk about what had just happened. Nobody did. 'Well, the offer's there.' He went on to outline the objective of the next patrol. 'Meanwhile get some rest. You've earned it.'

It was another furnace-like Helmand morning. I started the day with a boil-in-the-bag meal. Sausages and beans. I used the remaining water to make a brew. Nothing went to waste. Cent had a sweet tooth. He started the day with chocolate pudding.

'That's disgusting,' I told him. 'Your teeth will drop out.'

'Chill, Hooky man. You don't think this is real chocolate, do you? Besides, when you've got people shooting at you and planting IEDs, tooth decay is the least of your worries.'

I picked up my helmet, body armour and rifle. The Mastiffs' engines were running. We were about to move out. The drive took us to a series of compounds a couple of hours north. There was word of Taliban activity and an arms dump. As we moved through the compounds the enemy opened up.

Nugget was shouting: 'Contact! Contact!'

I was already running through the din of gunfire. I followed the line of a drainage ditch, ducking low. An RPG exploded overhead.

Cent cursed. 'That could have taken my sodding head off.'

A second RPG thumped into the wall behind us.

Cent observed that this wasn't funny. He was a master of understatement. Soon I saw muzzle flashes. The Taliban were raking the ground with their AK47s. Nugget pulled a grenade from his patrol vest. He had developed a different tactic from the rest of us. He didn't post the grenade into the doorway. He had one hell of a right arm, the product of long summers in the cricket field. He just ran forward, yanked out the pin and tossed it inside. Like a fielder. I followed him through the dust and smoke, spraying fire across the interior. There was one dead Taliban sprawled in front of me. A blood trail disappeared out of a door on the far side. A burst of bullets told us there was plenty of life in the enemy yet. The incoming rounds and rocket fire pushed adrenalin through my veins.

I stumbled into a compound the size of a five-a-side football pitch. The wounded Taliban fighter was backed up against the far wall. The AK47 was trembling in his hands. He had it pointed towards the floor. He was badly wounded. Nugget gestured for him to put the weapon down. The gunman smiled grimly and did the opposite. Nugget dropped him with a single shot. He checked that the man was dead then turned to me, anger showing in his face.

'I told him to surrender. You heard me.'

Cent took possession of the AK47. 'He chose death. Not your fault.'

I looked around the compound. 'So that's what he was protecting.'

I stepped over a filthy carpet, an empty ammo box and a few pairs of hurriedly discarded sandals then I examined the pot of steaming rice and meat, the half-eaten flatbread and the tea-making equipment in the corner.

'Still warm. Our friend over there wasn't alone. Somebody just bailed out.'

Whoever it was had left in a hurry. We looked at what the runner had left behind. There was a substance like molasses in half a dozen transparent plastic bags. There was also a row of drums full of a thick, brown stew and some bags of chemicals. An AK47 was propped against the wall. One last item confirmed what the compound was for. It looked like an alcohol still.

Cent shook his head. 'We're looking at a heroin factory.'

I wondered if any of this stuff made its way to places like London, Leeds and Bradford. I thought about Majid and his skinhead mates from across town. They were all one long production line.

Sergeant Laidlaw appeared. 'Don't touch anything, lads. Leave it to the ANP. They'll burn it.'

Nugget waited until Sarge was out of sight before giving his opinion. 'Burn it? Maybe. Either that or they'll sell it.'

I asked him what he meant.

'Simple,' he said. 'A fair few of the Afghan National Army guys I've met are brave men. The police aren't the same quality. Some of the beggars ... corrupt as hell.'

Nugget's words came back to haunt me before the week was out. We got intelligence of a substantial force of Taliban converging on the heroin factory. There weren't enough ANP to defend the compound. It meant a 0330 start to make the journey north before dawn. We left the transport on the far side of a ridge and moved down the slope under the cover of darkness. We kept noise to a minimum. Soon I spotted silhouetted figures moving against the background of the rising sun.

By the time we made contact with the enemy the heat was suffocating. Thoughts ricocheted through my mind like stray bullets. I wondered what Kelly was doing. What about Mum and Dad? I relived the moment when I saw the Taliban fighter in the cornfield. He had Imran's face. So what did I do? I killed him. Would I kill a man today? Or would he kill me?

A mortar landed, sending chunks of clay spinning by. There was no more time for memory. My mind changed gear, slipping into a permanent present where I was running, sweating, shouldering my rifle. I got the command.

'Rapid fire!'

The guys on the hill opened up with their .50 cals. Shards of brick, stone and mud flew. Nugget's voice whooshed past my ear like an RPG. He was saying words his mother wouldn't want to hear. I looked over my shoulder at him. His face was taut. His jaw was set. The

Taliban had retreated beyond the treeline. He told me to take cover.

'They're calling in fast air.'

I saw the first attack run. The plane flickered along the horizon, a silvery dance of menace. The bomb separated from the plane and punched into the ground out of sight. The smoke plume rose. The plane streaked in again and again.

Cent voiced unlikely compassion for the Taliban. 'I wouldn't like to be on the receiving end of that lot.'

I watched the awesome display of airpower and whistled through my teeth. 'How the hell does anybody live through that?'

Somehow the enemy did just that. It wasn't long before we were taking small arms fire from our right.

Nugget wanted to know what it took to quieten these guys. 'Nuclear weapons?'

The platoon got a radio message to return to the compound.

'What's up, Cent?'

'An Afghan National Army unit has turned up. The commander is interrogating a prisoner.'

The men had more respect for the ANA than the police, but we were all too aware of a couple of incidents in the past. Rogue ANA had been known to shoot up their allies and defect to the Taliban. We reached the compound and there was the same sense of surprise as when I first entered it. I stared at the kneeling prisoner. I recognised him instantly.

'He's ANP. He was with us when we found this place.'

Mac rolled his eyes. 'We left him and his mates in charge

of the smack. So what does he do? He sends a message to the local Taliban to come and collect. I wonder how much they were going to pay him.'

Sergeant Laidlaw strolled by. 'It gets worse, gentlemen,' he drawled. 'When I got here a couple of the ANA were dragging him down to the mouth of the wadi. I can't say for certain, but I think they were going to shoot him.'

Nugget shook his head. 'And they're supposed to be our allies.'

The Political Soldier

Three and a half thousand miles away Quade looked at the plastic bottles of clear chemicals. This was the fun part. The *what* had been decided. Now for the *how*, the technique. He had been experimenting with this stuff for years. He had started with *The Anarchist Cookbook*. He had played around with timers and fireworks.

Inspired by Soho bomber David Copeland, he had assembled several nail bombs. To be honest he could do it with his eyes shut. Now he had progressed to some grade A materials, employing the Middle Eastern bomber's chemical of choice, triacetone triperoxide, or TATP. Didn't this little baby have a kick?

He looked at the ingredients for his feisty Sharia cake and smiled. He returned to his emails. Aryan Reformation had given the operation the go ahead.

Whenever you're ready, Adler.

Twenty-Four

The White Leopard

The struggle has reached the crucial stage. In the early days I marched. I demonstrated. I interrupted meetings and heckled the unbelievers. I took my place among my brothers. I grew my beard and I was mocked for it. I heard the shouts of derision. 'Hey, did you see the ginger jihadi?'

The kuffar hooted and jeered.

I chanted my defiance.

Democracy, hypocrisy.
Democracy go to hell.
Freedom. Go to hell.
Behead the Kuffar.
Bomb bomb America.

When I chanted I felt strong but when the chanting died away the taunts remained. Still the onlookers picked me out among my brothers and pointed their fingers. Their laughter rang in my ears. I vowed to make them choke on their mockery.

My brothers trained me to be a sleeper. I slipped below

the radar of the security forces. They showed me how I could destroy the enemy from within. I did everything they told me to do. I lived the infidel lifestyle. I shaved off the beard that made me a figure of fun. I adopted the ways of the kuffar. There was no more leafleting. The chanting stopped. I buried myself deep. Now I am trusted. The time has come to make this country of disbelief pay.

Soon nobody will be laughing.

Twenty-Five

Chris

LATE OCTOBER 2010

I was beginning to understand how the aftershocks of the war on terror were rumbling beneath my feet.

Since the firefight in the maize field, I couldn't get the image of Imran out of my head. I imagined his face in every young Afghan male I saw. Tall or short, slight build or heavy, they reminded me of my first friend. The Taliban fighter I killed haunted me. Every time I closed my eyes I saw the crumpled form in the dirt and there was Imran lying at my feet. I knew it was crazy but the image wouldn't leave me. Sometimes I thought I was losing it completely.

I remembered the generous, mischievous friend of my childhood and I wondered how he made the journey to the man who confronted me in the city square and smeared my face with blood. I re-read my parents' letters.

But before I could find it in my heart to condemn him I remembered what Danny said. Was I ever like him?

There were plenty of occasions when I had failed to challenge people about their attitudes. I found myself questioning my own choices. Had I ended up in Afghanistan because of conviction, or was it just one of those chance conversations with Joe and Charlie?

I had begun to take immense pride in the uniform I was wearing. Whatever my misgivings about the conflict, every day I fought alongside heroes. The other men were asleep. I heard their breathing. On account of their courage, their selflessness, I would take a bullet for any one of them. That's what it was: not Queen, not country, them. My comrades were the cause I fought for, not this lousy politicians' war. Before I came out people always admired my guts. Then, in the same breath, they would ask what the war was for. Would anything I did bring democracy and freedom and women's rights to this ancient land? Was I ever able to give a convincing answer? Was I really keeping terror off the streets of my hometown?

When did life become so confusing? How did bright-eyed, excited kids like me and Imran end up on different sides? Danny Moncur and his kind weren't born racist. Imran's new friends weren't born spewing their own breed of hatred. What breaks inside the child that makes the man so flawed?

I rose before dawn. I couldn't have snatched more than two hours' sleep. Orders had been issued. I pulled on my body armour and picked up my SA80. The FOB was a hive of activity. The convoy left at 0500. Soon after dawn I was making my way through close-packed shops and houses. Past the usual open sewers and drains, picking through the rubbish.

Christ, it would take a miracle to turn this place into

a modern country. I noticed the pockmarked walls and wondered who caused this damage. There were plenty of potential culprits. Was it the Russians, the Americans, the Afghans, us? These people had been living in the shadow of war for, what, more than thirty years? There was the rusting hulk of a Soviet tank not far from where we were standing. It had been there since before I was born. That's the meaning of history: scorched, twisted metal and burned, twisted people.

I wondered how men like Mac, Nugget and Cent did this job every day. They'd seen it all before. All three of them were on their second tour. Tough as old boots. How would I feel if I had to do this all over again? I was almost halfway through my tour. Soon I would be on R and R. It would be a welcome break. But what would I feel when I found myself back on the ground at Kandahar? Suddenly a burst of automatic fire churned the earth in front of me. I realised that all thoughts of R and R were premature. I still had to get through the next couple of weeks in one piece.

Back at base we took advantage of a lull in the fighting to get ourselves sorted. We cleaned the vehicles. That took a good part of the morning. Then it was the equipment's turn. I cleaned my weapon and stocked up on ammo. I ate. It was real food, solid food. Nugget made a fry up. He devoured his meal and squinted against the laser-bright sunlight.

'Not such a bad ring of hell sometimes, is it?'

He'd spoken too soon. Half an hour later the doo-doo hit the fan. A driver had come roaring up to the base in a battered Toyota pick up. He had brought in his seven-year-old son. As he dropped the tailgate and lifted the boy down, the man's face was tortured by worry. He could see his boy's life slipping away. I looked at his frail, torn body. I swapped glances with Cent.

'I hope that's down to the Taliban and not us.'

The boy's hair had been burned away right down to the scalp. There was blood on his clothing. His eyes were dull and unfocused.

Cent shook his head. 'The kid's in a bad way.'

The guys stood around watching events unfold. Captain Forrester and Sergeant Laidlaw were in a flap.

Nugget had already made his mind up about responsibility. 'Look at their faces. This is down to us. I'll lay you a tenner on it.'

Mac grimaced. 'This is what the Yanks call collateral damage, Hooky. It's an accountant's name for an undeserved death.' He rubbed his nose. 'We try to take out the bad guys. Then there's a misfire, a cock-up, just bad luck and we end up maiming and disfiguring some poor bloody kid. Last time I was out the Americans bombed a house. They said they were targeting Taliban. The locals said it was a wedding. I don't know if anybody got to the bottom of it. War, eh? All I want is a straight clean fight with the enemy.'

Cent snorted. 'They're not going to give us that, are they?'

'I suppose not.' Mac took another look in the direction of the confusion around the boy. 'They make films and computer games out of this mess. Nobody shows you the truth though, do they?'

All the guys were depressed. Within the hour we watched the ambulance carry the kid to a waiting helicopter. They were going to airlift him out for surgery. The vehicle accelerated out of the gates in a cloud of dust.

Cent made an observation. 'Just when you think you could be doing some good, this happens.'

Sarge cut the muttering dead. 'We *are* doing good. Don't you forget it.'

As he strode away I met the eyes of my mates. Nothing was going to banish their doubts that easily.

Next day there was an unexpected chance to unwind. We pulled up by a river. There was a clear view across open ground. We stripped off and dived into the river in two shifts. We got to plunge into the water to freshen up. Suddenly we were just a bunch of young guys messing about. It was hard to imagine we were in the middle of a war zone. The sunlight teased the water. I rolled on my back and glided in its balmy caress. As I waded to the bank I told Cent I was feeling human again.

He asked me what I meant, *again*. 'I love water though,' he said. 'You?'

'My family say I'm half fish,' I answered. 'I used to go swimming with my mate all the time, and football.' I realised I was talking about Imran, not Joe. It felt strange. We'd hardly had anything to do with each other in seven or eight years, but say the word mate and it was Imran's face that came to mind. Every time. Maybe there is something magic about early childhood that you never recapture. Years went by when I hardly gave Imran a thought. Just lately his face was always there. There was another memory. 'There was one time ...'

'Yes?'

'It's what you were saying about water. I could have drowned.'

I told him about the day on the ice.

Cent pulled a face. 'It doesn't sound as if it was that deep. You sure you're not exaggerating?'

I shrugged. 'Maybe. It seemed a big deal at the time.'

Cent laughed. 'Back in the day.'

'Yeah, back in the day.'

But I knew what it meant. When I got home I was going to get in touch. We returned to base. It had been a quiet day. There weren't many of them. I'd only been back half an hour when Nugget dropped heavily on his bed.

'Life's a swine, you know that?'

Cent frowned. 'What's up with you?'

Nugget lay back. 'The little boy they brought in. He died of his injuries in the night. We're meant to be helping these people.'

Silence settled on us. We sat, each immersed in our own thoughts.

Mac was the one who gave voice to how we were feeling. He had two kids of his own. 'You see the mortars, the thousands of rounds, the air strikes,' he said. 'You cope with it. You see the blood trails, the suicide bombers. That you handle. Then some little kid comes along and ... that's what sums up war.'

'It's not like a bloody computer game, is it?' Cent added.

Mac shook his head. 'It's no game.'

That's the way I would always remember Mac: sitting on the bed saying war isn't a game.

Within a few months he would be dead and his kids would be fatherless.

*

'Chris!'

Through the Lathams' front window I could see Kelly scrambling off the couch and rushing to the door. She flung open the door and leapt into my arms, wrapping her legs around me.

'Glad to see me?'

'What do you think?'

I spun her round then I felt the eyes of her parents on me.

'Oh, hi.' I was blushing.

'Don't let us interrupt things,' Mrs Latham said with a grin. 'How are you, Chris?'

'I'm good. Killer of a flight from KIA though.'

Mr Latham nodded. 'I hate long haul myself.'

Mrs Latham jabbed an elbow in his ribs. 'I don't think returning from Orlando with a fluffy killer whale is quite the same, do you?'

He pulled a face. 'I suppose not.' His eyes strayed to Joe's photograph. 'What was it like out there?'

I didn't know what to say to a man who had lost a son. He didn't want to hear my doubts. Joe couldn't have died for nothing. 'We're doing a good job. I think it's calming down a bit.'

Kelly laced her fingers in mine. 'Haven't you been home yet?'

'No, I wanted to see you first.'

She told me she would come across the road with me. 'Your parents are bound to have seen you arriving.'

She was right. Mum and Dad were at the door waiting. Jess rushed up the drive and hugged me.

I laughed. 'When did we sign an armistice, sis?'

She punched me playfully. 'I've been waiting for somebody to fight with. Mum and Dad give in too easily.'

Mum wanted to know what it was like to be home.

Good, I told her. 'Do you know what struck me? I can't believe how green England is. All the way from the airport I was staring out of the window. It didn't feel real, being back. It was like being in the middle of a 3-D film. I can't explain it.'

I didn't need to. Home is your refuge. The moment you arrive everybody accepts you for who you are, what you are. No matter where you've been. No matter what you've been through. This was what I'd been waiting for.

I left it near to the end of my leave to bite the bullet and phone Imran. I suppose I was worried about how it would turn out. Finally I tried his number. He didn't answer. I told myself I was going to call at his house before I left.

Kelly and I were inseparable. She dragged me into town to go shopping. I visited friends, attended a few parties, revisited the life I had before Helmand. But it was a world peopled with ghosts.

Compared to what happened in the harsh light of Afghanistan this felt like a half-life. The people I met seemed to sense it. They wanted to know about Afghanistan. At least they did at first. They asked a few questions, mouthed a few platitudes, rather you than me, stuff like that. One or two of them voiced doubts about what we were doing out there before hurriedly adding that they backed us all the way. Of course. I don't know why and I don't know when it started but for the last couple of days I'd started to get impatient with all the questions. I didn't even like Kelly raising it.

'Something wrong?' she asked the next time I retreated into myself.

I told her no, not really.

'Don't give me that, Chris. I know you too well.'

I tried to explain. 'It's all these people asking about the war. I wish they'd stop.'

'Why? They're only trying to be supportive.'

I stared down at the floor. 'Well, it doesn't help. They weren't there. Only a soldier knows what it's like.'

She fell silent and I knew I'd said the wrong thing.

She told me she wanted to share it with me.

I pulled a face. 'This is one thing I can't share. I've seen stuff out there only another soldier can understand. It's like ...' I turned to look at her. 'I saw a suicide bombing. I had to watch an old man swimming round in his own blood. All he had left were these ragged stumps. He was floundering around, dying before my eyes.' I saw her face change. 'There, you don't want to hear it.'

'I do, Chris, only it's so horrible. You can't blame me for finding it hard to take.'

I held her gaze. 'Of course. Because of what happened to Joe. Do you want to hear the rest or not?'

She said she did and I told the story, every graphic detail. I tried to explain why nothing felt quite as sharp, quite as relevant as the brutal tension of the Green Zone. 'There, I've got it off my chest.'

She wanted to know if it helped. I said yes. I thought no. 'You'll be able to see what it's like for yourself.'

Kelly frowned. 'How's that?'

'When I go back we're going to have a film crew embedded with us. Some of us will be wearing helmet cams.'

Kelly grimaced. She had mixed feelings about it. 'Chris,' she asked, 'can I ask you something?'

I told her to speak her mind.

'Do you miss it? I mean, you've only been home a few days and you sound bored.'

I told her I wasn't bored. 'That isn't it at all. I'm ...' I struggled to find the words. 'I feel guilty. There's a job to be done out there. I feel as if I've walked away from it and left other guys to do my fighting for me.'

She told me that was crazy. 'You've got to have a break. Chris, you can't live for the regiment.'

I fell silent. Was that what I was doing, living for the regiment?

It was the day before I was due to fly back to Kandahar. I jumped off the bus and set off down the hill to the streets where I grew up. Kelly caught up and grabbed my sleeve.

'Slow down,' she said. She eyed me suspiciously. 'Don't you want me along?'

'I told you I was cool with it.'

I wasn't. She seemed to be keeping her eye on me. Maybe she was just curious about my past. We reached the new retail park. I stopped and stared.

'Something wrong?' she asked.

'They've built on it.'

She didn't understand the significance of the shiny new development. 'Built on what?'

I pointed at the bland retail units. 'We used to play here, me and Imran.'

'Things change, Chris. It's progress.'

I observed the *exciting new shopping experience* that was the same as every other shopping experience the length and breadth of the UK. I remembered Nugget telling me there was even a shiny new shopping mall in Kabul. I sighed. 'If you say so. But this was ours.'

'That's it?'

'That's it. There was nowhere else like it when we were kids.'

Football and swimming were great but there was always a coach or a supervisor. Adults set the rules. They were ordered, controlled. Down here we were wildly, joyfully out of control. We ran along the dirt paths roaring and howling and there was nobody to tell us to keep the noise down. We explored, sat, talked, dreamed until dusk gathered over the distant rooftops and we wandered home dirty, tired, happy. The Wilderness was what we wanted it to be: a dark forest, a land of giants, a sanctuary. Now it belonged to the planners, the chamber of commerce. It belonged to the sharp-suited lawyers, the marketing men, the politicians.

'I'm disappointed it's all changed, that's all.'

I took one last look. The day we moved out to the new estate was pretty much the end of my childhood. From then on I was ferried to football and boxing. I went on holidays abroad. There was an unwritten law that kids didn't foul the manicured lawns with football and cricket. There were designated areas for that sort of thing. My life was channelled into *designated areas* and I felt as if I was dying of boredom.

I turned into the old street and walked up to Imran's door. I glanced at Kelly.

'Here goes.'

Mrs Hussain answered. For a few moments she didn't recognise me, then a light caught in her face. 'Chris, is it you?'

'Yes, it's me.'

'You've grown into a fine young man.'

'Thanks. Is Imran in?'

'I'm sorry, Chris. He's gone down to London to stay with Rafiq for a few days.'

I asked about Rafiq. Mrs Hussain told me about his new start in London. I said I was pleased for him. 'You know, after everything.' She squeezed my hand. 'Imran will be so disappointed he missed you.'

I decided to be honest. 'Are you sure about that?'

She nibbled her bottom lip. 'You heard then? You know he got involved with those people?'

'Yes, my parents saw him in town. What happened?'

'He was unhappy. Things went wrong. I don't know exactly. He made contact with people through chat rooms.' She thumbed a tear from her right eye.

'But he's so intelligent, so level-headed.'

'Something happened after Rafiq went to jail. Imran retreated into himself.' She rushed out the next few words as if she was trying to convince me of something. Maybe she wanted to convince herself. 'He's put all that behind him. He's applied to university. He's got a good chance.' She told me to wait there and vanished indoors.

While she rummaged in a drawer I shifted my feet on the doorstep. For a reason I couldn't quite fathom I was glad Imran wasn't there. She returned with a scrap of paper. 'This is Imran's new mobile number. You've got to phone him. He will be so pleased.'

'Don't worry, Mrs Hussain. I will.'

Somehow I never got round to it. There was so much to do before I headed to Bastion. In the first week back on the ground in Afghanistan I trod on the IED.

Twenty-Six

Imran

JANUARY 2011.

Imran answered the phone.

'It's me.'

'Rafiq! How are you doing?'

'I'm good.' There was a pause. 'In fact, I'm more than good. I proposed to Sayeeda a couple of days ago.'

Imran teased him. 'No way! What did she say?'

'Watch it!'

'So it was a yes?'

'Yes, result. She isn't going to turn down a catch like me. I'm going to do this right. Her family is minted and Dad is going to step up to the plate. I'm going to have a horse and a doli, the whole shebang. I'm coming up to make arrangements.'

He sounded happy. It was about time.

'Put Abbu on, Imran. Is he there?'

Imran watched Dad's face light up as he discussed the wedding. His family was healing. His eldest son was getting married to a beautiful girl. Aisha appeared to have a glittering academic career before her. Imran was home. Safe. Back to his true self. He watched Dad talking animatedly, reconciled with his eldest, his joker in the pack. Imran tapped him on the shoulder. 'I'm going into town, OK?'

Imran was walking through the city centre deep in thought when he pulled up short. It was as if he had summoned his nemesis. He had stumbled across Arshad and the rest of his group. Imran couldn't believe his luck. He had been giving their usual pitch a wide berth, but the police must have moved them on. So here they were. The moment they saw Imran they strode forward shouting. Imran heard the insults.

Traitor.

Partial Muslim.

Apostate.

Arshad led the catcalls. 'You have turned your backs on the Muslims.'

'I've turned my back on you, Arshad. You don't represent the Muslims. You're nothing.'

He sneered. 'You will see who is nothing. You're going to feel the claws of the White Leopard.'

Imran remembered those words. He was no longer under any illusion. Arshad was no loudmouthed fantasist. He was the real deal. Imran made a decision. He started to watch the flat. Should he go to the police? He didn't even consider it. Imran, the radical, brother of a convicted rioter – he was only going to create more trouble for himself.

So he acted alone. He found an alley from which he could watch the door without being seen. A couple of children peered up at him A dog paused, cocked its head as it decided what to make of him and wandered off. Sometimes he stayed an hour. From time to time he was able to devote two. Once he hung around all afternoon but he didn't see anything. Nobody entered. Nobody left. On each occasion Imran walked away disappointed. Then he received confirmation of his worst fears.

Down the street came a clean-shaven white man in his late twenties. Imran was certain it was the same man he'd seen the day he broke with the group. The White Leopard had a key and let himself in. After half an hour a van pulled up. The Leopard appeared and let the newcomer in. Imran recognised Nabeel. He hung around, thinking maybe he should follow the White Leopard. After three quarters of an hour the Leopard emerged.

Imran trailed him at a safe distance. He hurried as the Leopard turned the corner. He waited for a bus. Imran let him climb aboard then he ran to catch it. The Leopard got off half a dozen stops later, completely oblivious to Imran's presence. Imran followed him at a safe distance. It was when he took the next left turn that he realised where the Leopard was going. The entrance to the Army barracks was at the end of the road. Imran saw him reach the barrier and flash a pass at the soldier on duty.

Imran

31 JANUARY 2011.

For the next few days Imran was desperate to think of an innocent reason for the sequence of events. But there was only one explanation.

Imran decided to confide in Rafiq. He would be home any time. He had set off from London early with Sayeeda. He would know what to do. Imran hung up his jacket and sat down at the table. Mum was making prantay, frying chappatis in ghee. He glanced in her direction. He had let his family down once. How could he tell them about his suspicions? No, Rafiq was the only one he would tell.

Would it be wise to go to the police? He'd heard people talking about forty-two days' detention. They were bound to treat him with suspicion. How much evidence did they need to charge him with something? But what if something happened and he didn't tell anybody? There was bound to be a law about that too. Fear clawed at Imran's throat. Did he check the street? What if somebody had got him on camera watching the house? Could that implicate him? What a mess. His imagination was working overtime.

That's when Mum turned and wiped her hands. 'Rafiq and Sayeeda are going to be here within the hour. They called from the motorway services.'

For the first time Imran noticed that Mum wasn't as happy as she should be. Her eldest son and his bride were due within the hour, but she seemed preoccupied herself. A moment later Imran discovered why. She had a copy of the evening paper in her hand. 'Have you seen this?'

'No, why?'

'So you don't know about Chris?'

'What are you talking about?'

She looked away and went on talking with her back turned. Imran knew this gesture. It set off alarms in his head. 'Tell me. Please.'

'Chris is in the paper, Imran. He is going to be in a

documentary later this month. They're going to show excerpts on breakfast TV in the morning.'

'A documentary? How come?' She didn't answer. 'Ammi-ji?'

'I don't know how to tell you this. Chris has been hurt in Afghanistan.'

'Hurt? How badly?'

'There is an article on page eight. It's very short.'

Imran's fingers fumbled to the right page. He raced through the words and winced at every detail. Chris had lost a leg below the knee. Imran's senses reeled. Chris had been transferred from Selly Oak Hospital in Birmingham to Headley Court in Surrey for rehabilitation.

He dropped the paper. 'I never even knew.'

Imran

1 FEBRUARY 2011.

Imran watched the item about the documentary. Rafiq and Sayeeda sat on the couch next to him. Mum was fiddling with the remote, recording it for Dad so he could watch it when he got home from work.

There was a film crew embedded with Chris's company. They had been present when it happened. Imran watched the grainy footage of the moment Chris stood on the IED. He saw the canal. He heard the command to stay still. The medic administered morphine, applied a tourniquet. Shouts crackled through the air: 'Get him out now!' The footage mingled in Imran's mind with images of the White Leopard entering Arshad's flat. He felt his mother's eyes on him but he didn't return her gaze. For some reason he remembered that day on the ice. The cracks were still spreading. But when Chris plunged through the ice he had been there.

Imran watched as the filmmaker charted Chris's rehabilitation. He saw the early despair, the moments of self-pity, the repeated question: 'Why me?' He saw Chris's girlfriend Kelly, how loyal she was, how unflinching in her support. Chris's parents used the words 'true as steel'. And what was I doing while Chris was suffering? Imran asked himself. I was acting as a ventriloquist's dummy for Arshad.

At one point Chris seemed to be giving up. He groaned and told the camera he was useless, a cripple. This time it was a young para called Jack who shook him out of his black mood. He demanded to know what Chris had got to complain about. Jack was in a powerful position to challenge Chris's slide into hopelessness. He had lost both legs and an arm. One of his eyes was permanently damaged. Inside his torn and shattered body his will was strong, his pride unbroken. He took to the circuit training and physio with gusto. He shamed Chris with his fortitude, his determination, his courage.

From that moment Chris climbed back out of the hole. Imran closed his eyes. You did it all without me. Chris established a routine, set his face forward, not back. He became practical, pragmatic, somebody who wrestled with, controlled and changed his own circumstances. Imran knew he should have been there. Chris's parents barely left his side. His girlfriend was there too. But, at the moment of Chris's greatest need, his oldest friend was nowhere to be seen. If only he'd known. If only the world had been different. Why did so many insane, chaotic events have to tear them apart? Why couldn't they have gone on being the people they were when they were boys?

The various episodes in the film flashed through his consciousness. He saw Chris in the rehab centre. He witnessed the setbacks: the time the wound started to weep, the first step using the stubby, the first time he got back on his own two feet, using the prosthetic limb to stand up in a frame.

Imran witnessed the moment Chris suggested he and Kelly get engaged. He heard him ask if she would marry him one day. There was no hesitation. She said yes. This girl didn't see somebody disabled. She saw the man she loved. Her arms folded round his neck. They kissed. Chris began to sob into her hair. Imran felt tears on his cheeks.

The clips were followed by a live interview with Chris and Kelly. Imran leaned forward and hung on every word. The interviewer asked what next?

'I set myself a target in Headley Court,' Chris answered. 'I'm not going to be in a wheelchair when I get my medal. I am going to walk.'

'And that's today?'

Chris squeezed Kelly's hand. 'Yes, and I'm all ready.'

Imran was smiling. Suddenly blood boomed in his head. He didn't hear the journalist's summary. He didn't hear her wish Chris and all the other young men the best of luck.

He didn't hear because his flesh was creeping. Horror roared through him. It was the medal ceremony. That was the target.

And it was happening in less than two hours.

Twenty-Seven

Chris

1 FEBRUARY 2011. 10.50 A.M.

I am at the eye of the storm. Nugget and Cent have gone to raise the alarm.

The regimental band strikes up. The order snaps across the parade ground. 'Remove headdress!'

The men stand at ease. The families produce their cameras, camcorders, mobile phones and get their record of the big day. I hear my name and march forward, eyes ahead.

Many men and women have made it possible for me to attend the ceremony today: the medics, nurses and physios. As I set off my pulse is racing. I think of the bomber on the loose close by. The people in charge must be aware of the emergency by now, though nobody would know it. There is an eerie calm. I wonder what the prince and the senior officers have been told. Somebody must have decided to continue with the ceremony. I am aware of the bright sunlight and the east wind skipping across the tarmac. Any minute I expect to hear the terrifying crack of an explosion. It takes me back to that sluggish canal, the dirt, the noise, the pain. My gut churns. Not again. Dear God, not again.

But I observe perfect discipline. I go forward to receive my medal. I keep my back straight and my eyes fixed on a point right in front of me. The prince pins the medal on my chest. He says something about courage and the horror of war. I can barely make sense of the words. They fly up and dissolve into the morning light. My mind is elsewhere, at the edges of the crowd, in the corridors, offices and storerooms of the many buildings. That's where the bomber prowls. Where is he? What are they doing about him?

Out of the corner of my eye I am aware of movement. The public is oblivious to what is happening but any practised eye would notice the beginnings of a systematic search of the buildings. There is the loud, chattering roar of a helicopter overhead, evidence of the desperate search. I salute, turn and march back to my comrades. I am delighted to have mastered my new leg. There is pride. But there is apprehension too. Where is he? Where the hell is he?

The ceremony continues. Each man goes up for his medal, salutes, returns. I turn left. I turn right. I glance over my shoulder. Nothing. I scan the buildings, the car park, the perimeter fence. My gaze is even attracted to the roof. Still nothing. Where is he? Who am I looking for?

I wonder about Imran. Where was he when he texted?

And where are Nugget and Cent? How many people have they told? A hand touches my arm.

'Would you come with me, sir?'

The newcomer introduces himself as a member of Special Branch. His name is Ruddock. I follow him to the corner of the nearest building.

'Have you found him?'

There is a shake of the head. 'No, but we have a photograph.'

'Can I see?'

Ruddock holds out a mobile phone. I see a security pass mugshot.

'He has been working in IT support. He adopts the name the White Leopard. We are undertaking a room by room search of the barracks.'

'What if he is already in the crowd?'

'We've carried out a thorough search. We're pretty sure he isn't.'

'And if you're wrong?'

His face twitches. 'We are in an impossible situation. It's a large crowd. If we make an announcement now, we could start a panic and make things even worse.'

I glimpse a couple of men with earpieces among the service police facing the crowd. I spot a couple more probables. There must be more among the onlookers.

'We are interviewing the individual who sent you the text,' Ruddock says. 'What do you know about him?'

'Imran? He's my oldest friend.' I glance at the photo. 'He put you onto this guy, this White Leopard, didn't he?'

Ruddock answers that he is not at liberty to say. 'We have surveillance footage of Imran Hussain.' He shows me a second photo. It features Imran in the front rank of a demonstration. I wince at the slogan on the placard he is holding. 'You're aware that he is an associate of known radicals?'

'I know he's been hanging round with some dodgy characters, but I would trust Imran with my life.' It sounds a strange thing to say after everything that has happened.

I would trust him with my life.

But it's true.

As true as a hand hauling me off the ice one winter's day all those years ago.

'If he says there's a plot, then that's what's happening.'

Suddenly I catch sight of Cent's shaven head. He is standing by one of the admin blocks. Ruddock is still talking, but I've lost interest. Talk won't stop this madman. I am already on my way over to where Cent is standing. I reach him. Nugget has his hands cupped round his eyes so he can see inside.

'What is it?'

Cent explains. 'Nugget thinks he saw a flash of light from that window.'

Simultaneously Nugget confirms the sighting. 'There!'

Ruddock is only a few metres behind. He says something about leaving it to the experts. Nobody's listening.

'If you're set on going in,' Ruddock says, 'this is the man you're looking for.'

Cent and Nugget look, nod, try the door. It's locked. Cent has the answer. He crashes his boot into it. The door bursts open and we are inside. My comrades remember their training. Cent is pounding up the stairs. Nugget follows. That's when I see the layout of the staircase. I take a step back, looking around.

Ruddock arrives behind me. 'What is it?'

I point. 'There's another stairwell through that set of double doors. He could go up this one and back down the other flight. We need to get down there to cut him off.'

'Leave this to me, sir,' he says.

I tell him no chance. 'Neither of us knows what we're dealing with. One man won't be enough to stop him.'

I know what Ruddock's thinking. He's wondering what good I am with one leg.

'Don't worry about me,' I tell him.

I ease open the double doors and set off along the corridor. There are light footsteps on the stairs at the far end. I flatten myself against the wall and point. Ruddock nods. I hear the whisper of a draught excluder on the tiled floor then fast, padding footsteps. The Leopard is wearing soft-soled shoes. He has entered one of the offices.

I reach the door. Through a glass panel I can see him. He is wearing the suicide vest. I know this scene. I've been here before. My eyes travel over the explosive-filled cylinders, the fragmentation jacket, the shoulder straps, the detonator. It was a device like this that left two ANP dead and an old man floundering in his own blood. I swap glances with Ruddock. There's a simple, recognised drill. Keep the bomber from the nearest people.

Ruddock clocks the detonator. 'We're in luck,' he whispers.

I look at him as if he's insane. 'Look at the detonator. He has to actively press that button. It gives us a chance. Some bombers use a squeeze clip. Take them out and they loosen their grip. Boom.'

'Christ!' I hiss a suggestion. 'We can isolate him in here.'

That's when I see something that makes my heart kick in my ribs. There's an emergency door on the far side of the office. It leads directly onto the parade ground. So much for the isolation idea. Where are Ruddock's security guys? There is a direct route to the crowd.

'That does it,' Ruddock says. 'We take him now, before he gets a chance to detonate that thing.'

To free both hands the White Leopard has let the detonator dangle from his sleeve by the wire. Ruddock bursts through the door and grips the startled Leopard's right wrist to prevent him triggering the device. But his left hand is free. I see the knife at the same moment as Ruddock. The Leopard slashes with savage force, slicing through flesh. The officer screams and goes down. Blood seeps through his shirt and patters onto the floor. There's no time to lose. I launch myself into the room.

My movements are awkward in spite of what they taught me at Headley Court. The rehab wasn't meant to prepare me for unarmed combat. They got me walking in no time but this is the first time I've tried anything remotely like running. I see the bloodstained knife. This time I'm forewarned. I slam into the Leopard clutching his wrists, trying to disable the knife, the trigger. I pound his wrist on the floor. Once. Twice. Three times. He is howling with pain. His grip loosens. I remember what Ruddock said about the squeeze clip. There's still a chance. I smash his arm down once more and he releases the knife. The greater danger remains.

Adrenalin pumps. My superior strength has given me the advantage. All I have to do is pin him down and yell until somebody comes. Nugget and Cent can't be far. The Leopard is writhing and twisting under me. I have to shift my weight to hold him. But I can't. Something is holding me back. I snatch a glance backwards and curse. My prosthetic limb is trapped. The overturned furniture has jammed it, reducing my mobility to zero. I try to unfasten it but the Leopard seizes the opportunity. He crashes his forehead into my nose. I see my blood spattering his face. I'm numb. Dazed. I'm a kid again being butted by Link. But I'm a kid grown up. This time I won't lose the fight. I refuse to lose. I've got his wrists but he is trying to flick the trigger into his palm.

'No!'

I cling to him. My damned leg is still trapped. His fingers are millimetres from detonating the belt. He might not manage the spectacular he wanted but he's going to get his revenge on me for thwarting his attempt at martyrdom. The frantic struggle continues. I'm losing my grip. Damn my leg. Come on, Chris. Hold on. For God's sake, hold on. His fingertips are on the detonator pad, clawing at the trigger. I squeeze my eyes shut and cling on with all the effort I can muster. We're both yelling.

I reopen my eyes and howl with terror. He's got the knife back. I've been concentrating on the detonator and I've let him recover the blade. He has it in his left hand and he is slashing down at my chest. He's right-handed so the lunges with his left are clumsy. I'm aware of a badly injured Ruddock trying to crawl over the bloody floor towards me. He isn't going to make it in time.

The blow never comes. There's a scream. For a moment I think it's me. Then the Leopard is on the floor next to me, face pressed against the tiles. Cent has got one arm forced up his back, the other crushed under a desert-issue boot. Nugget uses the knife to cut the vest off the Leopard. He rushes it across the passage to an empty room.

That's when I do something I've seen men do in the

heat of combat. I start to laugh. Within moments I'm laughing hysterically. Cent isn't even looking at me. He's seen it all before. He is busy tending to Ruddock, now that Nugget is back and has the Leopard. I look on fascinated. Nugget is dispassionate in the way he treats the Leopard. He restrains him, makes the room safe. Training over emotion. The next few minutes are a blur of paramedics, police, plain-clothes guys all flooding into the room. Doing their job.

One of the paramedics starts cleaning me up. 'What's so funny?' he asks in a broad Glaswegian accent.

'Everything,' I tell him. 'Bloody everything.'

He stares at me. 'You squaddies,' he says, 'you're mental.'

When I finally control the laughter I turn my head to watch Ruddock being stretchered out. 'How is he?'

'He's lost a lot of blood, but he'll live.' The paramedic tells me I've got a broken nose. 'You'll have to get that set.'

He starts to move and jumps as if he's been shot.

'What's wrong?'

'I just stood on your leg,' he says. 'Did you not feel that?'

I pull up my trouser leg to expose the prosthesis.

'Present from Afghanistan?'

'Got it in one.'

The police have a few questions. They say they will arrange an interview at a later date. When I finally stumble back outside, Kelly and Mum rush forward and fuss over me. I tell Kelly I'm sorry about the nose. She tells me forget it. It will give my face a bit more character. Which makes me ask what was wrong with it the way it was. She does the wavy thing with her hand: it was so-so. As we talk I realise what people mean by gallows humour. I fill the time with nonsense. If I didn't I would have to face how close we all came to the gates of hell. Dad is the only one who doesn't join in.

'What was I thinking?' he says, furious with himself. 'I wanted to ignore that message.'

I tell him to forget it. 'You made a judgement call. It's not the kind of situation you face every day.'

'All the same . . .'

'All the same nothing. It's over.'

But I'm wrong. So wrong. It is far from over.

Kelly suggests they get me straight to the hospital. I slide in next to Dad. He drives past the media scrum. Suddenly I pound on the dashboard.

'Stop!'

I unbuckle my seatbelt and struggle out of the passenger seat. I'm lurching out of the car by the time anyone understands the reason for my agitation. It's Imran. The police are bundling him and Rafiq into the back of a van.

'What the hell are they doing?'

I make my way to the police line and push against the burly officer who steps in my way. His face is a picture of bewilderment. What is a uniformed soldier doing defending a known militant?

I'm in no mood to explain myself. 'Where are you taking them?'

The policeman tries to brush away my protests. One of his colleagues tries to escort me back to the car.

I tell them to get their hands off me. I yell to Imran. 'I'm going to speak up for you.' When my friend turns to look at me I see the old Imran, not the embittered man who once painted my face with blood. I wrestle with the restraining arm. 'This is crazy. But for him there would have been a bloodbath.'

The van doors close.

'I've got to put this right.' I start thumbing a number into my mobile. 'I'm calling Imran's parents. They will arrange a solicitor. I'm going to do everything I can to get Imran and Rafiq out of the cells.'

They release Rafiq next day. I'm at the police station when he emerges. He embraces Aisha and his parents and a woman, who I learn later is Sayeeda. He exchanges a few words then he makes his way over.

'Good to see you, man. I heard about your leg.'

I shrug. 'Who said life was fair?'

He glances at Kelly standing beside me. 'This must be ...'

I introduce her. Briefly. 'Have you seen Imran?'

Rafiq shakes his head. 'They separated us. They didn't seem interested in me. Imran's the one.'

'But he stopped the Leopard. It was his call.'

Rafiq shakes his head. 'Like they're going to give him a medal.' He chuckles humourlessly. 'Do you know the bomber's real name?'

'No.'

'Nigel Lappin. Doesn't sound quite so cool, does it? He changed it to Usman Ahmed when he converted.'

I tell him I saw him being taken away by the police. 'He was weeping like a slapped child.' I ask the question that's been haunting me. 'They couldn't charge Imran, could they?'

Rafiq grimaces. 'These guys are capable of anything. By the end of the first interview even I thought I was guilty. I tell you, they're genuinely scary people.'

I tell him I've made a statement on Imran's behalf.

'You're a stand-up guy, Chris.'

I rub my forehead. 'You don't owe me anything. What a mess.' I stare into the distance. 'I wish I could turn back time.'

He rests a hand on my arm. 'Don't we all?'

It is another three days before the police finally release Imran. Rafiq calls me at home.

'He's out. There are no charges.'

'They took their time.'

'Only one thing matters, Chris. He's free.'

For a moment there is the same excitement I felt when he used to knock to play football. I grab my coat and reach for my mobile.

Dad asks where I'm going.

I tell him about Imran. 'Got a problem with that?' I head for the door, dialling a cab as I go.

He picks up his car keys. 'Don't call a taxi, son. I'll run you.'

I meet his eye. 'Are you sure about this, Dad?'

'It's a new world,' he says. 'I don't know what to make of it. Look Chris, they've both been released without charge. That's good enough for me.'

I finally agree to let him drive me. 'You shouldn't need the police to tell you they're innocent. Dad, they lived right next door to us. They saved lives. In my book, they're heroes.'

We barely exchange a word on the drive over. When we

pull up in the old street Dad wants to know if I will need a lift back.

I don't answer. I have a question first. 'Aren't you coming in?'

He shakes his head. 'I don't think so. Not this time.'

I watch him go then ring the doorbell. Mrs Hussain answers and leads the way indoors.

Imran rises to his feet. We shake hands. Awkwardly. 'Do you want to go somewhere to talk?'

I nod. 'The Wilderness is out. Have you been down there?'

'Yes, another retail park. Just what this town needs.'

We go out the back way. I notice the rusting basketball hoop. 'We wouldn't need to jump to do a slam dunk now.'

Imran taps the rusted metal. 'I should take it down.'

It's only a ten-minute walk to the hills above the streets where we grew up. We find somewhere to sit and look down at the terraced houses that cluster round the green-domed mosque. 'What was the interrogation like?'

Imran digs his hands in his jacket pockets and sucks in a breath. 'Not as bad as Afghanistan, I bet. Do you get much pain?'

I rub my knee instinctively. 'You know what's weird? It's the bit they cut off that hurts.'

Imran struggles to find the right words. 'Nobody deserves what happened to you. Are you bitter?'

'I was. Now I'm kind of resigned to it. Funny thing, some of the guys I met at Headley Court seem to love the Army even more since they got hurt.'

'Not you?'

I watch the progress of a car along the bottom road. 'I don't know if I ever believed in the war. It's something that happened to me, not something I chose with my eyes open.' I pick up a stone and throw it down the slope. 'You think you're in control of your life but you're not. Not really. It's like you stumble through the years with a hood over your head. Nobody knows where they're going.'

Imran is staring at me.

'What's wrong?'

'You could be describing me. I kind of drifted into Arshad's group. I went along with everything he said. I just wanted to destroy.'

'Is that how you feel now?'

'No, I'm done with that. It's easy to know what you're against. It's a lot harder to know what you're for.' He lies back and stares up at a hawk hovering against the racing clouds. 'Do you know what's stupid? I don't think I ever fell for Arshad's jihad. I boarded a rollercoaster and I couldn't get off. My parents' way was hard. Finding my own was even worse. Arshad's was easy. He gave me a home when I couldn't find one anywhere else. He gave me an enemy I could dump all my problems on. He even did my thinking for me.'

My mobile buzzes. It's Kelly wondering where I am. I tell her I'll be back in an hour or so. I end the call. I wave the phone and smile. 'Home.'

'Kelly? You've got a good one there. You should go.'

I tell him not yet. 'I think we've still got stuff to say.'

We talk for another half hour.

About the old days.

About the passing years.

About Kelly.

He walks me back to the taxi rank. I stumble a couple of times going down the slope. He steadies me. I'm about to get in the cab when Imran embraces me. I pat his back.

'We did good, Chris, well ... in the end.' He steps back. 'Don't leave it another eight years before you call me. You hear?' He closes the door.

I remember something. 'They got Arshad and Nabeel. It was on the news. The police will want you to give evidence. Are you ready for that?'

Imran doesn't say much. The prospect clearly worries him. He slaps the taxi with the flat of his hand and sets off down the street. He doesn't look back. As the cab pulls away I settle back in the seat. All the plotters are off the street. The town is finished with violence, at last.

Thank God.

Epilogue

A week later Imam Nawaz knocks on the mosque's security shutters. He hears the custodian coming to let him in.

'Thank you, Abdul. How is your daughter? Any better?'

Abdul tells Nawaz that she has to have a biopsy. He will have to leave immediately to get her to the hospital for her appointment. Nawaz tells him of course. Abdul is about to go when he glances over his shoulder.

'I heard something before. It might be the same hooligans that sprayed slogans on the shutters last week.' He glances at his watch. 'I will have to go. Ismail will be here soon.'

Ismail is the muezzin. He is always punctual.

'You go and attend to your daughter,' Nawaz says.

He starts to prepare for Friday prayers. Presently he hears the adhan, the call to prayer. Ismail has arrived. Nawaz hears the first worshippers doing their ablutions. He is about to enter the prayer hall when he hears the sound Abdul told him about. There are foosteps coming from the disused cellar. Nawaz goes to the top of the stairs.

'Is somebody there?'

There is no answer. He sees more people arriving. For some reason, his skin begins to prickle. What would anyone be doing in an empty cellar? He remembers what Abdul said about hooligans.

'Abdul,' he calls. 'Is that you? Ismail?'

Still there is no answer. He starts to edge down the stairs. He hears somebody behind him and turns. It is Ismail.

'Did you call me?' he asks.

'Yes, there is somebody down there.'

'Do you want me to come with you?'

'No,' Nawaz says. 'I don't like the sound of this. Get everyone to wait in the entrance lobby. Yes, stop them entering the prayer hall. I think you should call the police.'

Ismail nods and hurries away. Nawaz moves quietly but purposefully. Soon he sees somebody's back. 'Who are you?'

Quade spins round.

Nawaz demands to know what he is doing in the mosque. Even as he speaks he sees the device: metal, wires, a battery, chemicals. He starts to yell for Ismail to clear the building. Quade presses something and rushes towards him. Nawaz grabs him.

Quade throws a punch. 'Get off me!'

Nawaz struggles with the younger man. Quade interlaces his fingers and brings both hands down on Nawaz's neck. The Imam grunts with pain but clings on.

'Let me go,' Quade yells, 'it's going to blow in one minute.'

Nawaz thinks of the worshippers. Will Ismail have had time to clear the mosque? 'Get everyone out!' he yells up the stairs.

He sees the panic in Quade's face. There is no time to get clear. There is only one thing to do. Nawaz wrestles the intruder closer to the bomb. Quade screams. 'What are you doing, you lunatic?'

Both men fall heavily on top of the device. The explosion rips them apart. Fragments fly. The blast wave follows. There is enormous heat, deafening noise. Fire and metal burn and tear through skin, flesh, bone, muscle. The explosion shreds everything in its path.

Quade dies a reluctant martyr to his cause. He will be celebrated on a number of fringe neo-Nazi websites registered outside the United Kingdom. Their donations will pay for a grave next to his mother.

Nawaz dies to protect the innocent gathering outside the prayer hall. The mosque will be repaired by donations from the worshippers and from other faith groups and ordinary individuals.

The Hussains will be among the first donors. So will the Hook family. Nawaz will be buried and mourned by people inspired by the struggle he has put up in the final moments of his life on Earth.

It is an act of love.

Terror timeline

1995

- Mass graves containing executed Muslims found at Srebrenica, Bosnia.

1999

- Neo-Nazi David Copeland launches nail bomb attacks in Soho, London. The bombings kill three people including a pregnant woman and injure 129.

2000

- Palestinian Intifada starts.
- Death of a son: twelve-year-old Muhammad al-Durrah shot in his father Jamal's arms.

2001

- 20 January. George Bush Junior becomes president of the United States.
- 11 September terror attack launched in New York, USA. 2,995 people die.
- Bombing of Afghanistan.
- Bradford, UK – riots. More than 300 arrests are made.
- Shoe bomber Richard Reid arrested on commercial flight from Paris to Miami, USA.

2003

- 15 February. Big march against war with Iraq in London. Estimates of 2 million participants.

- 20 March. US attacks Iraq.
- 1 May. Bush makes mission accomplished speech.

- Abuse scandal at Abu Ghraib prison in Baghdad, Iraq.
- Bush re-elected for second term.

- 7 July. London bombings. Fifty-six people die including four bombers, in bus bombing and on tube.
- 21 July. Second series of London bombs.
- 8 October. Pakistan earthquake.

- Afghan war intensifies.
- John Reid promises UK troops will leave Afghanistan 'without a shot being fired'.
- 2 June. Forest Gate raids in East London.
- 12 July. Israel invades Lebanon.
- 30 September. Danish cartoons provoke outrage in Muslim communities across the world.
- 29 December. Saddam Hussein hanged in Iraq.

- Former BNP candidate Robert Cottage from Lancashire jailed on explosives charges.

- 8,000 UK troops in Afghanistan.
- Hammaad Munchi from Yorkshire convicted of terror offences, aged sixteen, the UK's youngest terrorist.
- Mumbai hotel siege.

- 30,000 more US troops sent to Afghanistan.
- 'Draw down' promised by 2011.
- Israel attacks Gaza.
- Afghan President Hamid Karzai wins disputed election.
- Andrew Ibrahim, a twenty-one-year-old British Muslim convert from Bristol convicted of preparing terrorist attacks.

- Twelve dead in Kabul bombing, January.
- Darren Lee Tinklin from South Wales jailed for three years for making a pipe bomb. He possessed Nazi symbols.
- Aryan Strike Force members Michael Heaton from Manchester and Trevor Hannington from South Wales jailed for total of four and a half years for inciting race hatred.
- Suspected commando-style attack like the one in Mumbai planned for a European city, according to security agencies.
- Prize-winning student Roshonara Choudhry was convicted in November 2010 of attempted murder. She tried to stab MP Stephen Timms to death because of his support for the war in Iraq.